PRAISE FOR THE BOOKS OF
AGATHA AWARD-WINNING AUTHOR
EDITH MAXWELL

"The historical setting is redolent and delicious, the townspeople engaging, and the plot a proper puzzle, but it's Rose Carroll—midwife, Quaker, sleuth—who captivates in this irresistible series debut."
— Catriona McPherson, Agatha-, Anthony- and Macavity-winning author of the Dandy Gilver series

"Clever and stimulating novel . . . masterfully weaves a complex mystery."
— *Open Book Society*

"Riveting historical mystery . . . [a] fascinating look at nineteenth-century American faith, culture, and small-town life."
— William Martin, *New York Times* bestselling author of *Cape Cod* and *The Lincoln Letter*

"Intelligent, well-researched story with compelling characters and a fast-moving plot. Excellent!"
— *Suspense Magazine*

"A series heroine whose struggles with the tenets of her Quaker faith make her strong and appealing . . . imparts authentic historical detail to depict life in a 19th-century New England factory town."
— *Library Journal*

"Intriguing look at life in 19th-century New England, a heroine whose goodness guides all her decisions, and a mystery that surprises."
— *Kirkus Reviews*

Books by Edith Maxwell

Quaker Midwife Mysteries

Delivering the Truth
Called to Justice
Turning the Tide
Charity's Burden
Judge Thee Not
Taken Too Soon

Lauren Rousseau Mysteries

Speaking of Murder
Murder on the Bluffs

Local Foods Mysteries

A Tine to Live, a Tine to Die
'Til Dirt Do Us Part
Farmed and Dangerous
Murder Most Fowl
Mulch Ado About Murder

More BOOKS BY EDITH MAXWELL

TAKEN TOO SOON

A
QUAKER MIDWIFE
MYSTERY

EDITH MAXWELL

BEYOND THE PAGE
PUBLISHING

Taken Too Soon
Edith Maxwell
Beyond the Page Books
are published by
Beyond the Page Publishing
www.beyondthepagepub.com

ISBN: 978-1-950461-54-7

For small historical museums and all the dedicated history fans who keep them running. I couldn't do this without you!

AUTHOR'S NOTE

Amesbury reference librarian Margie Walker is ever helpful with whatever I ask her. She accessed train information on traveling from Lawrence to Cape Cod for me in the blink of an eye. Believe it or not, the *Flying Dude* was the name of an actual express train, which ran on a subscription basis, from Boston to Woods Hole and back (Woods Hole was called Wood's Holl for twenty-one years, including during the period in which this book takes place). Thanks, Margie! In Wood's Holl, Rose and David see African-Americans on their way to Cottage City on Martha's Vineyard. This island community of middle-class blacks changed its name to Oak Bluffs in 1907. Gratitude is also due to Woods Hole Historical Museum archivist Susan Fletcher Witzell for her deep knowledge of the area in Rose's day and for help in finding old photographs.

A slight historic fudge: the Lawrence Meetinghouse wasn't built until 1895. Forgive my creative license.

Also forgive me if I have altered the personalities of any actual 1889 residents of West Falmouth, as I've wantonly stolen character names from the gravestones in the West Falmouth Friends' cemetery. I also invented another mansion on the scale of the Swift brothers' homes for the fictional Abial Latting, and located it next to one of them. The West Falmouth Public Library was a gold mine of useful information, and I particularly thank reference librarian Renee Voorhees for her help over the year during which I researched and wrote the book, including digging up a copy of *Traditions and Narratives of West Falmouth* by John Hoag Dillingham (1909). Local author and Friend Abigail Young also helped with historical facts.

The interior improvements to the West Falmouth Friends Meetinghouse happened shortly after this book, but I moved the date a bit earlier. Apologies, Friends.

I relied heavily on *The Book of Falmouth: A Tricentennial Celebration 1686–1986*, edited by Mary Lou Smith (Falmouth Historical Commission, 1986), for all kinds of details about the area in Rose's era and for maps. Many thanks to Linda Hollander, who loaned a stranger one of her copies until I could locate a copy of my own. In return, I stole her house for Tilly and Dru's home.

Suckanesett: A History of Falmouth, Massachusetts by Theodate Geoffrey, published in 1928, was also a useful history reference.

What is currently known as Old Dock Road in West Falmouth was named Chappaquoit Road on the 1880 map. The bridge leading to Chappaquoit on the current Chappaquoit Road was built in 1890, when Charles H. Jones developed the Chappaquoit area and built stately homes there. I slid its construction a few months earlier so Rose and David could travel that way to the beach.

The real Gilbert Boyce (who indeed managed the Union Store in West Falmouth) might not have invented the egg-carrying case—the first recorded egg cartons came a decade or two later—but who's to say what inventive solutions people came up with that weren't attested in the history books? I also invented a few places I couldn't find record of, including the Falmouth Opera House and the Cape Cod Burlesque Theater. Examples of both could be found all over New England during this period, including an opera house in Amesbury. Falmouth historically had neither at the time.

I visited the Mashpee Wampanoag Cultural Center for information about the Wampanoag tribe. Although I couldn't unearth any information about native midwives, they must have had them. I did my best to portray fictional midwife Zerviah Baxter with respect and dignity. I borrowed her name from the real nineteenth-century Native American Zerviah Gould Mitchell, an educated woman descended from Massasoit. In 1878, Mitchell published a monograph about him titled *Indian History, Biography, and Genealogy.*

Lynn Heidelbaugh, Curator at the Smithsonian's National Postal Museum, helped with questions about special delivery mail. Susan Koso of the Amesbury Carriage Museum once again assisted with carriage varieties.

I make reference to John Greenleaf Whittier's poem "The Meeting," written about his worship with Amesbury Friends. Thanks to Chuck Fager for sharing his research about details of Meeting for Worship in Rose's era.

As always, I consulted the Online Etymology Dictionary (www.etymonline.com/) for information about when particular words and phrases entered the language, as well as the *American Slang Dictionary from 1890*, originally published by James Maitland in 1891.

ONE

NOT A HINT OF MURDER tainted the air. It was the best marriage gift I could imagine. As it happened, the gift was an ephemeral one.

My new husband and I stood greeting our guests emerging from the Lawrence Friends Meetinghouse on this fine Ninth Month afternoon in the year 1889. Puffy clouds as light as my spirit floated lazily under a soft sun. Messages of grace and hope from the service filled my heart. David Dodge and I had had a long betrothal, which had ended not an hour earlier as we stood in front of family and friends and exchanged our vows, then affixed our signatures to the large marriage certificate.

Now we received blessings, kisses, and best wishes from those filing out, who then proceeded to bend over the low table nearby and sign their own names as witnesses to our union. I glanced up at David, looking splendid in a new gray suit, his dark hair set off against a snowy white collar. Beyond him, his mother Clarinda approached, outfitted in the latest fashion, of course.

"My fondest felicitations, dear son." She beamed and patted his cheek with a gloved hand. "And Rose, welcome to the Dodge family." She extended her hand, her smile dimming. As usual when she regarded me, it was a less-than-enthusiastic expression.

"I thank thee, Clarinda." I clasped her hand for a moment.

"I will be pleased to refer to you as Mrs. Dodge for the rest of my days." She extracted her hand and touched her hat, a brown velvet with ivory lace and a pink ostrich feather that needed no adjustment.

I swallowed. I would no longer be Rose Carroll. I hadn't considered how pregnant women who hadn't already engaged my midwifery services would find me. I'd already written each of my existing ladies a note and let them know of both my new name and my new abode. But I'd have to revise the advertisement I placed in the newspapers, too.

"Of course you'll be forgetting that silly hobby of yours from now on," Clarinda continued, arching her eyebrows. "As a wife, you understand."

I opened my mouth to object. She'd expressed this edict more than once in recent weeks.

"Of course she won't, Mother." David laid his arm lightly over my shoulders. "Midwifery isn't a hobby, and Rose is fully capable of being both a wife and an expert in all matters related to childbirth."

Clarinda's nostrils flared, but she kept her silence and moved on.

I whispered a thanks to my darling and smoothed down my new dress, a simple but lovely garment in a dark rose hue. Clarinda had thrown every obstacle she could onto the path to David's marrying me. He hadn't let her succeed. Nor had I. I was blessed with an enlightened and loving man with whom to spend my life, and I prayed I could find a way to soften the prickles Clarinda continued to present.

David's father Herbert was next. Here was a man who was truly happy for both of us. He embraced his son, then gave me a light kiss on the cheek, his eyes smiling, as always. "I am so pleased at this happy union, dear Rose. I hope you'll make me a doting grandfather with all due haste."

"Father," David admonished, setting his hands on his waist.

"It's all right." I touched his arm. "Herbert, we have every intention of providing thee with grandchildren, have no fear." Perhaps not immediately, but the time would be right soon enough.

Herbert moved on, and the Amesbury poet John Greenleaf Whittier — both friend and Friend — approached, with my niece Faith Bailey Weed at his side to make sure he navigated the crowd without mishap. At eighty-one, the famous Quaker abolitionist grew more frail with each passing month, it seemed.

"Blessings on each of thee for a long and happy union in the sight of God," John said.

David smiled. "Thank you, Mr. Whittier."

"I also thank thee, John," I said. "That means so much to us."

"Welcome to the Carroll-Bailey clan, David," Faith said. "I'm pleased to have thee as true uncle, finally." She held out her other hand to me. "My heart is full, Rose." Her eyes were, too.

"As is mine," I whispered as I wiped away a sudden tear of joy. Faith, nearly twenty, had been wed to her dear Zebulon Weed only last winter.

"A fine Meetinghouse this is." John looked up at the edifice, newly constructed within the year. "I'd say the Lawrence Friends building committee received some expert advice on the design." A smile played around his mouth, outlined by a white chinstrap beard. He had advised the building of our Amesbury Meetinghouse some years before and had been asked to contribute his thoughts to this construction, as well.

"I would have to agree with thee, Friend," I said.

"It is suitably simple and, as in Amesbury, supplied with generously sized windows to allow the Lord's light to stream over all of us as we wait upon His guidance." John touched his top hat. "Faith, if thee would be so kind to escort me to yon bench, I feel the need to sit."

In a brief lull between well-wishers, David leaned toward me. "We'll need to be getting to the reception soon, dear wife."

"I know." I wrinkled my nose, then pushed my spectacles back up. Clarinda had begrudgingly consented to our simple Meeting for Worship for Marriage after the manner of Friends but had insisted on a lavish reception immediately following at the Central House Hotel near the train depot. Those present here were invited, of course. Also included would be Clarinda's social circle, many of whom attended St. Paul's Episcopal Church in Newburyport with Clarinda. They were folks generally uncomfortable participating in anything Quaker. I, in turn, was not at ease around them. I sighed inwardly. But this would be my new life, straddling two different societies and expectations, and I had chosen it.

"Afterward we will have our lovely hotel room for the night, just the two of us." He winked.

"I cannot wait." I squeezed his hand. I was truly eager to deepen our intimacy.

"And our trip to Cape Cod awaits on the morrow. All we have to do is endure this evening, my sweet."

"Endure I shall, husband."

TWO

AT THE TABLE OF HONOR, as Clarinda had proudly put it, I glanced to my right at my father and mother. Daddy, otherwise known as Allan Burroughs Carroll, squeezed my hand in a sympathetic gesture. Two hundred people milled about the ballroom in front of us, enjoying rich delicacies served by passing men in livery. Our guests held glasses, sipping beverages both alcoholic and not.

We, the happy couple and parents, in contrast, had been relegated by Clarinda to our seated prison to receive even more well-wishes. Mother, at the end of the table, stood in deep and fervent conversation with someone who looked like one of her many suffragist compatriots. To my left, meanwhile, David was enjoying conversing with a fellow physician who had approached the table, while his father happily downed sherry after sherry. Clarinda, ever the appropriate hostess, smiled and chatted with the many Episcopalians approaching to greet and congratulate her. I imagined their disapproval if they knew the plans of the prized son's new wife to continue practicing her profession of midwifery. Or perhaps I was judging them too soon. Surely Clarinda's church included forward-looking women.

David glanced at my empty plate and signaled to a waiting hotel servant, who offered me additional dinner. I declined, instead sipping my glass of lemonade. I hadn't yet had a chance to chat with my dear pal Bertie and her Sophie, nor with Amesbury police detective and friend Kevin Donovan and his family. My niece Betsy and her twin brothers were exchanging jokes with several other children on the far side of the room. I longed to join them, but I knew Clarinda expected me to stay put for the duration of the supper.

"This will be over soon enough," Daddy murmured.

"I hope so. But this is only the first of the functions I'll have to endure as daughter-in-law," I whispered in return. "I want to be out there with my friends, with my nieces and nephews. Is this my new fate? Daddy, what have I done?"

4

"Now, now. Thee is having a case of the jitters." He gazed over his own spectacles at me. "Thee has acquired thy heart's desire. All the rest will sort itself out."

How fortunate in parents was I? Mother would have given me the same response.

As a string quartet played softly in a fern-embellished corner of the room, David's acquaintance departed. My husband turned to me.

"If only my brother could have joined us." He glanced at his mother, then back at me.

"A brother?" I frowned and tilted my head until a memory flashed in my brain. "I remember. Early in our courting thee mentioned a distant brother, but it never came up again. I had forgotten."

He let out a breath. "Yes, a distant brother. Currie is four years older than I."

"What an unusual name."

"It's a nickname for Herbert Currier Dodge, Junior. I sent him an invitation at his last known address but never received a response." My husband's tone was wistful.

"I didn't know. I'm sorry he didn't reply." I stroked his hand in what was clearly a moment of pain. "Thee and he must be estranged."

"It's my mother he's estranged from, but in effect he doesn't spend time with Father or me, either."

"Thee is sad about this." I rubbed my knee gently against his under the table.

"I am. Rosie, he was my world growing up. I adored him, I learned from him."

I thought back. Surely we had talked about David's childhood. I was certain he hadn't talked about a brother other than that one early mention. Perhaps the estrangement hurt him too much to dwell on those memories. Or had iron-willed Clarinda banned mention of him in the household? Herbert was a successful businessman and David had a thriving medical practice. Why were they so cowed by Clarinda?

"I would have done anything for Currie," David continued. "I tried to reach him. Father did, too."

"Of course thee would have."

"But he never responded. He must have felt too damaged by —" His eyes grew to resemble saucers. "My dear, has marriage transformed me into a conjurer?" He pointed at the entrance.

A man sauntered in wearing a fancy bowler and carrying a cane, looking as if he should be hobnobbing with the likes of the Carnegies and Rockefellers. He removed hat and gloves with similar flourishes and held them to the side, as if a servant would materialize to accept them. To my astonishment, one did.

I turned to David. "That's Currie?"

His eyes narrowed for a flash of a moment, but he quickly replaced the look with a sad smile. "That's my brother." He swallowed and stood, inhaling. "I must greet him, Rose, but I hate to leave you."

"Go, my dear," I urged.

A muffled shriek sounded from my left. Clarinda, staring, covered her mouth with a shaking hand.

Herbert slapped his hands onto the table and stood. "My prayers have been answered," he said in a thick voice to himself, as if overcome by emotion.

David hurried toward the newcomer. The crowd hushed and parted. The two met near the back and embraced, then pulled apart. They were too far away for me to hear what they said. David pulled at Currie's elbow, urging him toward our table. His brother shook his head, his gaze on their mother. Herbert joined them, wiping his eyes, and a minute later sat with his sons at a table near the door. The buzz of conversation in the hall resumed, along with the clinking of china and glass.

"A relative, I presume?" Daddy leaned close to ask.

"David's long-lost brother Currie." I twisted to see Clarinda, who smiled pointedly at a guest standing at her left, anywhere but at the rest of her family. "Who has been estranged from his mother, David told me only a minute ago." What I didn't know was what had caused the distancing. What had David been about to tell me when Currie made his dramatic entrance?

"This should prove an interesting party, doesn't thee think, my dear?" Daddy's eyes sparkled, as always.

"I expect so. I'm tired of being trapped up here. I think I'll go meet Herbert Currier Dodge, Junior, for myself." I made my way toward the Dodge men, smiling politely and thanking various acquaintances for their congratulations as I went.

"Ah, Rose." David leapt to his feet when I arrived. "May I introduce my brother? Currie, this is my wife, Rose Carroll Dodge."

Currie stood, a little unsteadily, and brought his heels together. He took my hand and bowed. "Very pleased to make your acquaintance, Mrs. Dodge." His words were ever so slightly slurred. He straightened and flashed me a white-toothed smile. "Or perhaps I should call you Sister now."

I reclaimed my hand but laughed lightly. "Only if thee wants to cast me as a nun, Currie, which I am most certainly not. A simple Rose will do. I'm pleased to make thy acquaintance. Thy scoundrel brother had not informed me thee would be joining us, but I am delighted thee was able."

A cloud scudded over the sunshine in Currie's gaze, but he shook it off. "Who would have thought my baby brother would wed before I did?" He widened his eyes in mock wonder.

"Your old pater might have entertained such a thought, but we don't want to dwell on that," Herbert Senior said. "Our David is a happy husband, my wife and I have acquired a daughter, and we've now regained a son, from all appearances."

"Where have you been keeping yourself, old man?" David asked his brother.

"Here and there." Currie gazed into the distance instead of at David. "Of late I reside in Wood's Holl on Cape Cod."

David and I exchanged a quick glance. A well-regarded science aquarium was situated in Wood's Holl, as was the Marine Biological Laboratory, established only last year. Both were only a few miles from our intended destination tomorrow. My two maiden aunts had been unable to come to Lawrence for our wedding, so David and I had planned a trip to see them and have a modest honeymoon at the same time.

"Does thee work at the aquarium?" I asked him.

"Me?" Currie scoffed. "Davey's the scientist in the family. I lean more toward the entertainment industry."

I'd ask David after we were alone what that meant. In the meantime, I gazed from one brother to the other. Currie was taller and leaner than my husband, and his hair was a lighter shade of brown. Around the eyes they were clearly brothers, but Currie's narrow nose and thin-lipped mouth resembled Clarinda's, while David's fuller features were every inch his father's.

"Come along son," Herbert began. "It's past time to greet your long-suffering mother." He held out his hand to usher Currie toward the front.

Currie folded his arms and refused to budge. "If you remember, Father, it was she who gave *me* the tip of her boot. I'm the one who has suffered, not Empress Clarinda." He shot a look full of sharp projectiles toward his mother, then turned his back.

What? Why did he come if not for reconciliation? David's family was turning out to be far more complicated than I'd thought. And my happy wedding day was not the completely blessed celebration I'd expected.

Currie was in for a surprise soon, too. Clarinda rose and moved, chin high, in our direction. David grimaced briefly. I thought about absenting myself, but she arrived before I could do so gracefully.

Clarinda clasped her hands in front her. "Herbert Junior?" She spoke softly. "I see you've done the right thing."

The unsaid "for once" nearly screamed itself. I was astonished to see a tic beating next to her eye. I'd never seen her nervous.

"I am glad for it," she continued, then waited for him to face her.

He rotated as slowly as the cylinder in a nearly spent music box. "Hello, Mater." He didn't smile, nor reach out for her.

"You are looking well," she said, her voice shaking.

Currie opened his mouth as if to begin a retort but clamped it shut again. Clarinda cast a look of desperation toward her husband. He shrugged, clearly leaving this volley to the two with the history of clashes. Was that smart of Herbert, or a sign of weakness?

"I hope you will return home with us this evening." Clarinda's voice was uncharacteristically hesitant, nearly pleading.

"I'm not letting him out of my sight," Herbert said, clapping his arm around Currie's shoulders. "The prodigal son and all that."

To my eyes, Currie looked torn between wanting to let the past be bygone and needing to finish whatever dispute had caused the rift in the first place. And Clarinda looked in all respects like a mother longing to reconcile with her son.

The hotel manager approached Clarinda holding a small tray with a yellow envelope and a letter opener atop it. "Forgive me for interrupting you, ma'am. I have a telegram for Mr. Allan Carroll from a Miss Drusilla Carroll."

"Allan is my father," I said. Daddy had also left the front table. I gestured toward him and caught his attention from where he'd gone to be with his grandchildren. I waved him over. "Dru is one of the two aunts we're off to visit in West Falmouth tomorrow," I explained to the group.

"Mr. Carroll, a telegram has arrived for you," Clarinda said when he arrived.

"I thank thee, Clarinda," Daddy said, slipping out the telegram. "Oh, my." The edges of his mouth drew down. He glanced up at David and me. "My sister wants thee to come to them right away, Rose."

"Now?" I asked.

"Immediately, is what she wrote."

"That's completely unacceptable." Clarinda pursed her lips. "Why, this is a wedding party, a happy occasion. I won't hear of it."

"What's the rush, Mr. Carroll?" David asked in a low voice.

My father fixed a sorrowful gaze on his new son-in-law. "She says no one but our Rose can help. Frannie has been murdered."

THREE

"WELL, I NEVER," Clarinda began. "This relation of yours has a lot of nerve."

David said, "Mother," at the same time as my father protested, "This relation is my elderly sister, and she is fully aware of Rose's expertise." Herbert looked somberly from David to me and back.

I cleared my throat. "If you'll excuse us, Clarinda?" I mustered a smile. "Daddy, may I?" I held out my hand for the telegram, then took David's arm and led him out into a corner of the lobby, Clarinda still muttering her objections behind us. David came along without protest. I faced him, held both his hands, and closed my eyes in a moment of silent prayer, waiting for discernment about the right path to follow. I opened my eyes to his blue-eyed gaze.

David squeezed my hands and dropped one, raising my chin with a gentle finger. "I will do whatever you wish, my dearest."

I read aloud from the yellow paper:

> *Frannie Isley found dead in bay STOP Sheriff says murder STOP Need Rose without delay STOP Tilly beside herself. STOP Hurry STOP*

"Poor Dru, and poor Tilly," I murmured. I pictured my elderly aunts, spinsters both. Dru, shorter, rounder, and more kindly—much like my dear father—than her austere, thin, crotchety younger sister. Still, they had lived together for many years, neither having married.

"Who is Frannie?" David asked.

"She's Tilly's ward. Frannie was orphaned when she was a toddler. I'm not quite sure why Tilly took her in, but she did. Frannie is sixteen—or she would be if she weren't dead. The poor dear girl, murdered. How, and why?"

David kept silent for a moment. "Rosie, we are legally married, and we have received the blessings and congratulations of nearly everyone we and our families know. I'm aware this reception wasn't going to be your favorite part of our wedding day. And neither is it mine. If you want to catch the next train to the Cape, I will defend you to my mother."

I shook my head in wonder at my good fortune in finding this treasure of a man. "We do already have our luggage here. But it's our wedding night, David," I said in a wistful tone, imagining the joys we'd anticipated in our luxurious room upstairs.

"We'll have it on Cape Cod, instead. I expect the Tower House Hotel in Falmouth, where we are to stay starting tomorrow, will have a room for us tonight, too. And, truly, every night with you will be the happiest of my life." He kissed my forehead. "We both know why they summoned you."

"Because of my increasing facility at solving cases of homicide, or at least helping the police do so."

"Helping the police do what, now?" Kevin Donovan appeared at my side. "Do I detect an emergency of some kind? I couldn't help but notice the arrival of a telegram, some degree of conflict between you both and Mrs. Dodge, and your sudden disappearance. I hope you won't think me too bold, Mr. Dodge, to ask if I might assist with any matter small or large." He straightened the coat of his best gray suit.

"Of course not, Detective," David said.

"Kevin," I began, "thee isn't being too bold, at all. In fact, I'm glad to see thee."

David continued. "Apparently Rose's aunt's ward has been murdered on Cape Cod."

"Oh, my," Kevin said. "Who says, and how?"

"The sheriff says, but I wondered how and why myself," I said. "The telegram doesn't include any details about that."

Kevin whistled. "What precise location on the Cape, may I ask?"

"In West Falmouth, the place where we aimed to travel to tomorrow," David said. "This relative has urgently requested Rose's presence."

"Aha." Kevin clasped his hands behind him and rolled on his heels. "I believe I have an acquaintance on the force down there. I'll make some inquiries, shall I?"

"Thank thee," I said. "I would appreciate it."

David looked at me and I inclined my head.

"We'll be taking the next train to Boston," David told him. "It's only half past four. I believe a train leaves Lawrence station at five sharp, and we can catch the evening express to the Cape from Boston."

"You can contact us, if need be, in care of the West Falmouth post office," I added to Kevin. "My aunts are Tilly and Drusilla Carroll."

The two men shook hands. I held mine out to the detective, too. He surprised me by enveloping me in a quick embrace, instead. We'd never hugged before, but we'd been through a lot together, the detective and me. And this was my wedding day.

Red-faced, he stepped back. "Many happy returns of the day to you both," he mumbled. "And you know what we say back in Ireland to the new couple." He rattled off words I didn't understand, then explained, "May you both live as long as you want, and never want as long as you live." He hurried back into the reception.

I blew out a breath and took my husband's hand. "Shall we brave the angry hordes?"

FOUR

As IT TURNED OUT, the hordes hadn't been particularly angry. Even Clarinda conceded that the reception was nearing its end, her mood perhaps buoyed by a possible truce between her and her older son.

Currie had made a valiant attempt to accompany us on our journey, saying he lived on Cape Cod anyway and could show us the sights. Thank goodness family members on both sides had prevailed to convince him we neither needed nor desired his presence on our wedding night. Clarinda seemed grateful to have his company. We were more than grateful not to.

"Rose, dear, is thee letting thy interest in solving crimes push too far into thy personal life?" my mother had asked me after taking me aside. "It's thy wedding night, after all." The fine lines around her eyes deepened as she gazed into mine.

"I suppose I am, Mother." I did regret this unpleasantness tainting my happy day. "But it would seem selfish not to go. Tilly asked for me. And David will be at my side."

She waited a moment before speaking. "I understand. Travel safely, then." She'd embraced me with a fierceness unusual for her.

I was her sole remaining child since my older sister's death, and I was now a married woman. Mother only wanted her daughter to be happy.

Now, at a few minutes past seven, David and I swayed in a plush seat for two along with the gentle movement of the Naushon drawing room car, one of two comprising the *Flying Dude*. It was an express train from Boston to Wood's Holl that operated by subscription. Herbert Senior had insisted we take his subscription card, which awarded us the two places always reserved for him. Herbert had also arranged for the hotel to pack us a picnic supper for our trip. The arched top of the car was as ornately decorated as the rest of it, and a chandelier rocked gently. Around us other travelers in upholstered armchairs also talked in quiet voices or read books or newspapers. One man snored lightly, his hat over his face.

"Is thee hungry, darling?" I asked David.

He leaned over to nibble on my earlobe and whispered, "For you, wife, always."

"Shh." My face warmed even as I snorted and pushed him away, murmuring, "Thee knows it's mutual, husband. In this case, however, I meant for food. Like pies and cheeses and sweets, whatever they prepared for us."

His stomach growled in return, prompting my laughter. I set the basket on the seat between us and we investigated its contents: meat and chicken turnovers, sweet red grapes and sharp cheese, tiny apple tarts, and wrapped dreams of creamy chocolate. I even tasted the port wine they'd included.

"My, that's smooth," I said, but I held my hand up in refusal of more. I'd gone astray earlier this year indulging in sherry with Bertie, and I didn't intend to become stupidly intoxicated on my wedding night, not with an unsolved homicide to complicate matters. I frowned down at my flaky chicken turnover.

"Are you thinking of the deceased girl?" David's tone was gentle.

"How could thee tell? I'm wishing I knew more about the circumstances of her death."

"The death of any young person is a tragedy. To die at the hands of another is shocking."

"I know. My heart is heavy at the thought. Why would someone accost a young woman of sixteen? I also wonder how she died."

"Do you think your aunts had any inkling of trouble?"

I could only shake my head. "How could they not? Frannie was young, she was Tilly's ward. But of course I have no idea."

"We'll find out after we arrive." He patted my hand. "In the meantime, tell me about the girl and about your aunts. We won't arrive at our destination for another eighty minutes, and that's only if they're running on time."

"I will, on the condition that thee then relates the essence of Currie's falling-out with thy mother."

"I promise."

I pressed my hand to the window to gaze out into the dark as we clattered along. As the lights of a village came into view, three long blasts of the train's whistle split the air, and then we were past it. I turned back to David.

"Neither Tilly nor Drusilla married. To everyone's surprise,

Tilly—at the age of fifty-eight—took Frannie in after she was orphaned when she was only two, fourteen years ago."

"Why the surprise?"

"Because of Tilly's age, of course, and because Dru is the maternal one, not her sister. Dru bakes and quilts and loves her cup of hot chocolate. She adores children and taught them for many years. These days she seems wistful around little ones."

"Wishing she'd had her own." He nibbled on a hand-sized meat pie.

"Like that, yes," I said. "You'll see."

"How old is Drusilla?"

"Let's see, she'd be seventy-five by now, and Tilly is seventy-two. Daddy was the baby of the family. Anyway, it was Tilly who insisted on taking in the poor tyke. Tilly's always seemed stern and critical. In fact, she never lets up chastising Dru for doing this or that the wrong way."

"How does Drusilla take it?"

"She smiles and ignores her sister. Daddy has hinted that Tilly suffered a deep hurt in her past. Some who have gone through that adopt a cold manner as a shield. Tilly wouldn't want to become wounded again."

"You're a wise woman, Rosie. Many people do precisely that, in my experience."

I patted out a wrinkle in my dress. "Tilly cared very much for Frannie in her own way. She has to be devastated by the current turn of events."

"Who would murder a girl of sixteen, though?" He drained his small glass of port.

"That would be the question of the month, wouldn't it?" I watched more dots of light flash by in the inky darkness. "Frannie went to school, Tilly saw to that. West Falmouth is teeming with Quakers, as thee will see, and they have an excellent town school."

"And an academy for older children?"

"I am not positive about that. I believe Falmouth town has one. We'll find out soon enough."

David tidied up our supper things and set the basket on the floor. "I suppose it's my turn to divulge family history."

"I admit to some curiosity." In fact, ever since he'd mentioned

Currie at the reception, the fact that he'd talked about him only once previously had been pecking at my subconscious. Why was that?

"Very well." He stretched out his legs and slung his arm lightly over my shoulders. "It's been, let's see, three years, I think—before I was fortunate enough to set eyes on your lovely countenance for the first time." He squeezed my shoulder. "My brother has had his share of troubles. I believe he has some kind of disorder with his eyes or his brain, which makes it difficult for him to read well. Mother wanted him to go into law, but Currie couldn't manage the studies, try as he might."

"I've seen that syndrome, too, often in people of high intelligence. It's more common than we think, and unfortunately such souls are often labeled as stupid or lazy."

"Yes, and my mother would be one of those labelers. Father was more understanding and offered to find Currie a suitable position in his shoe manufacturing company, but the damage had been done to my brother's view of his own capabilities. Currie fell in with an unscrupulous man who claimed he had a scheme to develop a malarial marshland in Florida into saleable properties. My brother lost a great deal of money and had the nerve to ask my parents for more, as a loan on his inheritance. Father was willing, but Mother insisted they not rescue him. She and Currie had the worst falling-out, with much name calling on both sides. It ended in her telling him to leave and never come back."

I laid my hand on his knee. "I hate to see families fall apart."

"It was painful."

"But that was her relationship with him. Didn't thee or Herbert communicate on thy own?"

David grimaced. "Currie insulted all of us before he left. By then I had my medical degree. My practice was keeping me very busy, so I had distractions. I now regret not trying to find him, to come to an understanding."

I nodded. I still didn't understand why he hadn't shared this story with me before, during all our many hours of talking and growing to know each other. Did David not trust me with his past? Was he uneasy about it? This wasn't the time to bring it up, but I wanted to before long.

"Mother threw herself into her charitable works with the church as well as into trying to find me a suitable wife." He gave a throaty laugh. "She didn't know I was fully capable of finding one entirely on my own."

"How did your father handle Currie's departure?"

"It cut him to the bone, Rose, but he wasn't able to prevail with Mother to mend fences. I don't know if he tried to reach Currie privately. Did you see how overjoyed Father was today?"

"I did. I know you didn't have much time with your brother, but did you learn what he's been doing in Wood's Holl?"

David twisted to face me. "I didn't. Perhaps during our stay on the Cape I can make some inquiries. I hope it's a legal enterprise, whatever he's up to."

"He mentioned the entertainment industry. I didn't know Cape Cod had much of one."

He laughed. "God only knows what he meant by that."

It had been a full day, and it wasn't over yet. Many questions had yet to be answered but they would have to wait until our arrival. The telegram had said to come urgently, but what we could do tonight about Frannie's death remained a mystery. I let the rocking of the train and the warm comfort of my husband's arm lull me into sleep.

FIVE

DESPITE OUR BEING ON AN EXPRESS TRAIN to Wood's Holl, David had prevailed upon the conductor to make a stop in West Falmouth, as it was dark and our wedding night. The tracks passed directly past the West Falmouth station, so the conductor agreed with David rather than force us to hire a conveyance at the train's terminus to come directly back to West Falmouth.

On our way, I kept hoping for a glimpse of moonlight shining on the ocean, but the tracks had been laid woefully inland. It was nearly nine when we stepped down from the huffing, steaming train. David carried both valises, while I managed my birthing satchel, into which I had wedged all manner of additional personal items, plus a new book each as gifts for my aunts. I also toted the dinner basket. We were fortunate to have arrived during a full moon. An owl made its "who-who-who-who whoo, whoo" query from a nearby tree and a cricket chirped away.

"Is it far?" David asked. He glanced around, perplexed. The railroad station was a small one, and ours hadn't been a scheduled stop, so no one was about. "Will we need to hire a driver?"

"Not at all. My aunts live in a modest house on Baker Street, and it's a mere fifty yards from here. If we'd stayed on the train, we would have ridden directly in back of their home in the next minute." On the train I'd studied the map Tilly had sent last month when I'd told her of our plans. I thought I knew my way, despite never having been here before. "I wonder if they'll have the local detective there to inform us of the facts of the case."

"The telegram was certainly urgent in tone."

Off we trudged, rapping the knocker shortly thereafter. Dru opened the door, spilling a flood of lamplight out onto the landing. Shorter than I, she was round of figure and her fluffy snow-white hair formed a nimbus around her face.

"My dearest Rose, I can't tell thee how glad I am thee made the trip. And this gentleman must be thy new husband, David Dodge." She extended a hand to each of us, but it was a bit awkward, as our hands were full, and David stood on the step below mine.

"I am pleased to meet you, Miss Drusilla," David said.

"Aunt Dru, can we come in, please?" I asked. My lids rasped against my eyes from my nap.

"Of course, dears. Silly me." She stepped back and out of the way. "Please enter."

We made our way into the sitting room, which was full with books, needlepoint supplies, and more tatted doilies than a person would ever need in two lifetimes. It was empty of any kind of law enforcement officer, however. We set down our burdens.

"Now, how about a proper greeting." Dru held out her arms to me and enveloped me in a bosomy, rose-water-scented embrace. She let me go and beamed up at David. "Well, isn't thee a handsome drink of water? Give an old lady a kiss, will thee?"

She was awfully chipper for someone whose sister's ward had been murdered. I hadn't seen Dru in years, since the last time she came up to Lawrence to visit. Her behavior seemed odd.

David leaned down to buss her cheek.

"Sit down, sit down, and I'll put on the kettle."

I cleared my throat. "Aunt Dru, I'd like to—"

"Oh! Visit the necessary, of course. Follow me, darling. It's just at the back. Tilly came into a spot of money and insisted we install one of the newfangled water closets. It's all the rage among the wealthy Friends around here. She did it for our comfort, of course, not for fashion's sake."

I followed her down a hallway. From the back I saw that part of her fluffy hair covered a bald spot almost like she was disguising a tonsure. She kept prattling on even after I'd closed the door, but I ignored her. I'd forgotten how chatty she was. She'd been to visit us in Lawrence perhaps a decade ago, and both she and Tilly used to come more often when I was small.

Much relieved and washed up, I returned to the sitting room to find my aunt fussing over David, offering him cookies, pouring his tea, and generally looking happy as a hen to have someone to take care of. One might think there hadn't been a violent death in the family at all. Had I dreamed the urgent telegram? Or maybe this was Dru's way of coping with grief, to simply shut it away and pretend it hadn't happened.

"David, do you want to freshen up, or whatever men call it?" I asked him.

He stood. "Good idea."

I pointed him down the hall. "Last door on the left. Dru, what happened to Frannie?" I asked when he'd gone. "How did she die? Was she in trouble?"

"It's all a confusion, my dear. There is so much to tell, and so little, as well." She blinked and smiled.

What? She had certainly confused me. "Where's Aunt Tilly?"

Her smile slid completely away. "The poor dear. She's a complete wreck. I summoned our friends Sadie and Huldah Gifford to fetch her. They know how to calm her better than I. We've lived together too long, Tilly and me. For someone who usually strikes others as cold and stern, Tilly's heart is broken over poor Frannie's death. Mine is, too, of course. We raised the girl together." She sniffed back a tear. "But my sister had a special attachment to her ward, and she's taking it hard."

"What about the detective working on Frannie's murder? Thy telegram was most urgent that we should travel tonight. I expected him to be here." I sank onto a love seat.

"That will have to wait until tomorrow, dear."

So we could have stayed in a plush hotel room in Lawrence tonight, after all, and enjoyed the physical delights of being married. I sighed inwardly but resolved to make the best of it. "I've never heard the story of how Tilly came to take charge of Frannie. My family never made the trip down here, more's the pity." I'd have to ask my father why we hadn't come to West Falmouth to spend time with his sisters.

Dru blinked her rheumy blue eyes, so much like my father's except for the rheum. "That's a tale for another time, Rose. And it's rightly Tilly's to tell."

I glimpsed a framed photograph on a side table. It portrayed a girl of about twelve with dark curls, big dark eyes, and a spirited smile. The cheerful expression was unusual in such posed pictures, where the subjects were normally instructed to maintain a solemn demeanor.

"That's our Frannie, before she finished growing," Dru said with a sad smile. "I wish we'd had a photograph made more recently. She was quite a beauty, Rose."

David sat next to me on his return. "Is the girl's death truly a case of homicide, Miss Drusilla?"

I smiled to hear him address her as "Miss Drusilla." All on his own he'd come up with the same convention the rest of the village also used, at least the non-Quakers. If people called both her and Tilly "Miss Carroll," there would be no end of confusion.

"Enough of this Miss business. Thee must call me Dru, David."

He smiled. "Perhaps I shall, by and by."

"At any rate," Dru went on, "homicide is what the nice policeman said when he came here."

A person's death caused by another person, whether purposefully or not. "Will thee tell us all about it?" I selected a gingersnap and nibbled at its perfect spicy, crunchy sweetness.

"I'll do my best. Thee will get nothing coherent out of my sister, that's certain."

"Dru told me Tilly is distraught and is being cared for by their friends nearby," I told David. "And we won't be able to speak with the detective until tomorrow."

He raised his eyebrows in return. I knew he was thinking what I had about not having had to rush down here. I could only shrug.

Dru poured tea for us and herself, then settled into what looked like her usual armchair. "They found poor Frannie in the bay."

"Today?" I asked.

"Yes."

"Could her death have been accidental?" David leaned his elbows on his knees and clasped his hands.

"Apparently not, but the fellow didn't give us any details."

Killed and dumped in the bay? Or attacked and left to drown. Whichever, it was an awful way to go.

"Tell us more about Frannie, Dru, if thee will," I urged. We would learn the horrible facts of the death in the morning, I was certain.

"It was like this. Dear Frannie had completed her school through eighth grade, what, two years ago? She didn't really have the aptitude to go on to the Lawrence Academy in Falmouth, even though other girls from our Meeting attend there. For the last two years she's been working for Mrs. Annie Boyce tying tags."

"What's that, pray tell?" David asked.

"Women formerly gathered in Annie's living room or at other

women's homes. They add strings to the tags that label all kinds of goods. It's become quite the successful industry for Annie and the ladies and girls she employs, and she has an actual factory now down by the train station."

"We must have walked past it on our way here. So Frannie made a bit of money," I said. "That's good. Tell us more about her. Was she social or retiring? What did she enjoy doing? What was she like? I'm sorry I hadn't seen her since Tilly brought her to Lawrence when she was little." I would have been in my teen years then, as Frannie had been about ten years younger than I.

Dru smiled sadly. "As I said, she didn't seem to have the brains to continue studying. But that girlie was life smart. She was a dab hand at fixing anything. Frannie could listen to a song once, pick up the words and tune, and sing it back in her lilting voice like she'd been practicing for a year. She had lots of energy, and she was a strong little thing, and so graceful, too. And my, oh my, could she read people. I've seen her tilt the dark curls on her pretty head, regard someone — anyone, of any age or stature — and say something full of wisdom about them, or confront them about a false statement."

"How about friends?" David asked. "Who did she spend time with when she wasn't working or doing chores? Girlfriends? A young man, perhaps?"

My aunt tapped the arm of her chair. "There's the rub, David. She'd been stepping out with young Reuben Baxter. Boy's a clam-digger. He's not a Friend and in fact is a full-blooded Indian."

"Oh?" David asked.

"Yes. The local tribe is called the Wampanoags. In a way, you would hardly know its members to look at them. They have regular names and wear conventional clothing, although their skin might be a bit darker than us palefaces. With all the people in this area who spend their lives near or on the ocean, though, we have some pretty dark-skinned white folks, not to mention the more swarthy newcomers from Italy and Portugal. So the Indians can pass, as it were, unless you know their heritage for a fact. The boy's father, Joseph Baxter, is a local businessman's handyman — one of several servants he employs, with all his riches — and his wife is a midwife."

An Indian midwife? That was a woman I wanted to meet.

22

"Was Miss Tilly happy about Frannie's beau?" David asked.

"Not particularly. Thee must understand, my sister was only concerned for Frannie's welfare, and rightly so, as it turned out. The Baxter boy has himself a temper."

"Thee is saying the police think Reuben killed Frannie." I leaned forward.

"They hinted as much." Dru bobbed her head.

"But why?" I pressed.

"That's why we asked thee down here, Rose. We need help getting to the bottom of this. It's going to destroy Tilly if we don't." Dru stood. "Now, if thee will spare me thy husband for a few minutes, I'd like him to walk me over to Huldah and Sadie's."

David, ever polite, also rose.

"To fetch Tilly?" I asked.

"No. She and I will be sleeping there tonight." My aunt blushed. "We thought, since you two missed your wedding night in a fancy hotel, the least we could do was give you this house to yourselves tonight. Sadie has plenty of beds."

David glanced my way with a confused expression. "We were going to continue on to the Tower House Hotel in Falmouth, Miss Dru."

I gazed back. "But we aren't certain they have a room for us tonight, and it's been such a long day."

He squinted at me. "It is late." He parceled out his words. "We may as well stay here."

I tilted my head and smiled. "It's a truly lovely gesture, Aunt Dru, and the best wedding gift thee could have given us. We both thank thee."

"First door on the right upstairs." She pointed up. "It's my room, but the sheets are freshly clean, and I left out clean towels. You'll find breakfast things in the kitchen, and an apple pie, as well. We'll see you at Meeting for Worship at ten o'clock tomorrow, I trust? Thee can't miss the Meetinghouse. It's down the lane from here, surrounded by the burying grounds. We'll save thee and David seats next to us in our usual pew. We sit in the front row, fair warning."

So we'd be on display. *Oh, well.* My aunts were longtime members and deserved their preferred seats. "We will be there," I said. "What about a key to the door of the house?"

She gave a laugh like small bells jingling. "It's in the keyhole, but no one bothers to lock their doors in West Falmouth, Rose. There's simply no need."

"But what about talking with the detective?" I asked. "Won't we be doing that early, perhaps?"

"All in due time, Rose." Dru turned toward the door. "I shall return, dear wife."

My breath rushed in and I clapped my hand to my mouth. If Frannie was indeed murdered, where was the killer? Had he fled town, or was he lurking outside to do more harm?

"Be careful, will thee?" I murmured to David.

He touched my cheek. "Yes, wife, I will." David held out his elbow to Dru. "Your carriage awaits, madam."

SIX

FIRST SUNSHINE PEEKED THROUGH lacy bedroom curtains at the same time as the first train rumbled by outside, rattling the windows. It didn't bother me. So what if we weren't to see the officer on Frannie's case until later? I luxuriated in the arms of my still slumbering husband, my hair loose on the pillow. What a true gift Aunt Dru had bestowed upon us, letting us cavort in our first marital bed free of cares.

And cavort we had. Both slowly and exuberantly, with care and with abandon, arousing sensations beyond limits. I'd examined nearly every inch of his fine body — the first grown man I'd ever set eyes on in all his naked glory — and he mine. I now slid quietly around to spoon my back with his front, stifling a laugh to see our clothing tossed around the room by the hurricane of our passion.

In the light of day I idly wondered why my aunts had summoned me. Did they already know the local force was not up to solving Frannie's murder? With any luck, the authorities would be competent and would solve the case promptly, and I wouldn't need to become involved except to help comfort Tilly in her grief. I could have spent a week not leaving this very room, as long as David was in it, too.

The man behind me stirred, then murmured the same sound he made while eating a favorite delicacy. He tightened his arms and kissed the hollow below my ear.

"Good morning, wife," he growled.

"Mmm. A fine morning it is, husband." I rolled back to face him, and an entire hour passed before we rose from the bed.

By the time I'd cleaned up, garbed myself in a day dress, and tidied our belongings and the bed, he had breakfast under way. He'd started the stove, found coffee supplies, and had a potful waiting. He'd also located milk, eggs, jam, and bread, and stood barefooted with an apron tied over his shirt and pants, stirring eggs in a bowl. Two plates, mugs, and forks were set on the kitchen table, which was already covered with a red gingham cloth.

"Madam, your breakfast will arrive shortly." His cheeks were rosy and his hair damp. "Please sit and I will pour your morning libation."

"My, what a fine hotel. But seriously, David, thee doesn't have to wait on me," I protested. I sat, anyway.

"I insist, Mrs. Dodge."

"Oh, now, let's not make a habit of that. In my mind Clarinda is Mrs. Dodge, not me." When I saw him pull his mouth to the side, I hurried to clarify. "I only mean the appellation is new for me, David. Of course I am Rose Dodge now, and I'm proud to claim the name. But as a Friend, thee knows full well we don't consort with titles."

"Of course I know. Rose Dodge it is." A minute later he loaded up my plate with a flourish, filled his own, and joined me at the table. After we joined hands for a moment of silent grace, he asked, "Odd, isn't it, that your aunts wanted us to hurry down here? There doesn't seem to be a bit of urgency in the air."

"I know. I thought at the very least they would have made an early appointment with the detective. And did it strike you that Dru didn't seem to be grieving?"

"I admit it did. She is elderly, though, and perhaps is suffering from a lack of mental acuity."

"I suppose so."

By eight thirty we'd eaten our breakfast and cleaned up the kitchen. "Fancy a quick walk to the closest water?" he asked, sitting to don his shoes.

"Please, as long as we leave here ready to proceed straight back to the Meetinghouse."

"I've got my pocket watch, so we won't be late."

I ran upstairs to grab my bonnet. I was about to run back down as quickly but slowed at an open door I hadn't focused on last evening. I peeked into what had to be Frannie's room. I didn't want to take the time now, but I promised myself to come back to it later. Perhaps a thorough search would at least give me a clue into her life and character, if not the identity of her murderer.

Not five minutes later we'd arrived at an inlet on Buzzard's Bay, which I could spy beyond a spit of land. The tide was out, leaving the inlet a shallow pool. Despite it being First Day, clam-diggers dug their wide forks in the mud for the delicious bivalves.

"Didn't Aunt Dru say Frannie's young man was a clam-digger?" I asked.

"She did. Reuben Baxter."

"I wonder if we're looking at him." In front of us were adult women, young men, children, and even a plodding old man, all digging in the mud. Most wore knit caps, old jackets, and high boots. But would Reuben be working if his sweetheart had died the day before?

David laughed. "I wish you luck identifying any of these searchers unless you already know them."

Two of the large saltwater raptors called fish hawks dipped and soared above, and the smell of salt water on the fresh breeze made me nearly swoon.

"Does thee love the sea like I do?" I asked, my hand tucked through David's arm as we strolled on.

"I do love it. I'll tell you, I'm surprised Currie has been living down here. He had quite the terrifying experience in the ocean during his young teen years, and I'm sure he has neither been in the water nor out on a boat since."

"Oh? Do tell." The floodgate on stories about his brother had lifted, apparently. I looked forward to learning more about David's childhood, and his brother's as well.

"We were out at a family gathering on Plum Island. My brother was fourteen and I was ten. True to form, Mother was paying attention only to the other ladies, Father played football in the sand with the older boys and my uncles, and Currie and I were left to get up to mischief with our younger cousins." He strolled on a bit, then paused at the West Falmouth dock. "It was this time of year. A big storm was either approaching or departing the area, and the Atlantic was high and rough."

"Let me guess. Currie decided to go for a swim."

David frowned. "Yes. He was a good swimmer, but conditions were treacherous. Do you know what undertow is, and riptides?"

"I've heard the terms. Explain them, please."

"Undertow pulls a swimmer underwater. Plum Island Beach in places has a steep drop-off, so the water becomes deep immediately. The conditions can lend themselves to undertow. A riptide is when, sometimes due to storms, a swimmer can get out beyond the breakers and not be able to swim straight back to shore. Many have drowned from both situations."

I kept my silence, but I stroked his arm with my other hand.

"We nearly lost my brother that day. He floundered and called out, but we children had traveled a ways down the beach in our play. I yelled and waved my arms at the adults. I couldn't get their attention. Currie was the oldest among us young ones. I wanted to swim out and save him, but I wasn't yet very tall or strong. I knew if I tried we'd both drown."

"What happened?"

"A passing fishing boat saw my brother's distress and was able to pull close enough to toss him a life preserver. My mother never bought fish from anyone other than that man again."

A clear sign that Clarinda was grateful for not losing her son, and that she loved him, even if she had trouble showing it. "The experience must have scarred Currie," I said. That, combined with difficulties in school and an overbearing and critical mother—despite her gratitude that he hadn't been lost—could have contributed to whatever trouble he was having as an adult.

"I believe it did, Rose. I do believe it did."

SEVEN

A BIT WINDBLOWN AND FLUSH of cheek after our walk, David and I slid into a front-row pew next to Tilly and Dru in the West Falmouth Meetinghouse at a few minutes before ten o'clock. After I squeezed Tilly's bony hand, she turned her black-bonneted head and gave me one of the saddest looks I'd ever witnessed. I bobbed my head once in understanding. She folded her hands in her lap and closed her eyes.

I gave a quick glance to my other side, where David's eyes were also shut, his hands resting loosely on his thighs, his body still. My heart nearly burst at having married this man—a person with few prior experiences of silent worship, an avowed Unitarian—who was willing to join me at least occasionally in seeking for God's Light after the manner of Friends.

Before settling into the silence, which was still full of shoes thumping and benches creaking as members hurried in, I gazed around the Meetinghouse. In construction, it was nearly identical to our building in Amesbury. It featured two sides full of pews with a center divider now raised but able to be lowered. It had a lofty ceiling and an upstairs balcony above the entry hall for additional seating. The lower part of the walls here, though, were lined with wood paneling where ours were plain, and the building had one fewer tall window on each side. Paned sliding windows could close off the upstairs, where ours was open above the half wall. The entire interior presented a more elaborate and darker face than Amesbury's simple, light-filled worship rooms. The differences didn't matter. I could sit in expectant waiting on God wherever I was.

When I worshipped in Amesbury, experiencing Friends' gradually quieting was something I craved. West Falmouth Meeting was no exception. Latecomers sat. The rustling of clothing stilled. Benches ceased creaking. The children of the community were ushered out by a couple for First Day School. All around me breathing slowed and, as John Whittier so eloquently put it, the outer world fell away and left us God alone.

A pang invaded my quieting. For eight years I had been worshiping with Amesbury Friends. I knew the women's business meeting planned to read me out—that is, expel me—because of my marriage to David, who was not a member of our religious society. The more liberal Lawrence Meeting, where I had worshipped growing up, had allowed our Meeting for Worship for Marriage to go forward under their care, but when I returned to Amesbury I would not be welcome in our beautiful and peaceful Meetinghouse. I could write a letter of appeal to be reinstated, and I planned to do so without delay. I knew John Whittier would argue my cause with the women. Still, I would have some weeks of empty First Days until they allowed me to return. I blew out a breath. That was neither here nor now.

But the rejection, on top of Currie bringing both strife and joy into our wedding reception and then my being called to solve a murder, tinged what should have been my day of joy. If I were a more negative person, I might wonder if it all added up to a bad omen for my marriage in the years ahead. On the contrary, I tended to go through life with a measure of optimism that things would turn out for the best. I would not let darkness shade my love for David and our life together. I settled my shoulders and my mind and returned to the worship at hand, beginning with holding Frannie's soul in the Light of God.

My reverie was interrupted some time later when a sonorous voice dropped into the silence. I opened my eyes. An older man had risen from the facing bench, the seats reserved for the elders of the Meeting. He clasped his hands in front of a plain suit but one cut from very fine cloth, I could see even from here. His flat-brimmed hat and chinstrap beard marked him as a Friend. The quality of his shoes, the cloth of his shirt, the cut of his suit, every inch of him revealed that this was a Quaker with considerable financial resources. Except . . . was a button missing from the coat? I peered. Maybe he'd simply forgotten to fasten it. I imagined someone like him wouldn't go too long without having a repair done, unless he was slovenly about his appearance.

"Some of us are blessed with long lives in which to do God's blessed work. Others are placed on this earth for a shorter period of time. Our Frannie was one of those." His voice was pious and somber. "May she rest in peace, and may we honor her memory as we continue without her." He sat with a thump.

He'd brought the outer world right back inside. Tilly's shoulders shook. Dru's arm crept around her and I took my angular aunt's hand in mine as I held Tilly in the Light. Being me, I also held the local detective in God's Light, whomever he might be, that his investigation proceed with truth and all due dispatch. Finding Frannie's killer wouldn't bring her back, but it might provide some measure of solace to her devastated guardian.

The rest of the worship reverted to silence and ended with Friends exchanging the handshake of fellowship. Quaker after Quaker approached my aunts to offer condolences. David and I were introduced to each. A couple who were about my parents' age hung back until the crush was over.

"Thee must be niece Rose," the woman said when she drew near. "I'm Sadie Gifford, and this is my husband, Huldah."

"I'm so pleased to meet thee, Sadie, and thee, Huldah. May I introduce my husband, David Dodge?"

They exchanged greetings, plus handshakes for the men.

"Rose, we hope thee and David will join us for First Day dinner whenever Tilly and Dru are finished here." Sadie smiled at both of us. "We'd love to get to know the newly wedded couple better." She lowered her voice. "And I don't want the grieving sisters even thinking about cooking at a time like this."

I glanced at David, who nodded, as I knew he would. "We would be honored, and I thank thee, Sadie," I said.

"That's settled, then. Huldah, shall we be off?" She took his arm and they bustled away.

I smiled to myself, resettling my spectacles on the bridge of my nose. She reminded me of my mother, warm and hospitable but with a no-nonsense air about her.

The man who had offered the sole message during worship came up to a still-seated Tilly and took her hand.

"My dear Tilly." His beard was rust-colored, with the pale green eyes that often accompanied that coloring. The skin was puffy around his eyes, not from sorrow, I thought, but from excessive indulgences.

"Abial, we thank thee for thy words," Dru murmured.

Tilly raised a gaunt face and stood, letting him help her up. "I don't believe Frannie's soul will rest easy anywhere until her murderer is apprehended."

Abial's eyebrows went up but he didn't react otherwise. "Of course, Tilly."

"May I present our niece, Rose Carroll, and her husband of less than a day, David Dodge? Or, Rose Dodge, I should have said. Rose and David, this is Abial Latting, one of this Meeting's stalwarts and benefactors."

"Many felicitations to thee, Rose, and to thee, David." He and David shook hands. "It is a great blessing that Rose came to provide comfort and solace to her dear relatives, and that thee accompanied her, so soon after the happy occasion." Abial didn't quite smile but his expression was welcoming.

Or at least it seemed he wanted it to come across that way. I shook off a feeling of unease. The man appeared to be a successful businessman, and he was certainly a Friend. I didn't need to indulge my suspicious tendencies. On the other hand, if the police were correct, someone around here had killed a young woman. Perhaps suspicions were exactly what I needed to dwell on.

EIGHT

BY HALF PAST TWELVE, I stood in the hallway of Sadie and Huldah's home with Tilly before we joined the others for dinner. I'd wanted a word with her alone.

"Aunt Tilly, I am so very sorry about Frannie. I wish I had known her better."

Haunted eyes gazed at me from a face the color of bleached linen. "I wish thee had, too, Rose. Thank thee for coming so quickly. I hadn't meant to interrupt thy marriage celebration."

I had to strain to hear her near whisper. "It's all right. We are glad to be here." I embraced her, feeling her bony shoulders through the black cotton of her dress.

She didn't hug me back, as if it would take too much effort.

"Let's go in." I took her hand.

"I can't eat," she said.

But she let me lead her to the dining table in a spacious room whose large windows faced the inlet. Sadie beckoned to Tilly to sit by her and I took a seat next to David. With my aunts, a middle-aged woman whom Sadie introduced as Marie Deorocki, and the Giffords, we held hands in silence around the table. No modest house, Sadie and Huldah's home was a new construction with a tasteful light hand in its woodwork and design. The decor—rugs, lamps, furniture—was understated and of high quality. It was the same effect David and I had tried to achieve in the new house he'd had built for us, which we would begin living in upon our return to Amesbury. It even had room for me to have my midwifery office. We had finished decorating and furnishing it shortly before we were married.

Sadie, to my right, squeezed my hand to signal the end of our grace. "I made a very simple seafood stew, and we have a lovely tomato salad courtesy of Marie's mother's garden."

Tilly murmured her thanks but sat slumped in her seat. David and I exchanged a look. At her advanced age, poor Tilly shouldn't have to endure the murder of a cherished young person.

"Marie's a fellow resident of Amesbury," Sadie now said as she ladled stew from a white tureen into wide bowls.

"Thee is?" I asked, surprised. I pushed up my spectacles. "I don't think I've seen thee there."

"I've lived in Amesbury all my life." Marie adjusted her own glasses and spread her napkin on the lap of her yellow dress. "But I'm a Roman Catholic, and my children are all grown now, so our paths haven't crossed. I've heard of your escapades, Mrs. Dodge."

Escapades? I grimaced inwardly. "Please call me Rose."

"I don't know about that," Marie said. "Mrs. Gifford has been after me to do the same, but it wouldn't seem right."

"I hope thee will," I said. "What brings thee to the Cape?"

"My mother is ailing. I came down a few weeks ago to nurse her back to health, if I can."

"Her mother Judith lives next door," Sadie said. "We thought we should at least introduce you three Amesburyites."

"And introduce thee to Judith's prizewinning tomatoes," Huldah added. "I try to garden, but the soil is so sandy, it's hard to grow what I'd like."

I liked the look of Huldah. He wore suspenders over a rumpled homespun shirt and, with his mussed hair, eyeglasses, and a pencil behind his ear, had the air of an absentminded professor. Aunt Dru had said he was a lawyer, and from the appearance of this house, he must make a pretty penny. He was also a Friend, and it showed in his plain dress and manner.

"I don't know how Judith does it, but these fruits pop with flavor," he added.

The plate of thinly sliced tomatoes above my knife was adorned with flecks of parsley and bits of black pepper, and had been drizzled with oil and perhaps something else. My eggs and toast were a long-ago memory and I was dying to try the salad. But the hot portion of the meal should come first. I waited for Huldah to pass a basket of warm rolls and Sadie to take her first bite before I dipped into the stew.

I'd opened my mouth to speak when David beat me to it.

"This is a most delicious stew, Mrs. Gifford," he exclaimed. "The broth is wonderful." He rolled the tastes around on his tongue. "I detect dill, parsley, and a hint of pepper. Perhaps a bit of citrus. Is it lime?"

Sadie laughed. "So thee married a chef, Rose? I had no idea."

David's cheeks pinked up, but he smiled. "I enjoy cooking for relaxation."

"He's good at it." I smiled fondly at him. "And he's a doctor, as thee might know, so the job can be difficult and tense at times."

"I hope you'll share your recipe," he said to Sadie.

"Only if thee promises to call me Sadie, not Mrs. Gifford."

"Very well."

Sadie cocked her head. "Thee is not a Friend, then?"

"No," David said. "I worship with the Unitarians, much to my Episcopalian mother's chagrin."

"One can only imagine." Our hostess smiled at him. "Thy faith doesn't matter to us."

"No, it certainly doesn't," Huldah agreed.

"But Rose, what do Amesbury Friends make of thy union with this man?" Sadie asked.

I scrunched up my nose. "The women's business meeting is displeased and informed me I would be read out of Meeting. I shall appeal upon my return and pray for their lenience."

Sadie cocked her head. "I would be happy to write thee a letter of support if thee wishes. I have clerked our women's meeting for many years. I am considered in some circles a rather weighty Friend."

I brought my hand to my cheek at this unexpected gift. "I would be most pleased for such a letter." I gave her the name of the clerk she could address her letter to.

"I shall mail it in the morning, and happily so. I hope it helps in thy reinstatement. It's been a decade since we in West Falmouth abandoned the archaic practice of shunning those who marry out."

Tilly sat at Sadie's right. The crevices in her face seemed to have deepened even since this morning. She'd at most poked at her stew. I hadn't seen her take a single bite.

"Aunt Tilly, the stew is quite good, and it will sit easily in thy stomach," I said gently. "Please try it."

She laid her spoon on the table. "How can I eat when my Frannie will never eat again?" Her eyes filled. "When she was taken too soon, her young life extinguished before her time?"

"Oh, Till, dear." Dru's voice was full of anguish. "We must go on. She would want us to, thee knows."

Sadie and Huldah murmured their agreement. I'd only met Frannie once when she was a wee thing, so I kept quiet.

Tilly fixed her dark eyes on me. "Rose, thee must promise to find my girl's killer."

I swallowed. "I will do my best, Aunt Tilly." It was a heavy responsibility to take on, but what else could I do?

"Please eat, Friend Tilly. I used one of the fish thee caught last week," Sadie said, also softly. "Remember thee had too many? I kept it on ice. And I added the scallops thee likes and some clams, too."

"Tilly likes going out in her boat alone to fish," Dru explained to David.

"I fish, too, every chance I get." Marie gazed at Tilly. "I think I know what you're going through, Miss Tilly. Let's go have a rest, shall we?" She stood and whispered something to Sadie.

I was surprised to see Tilly agree to let herself be helped up and ushered out by a near stranger. After I heard a door click shut somewhere in the house, I glanced at David.

"All this might be overwhelming for her," he said. "Attending worship and being in a social setting is a great deal to handle for someone in deep grief."

"Marie lost her father last year, whom she was very close to," Sadie said. "And she works with the less fortunate in Amesbury. She's a keenly empathetic woman. She'll get a bite into Tilly, mark my words. Please excuse me while I dish out a bowl of broth for our grieving friend."

"I thank thee," Dru said. The level in her own bowl was steadily dropping. She was a woman who didn't let sadness come between her and her appetite.

NINE

AFTER SADIE RETURNED from delivering the soup, I asked, "The man who spoke in Meeting, Abial Latting. Is he a businessman? He appears to be quite wealthy."

"Thee could say that." Sadie frowned. "He owns a fleet of ships and has his finger in several other enterprises, as well."

"Sadie doesn't approve of Abial's ostentatiousness, but he has been quite generous with the Meeting," Huldah added. "He's donated money to maintain the building and to assist in improving the graveyard."

Dru raised a single white eyebrow. "If I may say so, Tilly and I, and several of the ladies at the library, also harbor a concern for his interest in the accumulation of funds and material possessions. It perhaps exceeds the bounds of Friendly propriety."

"Oh?" I asked.

"Yes," Sadie said. "As thee knows, Huldah and I have been blessed with a comfortable income, but we still try to live modestly. Abial? Not so much. He's quite lavish."

"People in our town perhaps imbue him with a power he doesn't deserve," Dru added.

"He also does not always conduct himself with modesty," Huldah said. "One hears rumors of his proclivities from many corners."

"What do you mean by proclivities?" David asked.

Sadie and Huldah exchanged a look. Sadie spoke. "He's been known to—"

A knock sounded on the front door. Huldah rose to answer it.

Known to what? I snuck a quizzical glance at David, but he only shrugged. Of course he knew no more than I.

Huldah returned, frowning, with a neatly dressed man following him. Our host cleared his throat.

"Pardon me, everyone, but this is Detective Merritt with the County Sheriff's office. He wondered if he might have a word with Tilly, but I told him she was indisposed. He, ah, rather insisted on coming in, anyway."

"Tilly is most certainly indisposed, Edwin," Sadie said. "Would thee like to sup on First Day fish stew with us?" Sadie clearly knew him personally, but then, West Falmouth was a much smaller town than Amesbury.

A stocky compact man with wavy hair the color of beach sand, the detective blinked. "No, thank you, Mrs. Gifford. I have dined. Miss Carroll, perhaps I might speak with you, instead."

Dru finished buttering her bread before answering. "Sit thyself down, Edwin. Whatever thee wants to ask me, thee can say it in the company of my friends and family. I harbor no secrets." She cupped her hand around her mouth and said to me in an entirely audible whisper, "I taught him when he was in short pants."

Edwin's color rose, but he sat where Tilly had been. Sadie introduced David and me. Edwin peered at me when he heard my name.

"Would you be Miss Rose Carroll of Amesbury?"

Kevin must have acted fast.

"I am the former Rose Carroll, still of Amesbury. David and I were married yesterday, and my surname is now Dodge." I peered back at him. Curiously, the man had one blue eye and one green, a sight I'd never seen until now.

"I was going to pay you a visit tomorrow, ma'am," he said. "Your friend Donovan suggested I seek you out."

"Here I am," I said. "Can thee tell me what time of day is Frannie supposed to have died, and how?"

The detective blinked. "Perhaps we can discuss that at a more suitable time, Mrs. Dodge."

"Very well." I assumed he was taken aback by my forthrightness. I didn't mind. If I stopped investigating every time someone wasn't pleased by my questioning, I might as well not even begin. "How can I help thee?"

"I'm not quite sure. We're still gathering the facts, as you might imagine. But it's good to know someone with such honed detecting skills is in town and is also intimately familiar with the family in question."

Huldah cocked his head in interest, but he kept quiet.

"Which is why my sister desperately wanted Rose to come early." Dru popped in another bite of bread. "What did thee want to talk with Tilly about?" she asked Edwin after she swallowed.

"We are looking into the character and whereabouts of a Reuben Baxter," Edwin said. "Has he been at or near your house since Miss Isley disappeared?" he asked Dru.

"I told thee yesterday." Dru waved her bread in the air. "She didn't disappear. She went off to the tag shop like she always did on Sixth Day."

"But you said she didn't come home."

"She didn't." Dru calmly buttered another piece of bread.

"Weren't thee and Aunt Tilly worried when Frannie hadn't appeared by nightfall?" I asked.

The detective shot me a look of annoyance, which didn't seem quite fair, as he had as much as asked for my assistance.

"Not really, dear," my aunt said. "She sometimes spent the night with a friend from the tag shop."

Edwin checked his notebook. "A Miss Hazel Bowman."

"Yes, as I told thee yesterday. They'd been school chums."

"We have learned that Frannie was, in fact, not with Miss Bowman on the night in question at all," Edwin said.

"I suppose that explains it." Dru lifted a shoulder and dropped it.

"Explains what, Aunt Dru?" I prodded. The detective looked to be growing frustrated, and with good reason. I was, too.

"Well, she was dead, of course."

My aunt was not making sense. Was senile dementia affecting Dru? She'd acted normally up to now, although her lack of sorrow about Frannie's death both last night and today seemed odd to me. I hadn't spent time with my aunts in recent years. They were both getting on in age, which is why I wanted to bring David to meet them. Or maybe Drusilla was the kind of person who shut away her feelings and grieved in private later.

Edwin chose to ignore her circular logic—or whatever it was—and returned to his earlier question. "Miss Carroll, has Reuben Baxter been at or near your house since Friday morning?"

"I haven't seen him. Doesn't mean he wasn't there. I was returning books to their proper shelves at the library most of Sixth Day. Thee must know, Edwin, that we Quaker ladies founded the lending library not so long ago."

The detective's smile was a thin one. "Yes, Miss Carroll, I know. An excellent library it is, too. How about Joseph Baxter?"

"Abial Latting's handyman?" Dru asked. "What about him?"

"I would like to know if he has been around your abode in the same time period." Edwin leaned forward a bit.

"Why would he come to our house?"

Sadie cleared her throat. "If everyone is finished eating, I'll just clear. And, Detective, perhaps thee could postpone further interrogations until tomorrow. Of course we want Frannie's killer to be apprehended, but this is our day of rest, after all." She smiled genteelly, but there was no mistaking the steel in her voice, again reminding me of Mother. The two of them would get on famously.

"Yes, of course, Mrs. Gifford." He pushed his chair back so fast he had to catch it from falling. "Please forgive my intrusion. I thank you for your time, Miss Carroll. Miss . . . I mean, Mrs. Dodge, might I have a word with you in the hall?"

My hostess signaled for me to go. "I'll be right back to help," I said to Sadie.

"Let me." David stood and began to collect my dishes and his.

Near the front door, Merritt donned his hat. "Mrs. Dodge," he began.

"I don't suppose I could prevail on thee to call me Rose?"

"I'm afraid not. My pitiful brain needs the tidy order of social convention or it gets mightily confused. To start again, I hope you will consider keeping your eyes and ears alert for any information pertaining to this case. The only possible suspect we have is the beau, but it's a long shot."

"I will, in exchange for information. For example, how did Frannie die, specifically?" I kept my voice as soft as I could, both so it wouldn't carry to the dining room but also so Tilly wouldn't hear, since I had no idea which door she and Marie had disappeared behind.

"From a preliminary examination, the girl appears to have died from drowning. But we also discovered a laceration on her head. The state medical examiner is coming down from Boston to perform an autopsy tomorrow."

"Good. Her body washed up on which beach?"

"On our own Chappaquoit, yesterday morning."

"And was she at work all day on Sixth Day?"

"Yes, so says Mrs. Boyce. Time of death has as much as an eighteen-hour span, though."

"How unfortunate. Thee will keep me informed of the autopsy results, I trust. My aunts will know where to locate me."

"I promise to. Good day, Mrs. Dodge. And you can find me at Mr. Gifford's law office. He's agreed to give us a suite for the duration of the investigation, as there's no police department in town, nor in Falmouth at all. There's only the Cape District, so the Barnstable County Sheriff handles all matters criminal."

"Has thee investigated many homicides, Edwin?"

He grimaced. "Only two in the last decade. This area is generally peaceful and not rife with murderers." He let himself out.

I stood in the cool quiet of the hall, barely taking in the fine Oriental carpet runner, the mirror edged in teak above a small table for gloves and calling cards, the burnished mahogany of the newel post, the ticking of the tall case clock. What I saw was a spunky girl with a bashed head washed up from the bay with the incoming tide. Had she fallen or was she thrown overboard? Was she alive or dead when she hit the water? Was her death purposeful, violent? Or accidental? Did Edwin even have the skills to find the person who ended her life? I closed my eyes and held her memory in the Light of God, that it might lead me to assist the detective in his search for the truth.

TEN

SADIE REFUSED ALL HELP with the washing up, saying she found it relaxing and that she had a kitchen girl coming the next morning to do the pots and pans. Dru retired for a nap, so David and I took ourselves off for a tour of the town, such as it was.

"How did Dru seem to thee, David?" I asked as we strolled arm in arm in the fall sunshine. "Did she seem to be losing her senses a little?"

"A bit, yes. Or perhaps she was evading the detective's questions on purpose."

I glanced up at him. "On purpose? But why?"

"I don't know, Rosie. A girl the aunts raised was murdered. Drusilla doesn't seem particularly broken up about it. Please don't take offense, because I know she's your beloved aunt, but I wonder why she isn't grieving at least partly as much as Tilly is."

"It is perplexing, and I wondered the same. It could be senility setting in, rather than guilt about something."

"It certainly could be. She is, what, seventy-five? Although many old people remain clear of mind until they die."

"Like Orpha," I said, referencing my dear midwifery mentor who, blessedly, was still very much alive, albeit increasingly frail. "And John Whittier, of course."

"Precisely. Still, as you well know, senile dementia is common among those with seventy or more years behind them."

We passed a large mansard-roofed house and then a more modest home.

"Last night Dru refused to tell me how Tilly came to take in Frannie," I said. "I think thee was out of the room when I asked her. She said it was Tilly's story to tell, which makes me wonder if there's something unsettling or revealing about the history. I've never known the facts about it, and it didn't matter when I was younger. Now I'm thinking the story might hold a clue of some kind."

"Will you ask Tilly?"

"I'm reluctant to. I don't want to upset her. Remind me in the morning to send a telegram to Daddy. I'm sure he knows."

"Consider me your personal secretary, my dear."

I laughed at the notion, but squeezed my arm more tightly through his. "Oh! Before we left, Sadie said she would insist on my aunts staying with her and Huldah during our sojourn here. That way she can look after both of them and they won't feel they need to take care of us even as they mourn. So if we want, we can forgo the costly hotel room and stay right here in West Falmouth."

He pulled me to a stop and turned to face me with a tender smile. "My thrifty Quaker. Don't you want the luxury of a fine room, breakfast prepared for us, the bed made up every morning and turned down every night? I can easily afford the price."

"That all sounds delicious, of course." I bit my lip. He clearly wanted to treat me to a fine experience.

"But you want to be close at hand in West Falmouth, to your aunts and to the investigation. I see that, dear wife."

I nodded slowly.

"Then we shall avail ourselves of Tilly and Dru's hospitality and Sadie's generosity to allow us privacy." He took my face in both hands and bestowed a kiss.

"You are the best, dear husband. And this afternoon . . ." I looked up at him with roses blooming on my cheeks.

"We can enjoy our hearts' desires?" His husky tone matched the desire in his eyes.

"Something like that." I leaned my head against his arm as we came to a well-appointed house with a wide wraparound covered porch. The pink blooms of Rosa rugosa smelled sweet even from the walkway.

"It's all I can do not to sweep you into those bushes right now, darling wife," David murmured.

"Thee knows I can't wait for our next mutual sweeping. But those bushes?" I snorted. "They feature an immensity of prickles, my darling. I daresay we both would rue the experience."

"So true." He laughed. "Then let's make all due haste back to our temporary marital bed, shall we?"

"Mmm," was my only response, because I spied a girl in her teens sitting in a porch swing to the side of the wraparound veranda. She was reading, and I waved in greeting when she looked up from her book.

A woman approaching called a greeting to the girl. "Good afternoon, Miss Bowman."

Miss Bowman? Perhaps this was Hazel, Frannie's friend. I tugged on David's sleeve and whispered, "I think this might be the girl Frannie worked with. Do you mind if I speak with her?"

He paused for a beat, then said, "Of course not."

I could have kissed him again. Instead, I reversed course and started up the walkway to the porch, with David close behind.

"Hazel Bowman?" I inquired, smiling.

She set down the book. "Yes. May I help you?"

I ascended the stairs. "I'm Rose Car— I mean, Rose Dodge, niece to Tilly and Drusilla Carroll."

Her mouth tightened for a flash of a second. She replaced the look with a welcoming smile. "Please come and sit with me."

"This is my husband, David Dodge." We sat on the wicker chairs to which she gestured. "I'd like to offer my condolences on the death of thy friend, Frannie."

Hazel, about sixteen, like Frannie had been, had large gray eyes and flaxen hair worn in a knot with stylish frizzed bangs. She studied me as if trying to discern my motives.

I studied her back, curious about her pupils, which seemed overly constricted even for the sunny day.

"Thank you," Hazel said at last. "It's awful that she was killed. Frannie was my good friend throughout our school days and more recently at the tag shop. I still can't believe she's gone. In a poof, just like that." She touched the neck of her summer dress, made from a lawn sprigged with tiny red blooms.

Interesting. She didn't seem broken up by Frannie's death. "It's a hard thing to take in, isn't it?" I asked. "My aunt said Frannie sometimes spent the night with thee."

Hazel laughed lightly. She gestured at the house behind her. "Look at this place. I'm the only offspring, more to Father's chagrin, and we have bedrooms to spare. Of course, when Frannie and I had our girl parties, we shared my bed. It was cozier."

As many girls did. "But she didn't sleep here the night before last?" I tried to keep my tone as light as her laughter had been. My tactic didn't work.

She narrowed those gray eyes. "The detective asked me the same question. Are you working with him? Frannie used to tell me about your investigations up north."

Interesting. Daddy must have written to Tilly and Dru about the several homicides I'd tangled with of late, and they'd told Frannie.

"I'm merely trying to set my Aunt Tilly's mind at ease about her dear ward's sudden demise."

"You could ask Brigid McChesney what she knows." Her lip curled. "She hated Frannie. I'm not sure why. If anyone murdered my friend, it would have been that Irish trash."

ELEVEN

AFTER AN ENTIRELY DELIGHTFUL AFTERNOON REST sequestered in our room at my aunts' house (much of which rest was spent energetically rather than in slumber), David suggested a swim in the bay. I'd acquired a bathing costume as part of my modest trousseau, my first such getup since I'd outgrown my childhood one. Today was the fall equinox, with a full moon to rise tonight, and the air was sunny and mild. Sadie sent over a note with a boy, inviting us to supper. I wrote back to thank her but said we had enough left from our train supper to dine on tonight. I also added particularly to give my love to Tilly and Dru, and said we'd come over in the morning to spend time with them.

"I feel guilty I'm not there comforting Tilly or out investigating the murder," I told David after the boy ran off, David's coin in his pocket.

"They are being well taken care of, darling. I expect you'll solve the murder tomorrow. Doing so might well prove more comforting for Miss Tilly than you hovering over her this evening. Come on. We have a sea to explore and a sunset to witness."

We found two bicycles in decent repair in Tilly's shed and rode them toward the beach, with our picnic supper, bathing costumes, and a blanket strapped to the back of David's steel steed. We bumped over a short bridge that must have been recently built judging from the smell of freshly sawn wood. We rode on along the sandy path. On either side the terrain was lined with scraggly windblown cedars, scrub oaks, and not much else.

After leaning the cycles against a post on the bluff above the beach, we made our way hand in hand down the slope. The tide was out, and the small waves of Buzzard's Bay lapped gently onto the expanse of westward-facing sand. The water was clear and a pale greenish blue, gradually darkening the farther out I looked.

A changing house was available, but even so I emerged somewhat nervous to expose my body so thoroughly in public. I tugged the short black dress down over the bloomers. The top garment didn't even reach my knees. The bloomers weren't much longer and my calves were bare. I hugged my naked arms as I waited for David to appear, the cap sleeves of the dress both too ruffled and too short for my tastes. Children dashed around me, and a seagull dipped and wailed. All around bathers strolled, swam, sunbathed, or sat sedately and fully clothed under umbrellas. I waited and waited, finally hearing a shout from the water.

"Rosie, join me!" David popped up from the shallows. He must have changed quickly and dipped into the sea already. He ran toward me, dripping and grinning.

Despite having seen him without a stitch on only an hour ago, I blushed. Even without my glasses, which I had left with my dry clothing, I could clearly see the sleeveless wet black knit suit clinging to his manly form over his bare arms and legs. As we were out in public, I resolutely gazed up into his face with his hair slicked down straight from the water—instead of farther down his torso.

He ignored my struggle, grabbing my hand to run back to the sea. Within seconds we'd both waded in up to our waists. When he dove, I followed. I'd learned to swim in the pond at home as a child, but I'd never swum in the ocean as an adult. Bertie and I rode our horses to Salisbury Beach on occasion but we didn't go into the water there.

"This is splendid," I exclaimed when I surfaced. The depth dropped off gradually so I could easily stand. "It's entirely refreshing and not too cold at all." I licked the salt water off my lips.

"Isn't it?" David came up behind me and wrapped his arms around my waist. My body still tingled from our last expressions of love. The tingling now increased to a throb.

"Wouldn't thee like to have amorous congress with me right here in the water?" I murmured.

He let out a moan and let me go. "Don't tempt me, woman."

I laughed and swam away in an attempt to cool my fevers. I stroked back, but David had swum away from the shore. I tilted back my head, stretched out my arms, and floated face-up. I had to distract myself from thinking about the delights of the flesh, so instead I pondered what Hazel had said.

Had I imagined a suspicious reaction when I'd mentioned Tilly and Dru? Hazel didn't seem sad about the loss of her friend, certainly. I wished I'd asked her about Reuben. She must know him, the town being the small size it was.

This Brigid whom Hazel had talked about was a new unknown. Not a soul had mentioned her so far, other than Hazel. While I would have preferred to enjoy a honeymoon free of murder, Tilly had asked for my help. I had to admit to myself I was intrigued to find out who Brigid was, and why she apparently disliked Frannie. Tomorrow I could poke about town asking questions.

Except . . . I wasn't at home in Amesbury with a good reason to patrol the streets on my midwife's bicycle. I was on holiday with my beloved, I was acquainted with nearly no one here, and I barely knew my way around.

Becoming cold, I swam toward shore until the water was again only waist-deep. Where had my new husband gotten to? The sun was sinking and it was difficult to search the horizon for a bobbing, swimming head, but I shielded my eyes and tried. I couldn't spy him. It didn't help that I wasn't wearing my spectacles. Still, a chill for his safety came over me. *"David!"* I wanted to cry out. I urged him silently to come back to me. After what he'd told me about Currie's near death in the ocean, I was terrified to lose my beloved in a similar manner. I stood there, swaying in the gentle swell, and shut my eyes. In my mind—and heart—I surrounded him with the glow of God's Light to guide him back to shore.

Something grabbed my foot. I let out a little shriek, kicking to loosen the grasp. David popped up in front of me from underwater.

"I got you!" His delighted smile stretched to the island of Nantucket.

"Thee near got me a heart attack, silly man." My mouth pulled down and my eyes welled with tears.

He sobered immediately. "I'm sorry, my darling. Did I scare you? I didn't mean to. Currie and I used to play at that game." He set his hands on my shoulders and peered into my face.

I covered my mouth with my hand and swallowed down my emotion. "I couldn't see thee. Thee hadn't swum back. I was afraid, David. Afraid a shark had bitten you, that you'd hit your head on a rock, that . . ."

"There, there, beautiful Rose. I am here, with you. I was

swimming circles around you as you floated in thought, feasting my eyes on your loveliness."

Now I was able to laugh. "Oh, thee is an exceedingly silly man. Come, let's extricate ourselves from this primordial brew and dry off so we can watch the sun set in comfort, shall we?"

TWELVE

DRIED, DRESSED—although not shod—and seated on our blanket, David and I settled in to sup and watch the unusual sight, for Massachusetts, of the sun setting over water. We in the Commonwealth were far more accustomed to seeing the light-giving orb rise daily over the Atlantic and set over whatever land lay to our west. Instead, here the vagaries of geography had plopped us squarely on a patch of sand facing westward—with an eighteen-mile-wide body of salt water between us and the next land. Specks on the opposite shore had to be buildings in the bustling port of New Bedford, with the tip of Rhode Island visible beyond. Curving around to our left was the peninsula of Wood's Holl followed by long, thin Naushon Island reaching into the sea.

Puffy clouds the color of my name arrayed themselves in a giant tower as I drew out the remains of the wedding supper and set them on the cloth between us. "The pickings are a little slim, it seems."

David reached for a bag he'd tucked in the corner of the basket, one that hadn't been there on the train. He drew out a squat little jar and an unopened packet of water crackers. "Caviar, madam?"

"Caviar? I've never had it. Isn't it quite dear?"

I must have been frowning, because he reached over with his thumb and gently stroked upward between my eyes several times, smoothing out the worry lines.

"Don't worry, Rose. The caviar was a gift to my father from some client. And now we can enjoy the delicacy before our meager meal. Which pickings, by the way, aren't really all so slim." A moment later he proffered a cracker topped with tiny black pearls of roe.

I savored the rich, slightly sweet flavor, the subtly salty eggs popping on my tongue. The topping went perfectly with the crunchy freshness of a cracker seasoned with pepper and rosemary, if I wasn't mistaken.

"That is very nice, sir," I said after I swallowed.

He threw his head back and laughed. "It is at that."

I gazed at the sky again and at how the colors of everything appeared more vibrant than at home. "The light here is remarkable, isn't it?"

"It's the reason artists are drawn to Cape Cod, especially at this time of year. I've heard of a young fellow named Herman Hartwich whose work is impressing quite a few collectors. Perhaps we can acquire one of his Cape landscapes while we're here."

Around us others were also dining, some more simply than others. An older couple not far away had opened a can of sardines and ate them on bread. A family down the way had lit a fire of dry driftwood and were roasting corn and small whole fishes on skewers, which smelled divine. And a group of ragtag young men seemed to be taking their meal solely from bottles of ale, with the occasional munch on a piece of pemmican.

"You know, Tilly said something to me before we went in to dinner. She said she hadn't meant to interrupt our wedding festivities. As we saw, there was no reason for us to hurry down here last night."

"Yes, I noticed."

"I think perhaps Dru magnified the urgency."

"We're here now, together and in paradise." David tucked a strand of hair behind my ear.

The simple but intimate gesture flooded me with warmth. I savored a chicken turnover while I watched a low open boat being rowed toward shore. It now bucked the last gentle waves and ground onto the sand near us. A man in high boots hopped out and pulled the boat farther onto land. His ruddy face was as weathered as the boat.

A tall young person in trousers, rubber boots, and a ragged pullover climbed out. I might have thought it was a young man, except she wore a long red braid down her back and had not a trace of whiskers on her face.

"Brigie, why're yeh after dawdling, now?" the man growled to her.

Brigie? Maybe this was the girl Hazel had spoken of.

She grabbed the rope at the prow and pulled the boat the rest of the way out of the water.

The man commenced to tossing wriggling sacks onto the wet sand. "Get yerself a-hustling, daughter."

They were close enough that I could see the girl, indeed no older

51

than Hazel or Frannie, roll her eyes at her father's impatience. But she moved, and with strength and efficiency. He'd brought down a wide wheeled cart, which soon enough was loaded with the day's catch. Of what type of fish I couldn't discern, other than they were still alive.

The father grabbed the cart's crossbar and leaned into it. The girl began tying the boat's rope to a thicker rope running down from a post anchored in the bluff, a rope ending in a float. I sprang to my feet, told David I'd be right back, and hurried over to her. If I wanted to speak with her, I'd have to act fast. Her father was already impatient.

"Would thee be Brigid McChesney?" I asked her in a soft voice.

She straightened. "Who wants to know?" Her brown eyes bore into mine out of a tanned face.

"My name is Rose Dodge." I barely escaped saying Carroll again. "I was Frannie's, uh, cousin." Or close enough. If Frannie had been like a daughter to Tilly, it meant the girl had been my cousin. That was another question, but not one for now: why hadn't Tilly adopted Frannie?

Brigid glanced at her father, whose back was turned. She faced me and crossed herself. "May Frannie's sweet soul rest in the arms of our Lord. It's a terrible thing, what happened to her." She sniffed. "I'm going to miss her that much, I am." Her brogue wasn't as pronounced as her father's, but it was there.

"We met a Hazel Bowman today. She claimed thee very much disliked Frannie."

The girl spat in the sand. "It's because that Hazel, she hates me."

"Why?"

"Brigid Siobhan McChesney, fer the love o' God!" Her father scowled at her, a scowl now including me.

"I need to go. Find me at the Union Store tomorrow, I'll be telling you more." She jogged over to her father and pushed the back of the heavy cart the rest of the way up the path.

I plopped back onto the blanket with David, who gave me an inquisitive look.

"The Brigid we heard about this afternoon?" he asked.

"The same. She is the first I've encountered, besides Tilly, who seems truly sad about Frannie's death."

"And the part about this fisherman's daughter hating Frannie?"

"She claimed it's because it's Hazel who hates her, Brigid." I drew my knees up and wrapped my arms around them. "She told me to find her at the market tomorrow. She must work there."

"The Hazel we met this afternoon. Did you notice her pupils were quite constricted?"

"I did."

"I wonder if she indulges in laudanum. That's a common effect of the drug."

"And it can cause erratic behavior, can't it?" I cocked my head.

"Yes. There is an initial euphoria, but as the opiate dissipates, people can become agitated and irritated, and they often experience dysphoria."

"It sounds awful."

David cleared away the food between us and scooted over to sit next to me. He took a bite of a berry tart, then held it to my mouth. "Your dessert, wife. That, and the moving picture show in front of us."

I let thoughts of murder slip into the ocean along with this glorious orange ball paying witness to the turning of the globe. I was happy to focus on nothing but my husband for the rest of the night.

THIRTEEN

I SAT WITH TILLY in Sadie's marvelous screened-in porch the next morning at nine. I nestled comfortably on the chintz-covered cushion in a wicker chair, while my aunt leaned back in a matching love seat. This room off the back of Sadie and Huldah's house faced their garden, and they'd lined the outer walls with screens to keep out the mosquitoes. We'd acquired the newly invented screening material only the year before on our windows at the home I'd shared with the Bailey family.

"The design of this porch is ingenious," I said to Sadie as she brought me a cup of coffee and Tilly a hot tea. "Thee has the benefits of the out-of-doors without the biting insects."

"We replace the panels with glass for the winter," Sadie said.

"I thank thee, Sadie," Tilly said. Her face was still pale and drawn, but she appeared more rested and less stricken than yesterday.

I thanked our hostess, too, and she bustled off. Tilly and I sipped in silence for a moment, watching chickadees flit around a plate of sunflower seeds sitting on a small iron table. Rudbeckia and zinnias bloomed in yellow and red profusion in front of us.

"Where has thy husband got himself off to, Rose?" Tilly asked.

"He has a physician acquaintance in town, a man doing an innovative procedure. David is currently treating a patient with the same condition and wanted to consult with this doctor somebody or other." He'd asked if I minded, saying conducting a spot of business wasn't exactly in line with a romantic honeymoon. I'd responded, "Neither is helping find a killer." One of the many reasons David and I got on so well was that we were both practical people.

"That's industrious of him."

"Did thee rest well last night, Aunt?"

"I did, my dear, to my surprise. Neighbor Marie recommended a calming tea, which helped greatly." She reached for my hand. "I'd like to pray with thee for a bit."

I joined my youthful, strong hand with hers. Soft, age-spotted parchment skin covered her knobby knuckles. Still, her grip was firm. I closed my eyes, letting the grace of the divine wash over me.

Sometime later I started when she spoke and let go of my hand.

"Thee didn't know Frannie, Rose." Her keen blue eyes regarded me from under still-dark brows. "May I share some memories of her?"

"Please, Aunt Tilly." Perhaps I would hear the story of how Frannie came to live with her. I hoped so.

"She was a lively girl, from the age of two onward."

I wanted to ask how the girl's parents had died, but decided to let Tilly's story play out. Perhaps she would mention the circumstances.

Tilly folded her hands in her lap and gazed out at an aster's spiky orange blooms. "She was so very curious, Rose. 'Why' and 'how' were her favorite words."

"Aunt Dru told us Frannie could fix anything."

She laughed softly. "She could. I think if she'd been a boy she might have become a mechanic or even an engineer. Not an appropriate profession for a woman, of course, but our Frannie had the aptitude, without a doubt."

"Besides tinkering, what made her happy?" I cradled my coffee in both hands after taking a drink.

"She was athletic and would go off riding on the bicycle as soon as she was big enough to reach the pedals." Tilly smiled as if at a sad memory. "She even tinkered and invented a guard to go over the back wheel so her skirts wouldn't become caught in the spokes."

"Did she enjoy swimming in the bay?"

"Very much. She was a veritable fish."

"David and I bathed there yesterday. It was quite pleasant."

"To my disappointment, Frannie never became enthralled with reading." Tilly sipped her cooling tea. "The girl loved to garden, though. Judith next door was teaching her a few tips about nurturing plants. Then that—" She stopped abruptly and turned to face me. "Rose, we Friends are taught that all are equal in God's eyes. But that boy, Reuben, he was a bad influence on Frannie. She thought he was going to share his Indian wisdom with her." Her narrow nostrils flared.

"What kind of wisdom?" I kept my voice gentle.

"His mother, Zerviah, was teaching her the traditional ways of fertilizing the garden by burying fish and whatnot."

"Zerviah is the midwife?"

"Yes. Drusilla must have told thee. I didn't mind our girl associating with Zerviah. She is a kind and modest woman. But after Frannie met the son, she started staying out too late, coming home flushed. I spoke to her about the dangers of passion, and she didn't heed my words. Not a bit. Once she even returned home reeking of alcohol. I have heard Reuben has a temper when he's drinking."

"And thee knew she'd been with Reuben? Did thee ever see him imbibing?"

"No, but there is talk." Her eyes filled. "Rose, I think he killed her."

Precisely what the detective had hinted at. "Tilly, why does thee think so?"

"Let me revise that." She was adamant. "I know he did. You see —"

I leaned toward her. Sadie hurried in. Tilly pressed her lips together.

"Excuse me, dears," Sadie said. "Rose, thee has a caller in the person of Zerviah Baxter."

"The midwife," I said. And Reuben's mother, of course.

"The very same," Sadie said. "Shall I show her in?"

"Thee shall not." Tilly straightened her spine. "I have no quarrel with Zerviah, but she is the mother of Frannie's killer."

Sadie's eyes widened, but she kept her silence.

"I shall not be in the same room as that woman," Tilly continued.

I stood, shocked that my aunt would be so judgmental and negate her own Quaker beliefs. It had to be her grief that was making her speak irrationally.

"I'll meet with her elsewhere." I worried Tilly might take offense, but I would not judge the local Indian family with malice. Tilly waved me away.

"Of course. Come with me." Sadie showed me to the front hall, where a dark-haired woman waited. "Rose, this is Zerviah Baxter. Zerviah, thy fellow midwife, Rose Dodge. Please, ladies, sit in the parlor here."

I smiled at Zerviah but didn't speak until Sadie had left us and we were seated. "I'm so pleased to make thy acquaintance, Zerviah. I'm always eager to learn from others who practice the art of midwifery, especially those who have assisted with many more births than I."

Zerviah, who was from her appearance probably on the far side of thirty years of age, perched on the edge of a straight chair as if ill at ease. Her cotton dress in shades of muted green and gray was as plain as a Quaker's and her green brimmed hat as free of adornment. Her hair was not pinned up in any kind of do but instead fell in a single black braid down her back.

"Thank you for seeing me, Mrs. Dodge."

"Might I prevail upon thee to address me as Rose?"

Her eyes warmed. "I know you Quaker women don't stand on titles, and you don't take offense at familiarity from the likes of me. But be aware, Rose, I will address you appropriately should we be in the company of those not of your faith. I cannot afford to be publicly castigated, not now, not ever." Her English held only the hint of an accent, mainly in the shape of the vowels.

Her calm statement saddened me. I was certain Indians underwent a great deal of unfair treatment solely on the basis of their heritage and coloring.

"I understand." I folded my hands and waited for her to continue.

She also kept her hands clasped in her lap. "I have several things to relate to you. First, I have a woman, a first-time mother, who is due to deliver soon. Her baby is in the breech position. Perhaps you have methods I have not heard of to assist with such a birth."

"If her labor begins while I am still in town, I shall be glad to help if I can. I also suspect thee knows techniques traditional and otherwise I can learn to enrich my own practice."

She bobbed her head once in acknowledgment. "Second, perhaps you have heard that the authorities appear to believe my son Reuben caused the death of Miss Tilly's ward."

It was my turn to signal that, yes, I had heard.

"This cannot be true. It cannot. Let us leave no doubt." Her dark eyes flashed in a face with full features, which might have come from her foremothers intermarrying with the Negro race, despite her straight hair. "He's a good boy, Rose, and an innocent one. Will you help me clear his name?"

I sighed inwardly. How could I say no? Yet this trip was intended to be a joyful respite with David, not a stay full of such strife, and this was the second such request of me.

"Doing so is the purview of the detective, of course," I began. "I'm not sure what I could accomplish."

She leaned forward. "Please, Rose, do whatever you can. Frannie told my son you have a gift for such things." Her gaze beseeched me. "And if a member of your faith does not help us, no other citizen of Falmouth will."

"I cannot promise, thee understands. But I will see what I can find out."

"Very well." The midwife sat erect and cleared her throat. "My last piece might be of interest. You and I, we know women's gravid bodies sometimes better than they do themselves. I do not have proof of this, but I am certain Frannie was with child."

Frannie, pregnant? With Zerviah's own grandchild, perhaps? I could only stare at her. I glanced away at the door, praying Tilly wasn't listening.

"She was a fully matured girl of sixteen," Zerviah continued. "She exhibited all the signs of pregnancy we are so familiar with. A thickened waist, full bosom, heightened color, an unease in her stomach."

"Does thee think she knew she was with child? Sometimes girls don't."

"I do not know." She gazed out the window at the road, where a wagon filled with salt marsh hay rumbled by. "I did not speak with her about her condition."

I spoke slowly. "I've heard Frannie and your son were friendly. Perhaps more than friendly. Could he be the father?"

"No." Her eyes became harder than obsidian. "And, for certain, he also is not a murderer."

FOURTEEN

ZERVIAH LEFT SADIE'S shortly after delivering her opinion that Frannie had been pregnant. She said she had no idea who the father might have been, only that it wasn't her son. How could she be so sure? I was well aware how many mothers refused to believe the worst about their children, and I prayed I myself would never be put to the challenge. I wondered, too, where Zerviah had trained as a midwife. She was clearly in command both of her profession and the associated vocabulary, using a word like "gravid," which was not in the common lexicon.

Tilly had laid down for a rest by the time I returned to the sunroom, so I set off meandering through town, as David was occupied until midday, about an hour from now. I strolled deep in thought down the main street of the town, passing a barbershop and a milliner.

Today the glowering sky put a damper on my mood. Gone was yesterday's lighthearted weather, which had let a newly wed couple splash in the bay and enjoy an al fresco picnic at sunset. Now the air was a swamp of humidity, dampening the neck of my dress with sweat simply from the exertion of walking. Today's cloud cover was an oppressive ash-colored blanket, reminding me a murderer walked these streets, too.

I paused at the railroad station, which also contained the telegraph office. I'd wanted to write to my father. I pushed through the door and made my way to the telegraph counter.

"I'd like to send a telegram, please."

The elderly clerk silently passed me a slip of paper and a pencil. I thanked him and stepped to the side to compose my message. I considered how to word it, in light of Tilly now being associated with a homicide investigation.

PLS INFORM HOW TC ACQUIRED F WHY DIDN'T ADOPT. R

There. I'd avoided using names, in case the clerk might gossip. It was exactly ten words. One had to pay for ten words even if the message contained fewer. A line had formed at the window by now, so I took my place at the end. The two women in front of me obviously knew each other.

"The Baxter father isn't much better than the son," the taller one said.

She was talking about Reuben and his father. I sidled a half step closer so I could hear better.

The woman continued. "Why, my husband saw him swilling the hooch and doing his redskin dance up in the hills last week." She pursed her lips and gave a shake to her head.

"I don't know why we even allow Indians to live here in West Falmouth among decent white folks," the other one said. "The government should keep them in Mashpee where they belong."

"Especially if they're going to go around killing poor girls. None of us is safe, mark my words."

"I certainly didn't let my daughter be delivered by that midwife, either," Shorter said. "The German one in Falmouth was properly trained and doesn't try to give ladies any strange concoctions like the ones Mrs. Baxter forces on them during their travails. She probably performs savage incantations, too. One can't be too careful."

"No, indeed one can't." It was Taller's turn at the window, and the conversation ended.

I shook my head at such judgment against the Indians from these two. Concoctions, indeed. What midwife didn't make up herbal remedies to assist her women during labor and afterward? Herbs were certainly part of my practice. I hadn't met Zerviah's husband or son, but she seemed a most competent and sensible woman. Of course, these women's prejudicial views were commonly held in our nation. Why else would Indians have been pushed off their native lands and forced to move or to go into hiding? It made me glad all over again to have been raised in the Quaker faith, where we are taught all are equal in God's eyes.

Finally I slid my telegram to the clerk and paid the seven dollars and forty cents, wincing as I did. David was well situated financially, but I wasn't used to spending money so wantonly.

The man squinted up at me after he read my words. I feared he was about to question me, but he didn't. I was sure he wasn't fooled by my enigmatic use of initials.

One purpose of my walk being accomplished, I headed out. I smiled at the very small library building across the street. Dru had said plans were in place to build a new library across from the Meetinghouse, but they hadn't broken ground yet. I made my way to the Union Store to talk with Brigid. As promised, she stood behind the counter, today clad in a blue sprigged dress with her hair pinned up. She was quite a pretty girl, especially cleaned up and out of her mannish seafaring garb.

I wondered if I should purchase something in case she had a boss who might disapprove of her spending time speaking with me. I spied a small tin of sweets and brought it to the front. I could give it to Sadie as a gesture of thanks for the meal yesterday. I was sure Dru would enjoy the candy, if not Tilly.

"Good morning, Brigid," I said.

She had turned her back and was running a feather duster over a shelf of tonics. She faced me, a smile already on her face, but it slid away when she saw who I was. "You're the lady from the beach, Frannie's cousin. You wanted to know about Hazel."

"Yes, I'm Rose Carr— I mean, Dodge." I laid the tin on the counter. "I'd like to purchase this, please, and I would very much like to know why Hazel harbors ill feelings toward thee." I kept my voice low.

She blinked at my use of "thee." "You're after being one of those Quakers, are you?"

"Yes, I am."

"Frannie attended your church, too." When her eyes welled, she swiped at them with the back of her hand. "I wanted to go with her once to see what it was like, but me da forbade it. Said walking into a pagan church would be considered a sin or some such twaddle."

She told me the sweets would be five cents. She pressed the keys on the big ornate cash register, making the drawer pop open with its dinging bell. As she accepted the coins I proffered, Brigid said, "Hazel hated me because I wouldn't do what she said. She's a one for going on and ordering her friends about."

Interesting. "Did Frannie obey her?"

"Not since she was taking up with Reuben Baxter, she didn't."

"I gather Frannie and Reuben were openly courting."

"Yes, ma'am, and Hazel was a right spitfire about it, I'll tell you."

"How do you know Hazel?"

"Ah, you know, we all live here, we're all of an age. I suppose Frannie introduced us first."

The bell hanging from the door jangled as another customer entered.

"One more quick question." A thought occurred to me. "Hazel told me she had no siblings, and she lives in a quite large house with her parents. Why does she work at the tag factory if her family is wealthy?"

She tossed her head and leaned toward me. "I think her da won't give her spending money. Hazel has a weakness for laudanum and the tonics, she does. She'd spend her entire inheritance on it if she could."

Laudanum, the potent mix of brandy and opium that was a favorite of women of a certain class who were eager to escape the prison of their idle lives. Tonics were often also laced with substances like codeine, cocaine, and alcohol. All were readily available for purchase at the druggist.

"Her mama doesn't like her associating with us working types, but her father indulges her and lets her earn her pin money," she murmured, then glanced at the newcomer. "Can I be helping you, Mr. Latting?"

I turned toward my fellow Quaker as he approached. "Good morning, Abial."

"Hello. Rose, wasn't it? Brigid, I'd like a word with the owner, if thee pleases."

"I'm sorry, but he's out, Mr. Latting."

Abial pursed his lips. "This is most unfortunate. I am obliged to raise an unpleasant issue with him. Tell him to contact me at my office at his earliest convenience. Good day, ladies."

The screen door whacked shut behind him. Did the market owner owe Abial money? Or was it a personal matter?

"What was that about, Brigid?" I asked, still staring at the door. Gone was Abial's solicitous tone in Meeting for Worship. Instead I had witnessed a haughty businessman. Perhaps this was the cause of some of those rumors Huldah had referred to. "Does thee know?"

"I don't, ma'am, and I'm glad of it. You don't want to be getting in that man's way, Quaker or no Quaker."

FIFTEEN

POINTING MYSELF BACK to Baker's Lane, my feet were heavy thinking about Abial Latting and what Brigid said about him. His behavior in the store had not been at all peaceable. I wanted to learn more about the man on the off chance he had some connection to Frannie's death. My thoughts harked back to a tragic case in Amesbury over a year ago, in which Hannah Breed, a Quaker mill girl, had been murdered by an unscrupulous person. She had also been pregnant and unmarried. Between Kevin and me, we'd caught the villain, restored the reputation of the first person accused, and uncovered quite a tangle of lies. Would it also be the same with Frannie's murder?

A sign on a brick building reading *H. Gifford & Co, Attorneys at Law* caught my eye. Huldah's office. I slowed. Should I see if the detective was in and relate to him what Zerviah had said about Frannie's condition? If I were home I would certainly tell Kevin. And Edwin had asked for my assistance. In I went, and told the tired-looking clerk I was seeking the temporary office of Detective Edwin Merritt. He waved me to a door on his left.

Inside, a fresh-faced young officer sat behind a desk with nothing on its surface. Another door was at his back.

"Good morning. My name is Rose Dodge. I would like to speak to Detective Edwin Merritt, if thee pleases."

He looked me up and down from my bonnet to my shoes and back. "What's your business with him, miss?" His tone was one of bantering rather than respect.

"It's of a confidential nature regarding the recent death of Frannie Isley." I had no plans to correct him on my marital status and wasn't about to start introducing myself as Mrs. David Dodge. I had a perfectly good name that needed no title.

"Oh, confidential, is it?" He folded his arms and cocked his head as if not believing me. "What's a Quaker lady like you doing consorting with a sergeant?" He snickered.

I pulled myself up tall and straight, erasing my friendly smile.

"Young man, what I have to relate to Edwin Merritt is confidential, and the detective specifically requested my assistance in the case. I would appreciate thee fetching him with all due haste. He will be well displeased at thy insolence."

The boy's eyes widened and his skin paled under his freckles. "Yes, miss. Right away, miss." He jumped to his feet and disappeared through the door. A moment later he reappeared, sheepishly following Edwin.

"You wanted to see me, Mrs. Dodge?" the detective asked.

The fresh-faced one, a scant twenty if that, turned even whiter at hearing I was married, which, in society's eyes, brought a certain degree of respectability.

"I am in possession of a few bits of information in which thee might be interested, Edwin," I said.

My rude greeter gaped at my use of the officer's Christian name.

"Certainly. Please come back to my office." To the boy, he added, "As you were, Larkin."

Larkin's relief was tentative at best. He had no idea what I would or would not relate to Edwin about his behavior toward me. Indeed, I planned to speak to the detective of our interchange. A young patrolman should not be treating women with disrespect—not me, not any woman. He was young enough to learn differently, given proper guidance.

A few moments later I sat across from Edwin. The desk occupying the space between us could have been Kevin's, with its stacks of papers and maps and scraps of notes everywhere. A tall bookcase held only two reference volumes for officers of the peace next to a stern-faced photograph of Edwin and his wife.

He must have seen me studying the photograph because he gestured at it. "I kind of hoped to have a passel of children by now, but we're finally getting our family going, so perhaps one day I shall." He flipped open his palms as if he didn't really care. "The medical examiner is due to arrive on the noon train, and I have a number of other pressing issues with which I must deal. Please tell me what you've learned."

"First, the Wampanoag Indian midwife, Zerviah Baxter, is certain Frannie Isley was carrying a child." I adjusted my glasses.

Edwin stilled the pencil he'd been fiddling with. "Do tell."

"Zerviah had not performed a physical examination. But there are signs no experienced midwife can miss. Please instruct whomever will be performing the autopsy to confirm Frannie's condition and to assess how old the fetus was when she was killed."

He scribbled furiously on a piece of paper. He glanced up. "How do you know you can trust the word of an Indian?"

I mentally rolled my eyes. I'd done my fair share of schooling Kevin over the last few years on judgmental attitudes. Apparently I'd have to do it here, too. "Edwin, Zerviah is a human and a woman with a profession, like mine, of caring for pregnant women. She knows of what she speaks. Why would I not trust her simply because she comes from a different geographical region — right here, in fact — than your ancestors or mine?"

"But some Indians act savagely."

"So do some Europeans, where most Americans originated." I shut my mouth and folded my hands. Rome wasn't created in a day, as they said, and neither was God's green earth. I would not change his beliefs in the span of a few minutes.

"Very well," he consented. "I will ask him to ascertain the victim's condition."

"If she was, in fact, with child, whoever the father was could have been angry about it. Or someone else displeased with Frannie, an unwed sixteen-year-old, bearing what society terms a bastard child."

"This could be the motive for the homicide." He nodded sagely.

"An excellent thought." I smiled to myself, since it had been mine.

"What else do you have?"

"When I spoke with Hazel Bowman, she mentioned a Brigid McChesney. I've had occasion to speak with the Irish girl twice in the last twenty-four hours. She was quite fond of Frannie. She told me Hazel is addicted to laudanum and that Hazel was quite displeased when Frannie began spending much of her time with the Baxter lad instead of with her."

"She, Miss Bowman, was displeased?"

"Yes. Brigid also mentioned that Hazel likes to be in control and always tells her friends what to do. I thought if Hazel had taken too much of the potent drug, perhaps she went mad and found a way to kill her friend."

Edwin blinked his mismatched eyes, as if thinking. "The idea is a bit fanciful, but I grant you it's possible, although I believe it makes the person who consumes the drug passive rather than crazed." He scribbled some more. Folding his hands on the desk, he shot his gaze to the wall clock, which read five before noon.

"I believe I've told thee all I've learned about the case. I thank thee for listening." I stood.

He rose, too.

"I need to say one additional thing." I cleared my throat. "Please instruct thy employees to treat everyone who enters here with respect. Young Larkin, as thee addressed him, was cavalier and rude to me. He's an officer of the peace, and his tender years make him still teachable. I do not intend he be punished, but thee could take this opportunity to direct him on appropriate behavior. I might have mentioned to him that you would be most unhappy to hear of the ungentlemanly and unprofessional way he first dealt with me."

Edwin smiled for the first time, displaying a set of astonishingly white and well-shaped teeth. "I shall proceed with his education forthwith." The smile ebbed. "I need to speak with your aunt again, Mrs. Dodge, as soon as I show the medical examiner Miss Isley's body. I can't delay my interview with Miss Tilly any longer."

"And why can't thee?"

Edwin gazed at the desk for a moment, finally focusing on me again. "It seems a witness saw Miss Tilly and another person out on her boat very early in the morning of the day Miss Isley's remains were found. The wharfmaster reported Miss Tilly returning her boat to its mooring alone."

My core stilled and chilled. "Does thee mean . . ." I let my voice trail off. I couldn't say the words. I covered my mouth with my hand, my brows pressing down on my eyes as I waited for him to utter them.

"That she might have killed her ward? Yes, Mrs. Dodge."

"She would never hurt Frannie!"

"Nevertheless." He took a deep breath and exhaled noisily. "We are considering it a possibility."

SIXTEEN

I EMBRACED DAVID with arms flung tightly around him when we met back at Tilly and Dru's at twelve thirty.

"Whoa, what's this all about?" he asked once we separated.

"I have so much to tell thee."

"Wait. If I don't eat a bite, I swear I will faint dead away." He smiled but his face was strained.

"Is thee feeling well?"

"I am hungry, that's all, and have a bit of a headache."

I planted a quick kiss on his cheek, then pulled open the icebox while he pumped us each a glass of cold water at the sink. Several minutes later we sat across the small kitchen table and dined on cheese and bread, the rest of the caviar, and slices of apple.

"We'll have a nice meal in Falmouth this evening to make up for one more picnic, I promise you," he said.

"I look forward to the prospect." I munched on a bit of apple. "Look at that picture." I pointed to a framed photograph atop the pie keep. It showed two girls, one slender and one round, wearing old-fashioned dresses.

David stood and brought it to the table. "It must be Drusilla and Tilly at around, say, eleven and nine, don't you think?"

I took the frame and examined the faces. "I do. Dru, with her big smile and round face, and Tilly has the narrower visage and curly dark hair. Despite Dru being older, Tilly is nearly as tall as her." Something appeared familiar about Tilly, but I couldn't place it. If anything, it was Drusilla's picture that reminded me of a picture of my father as a boy. "Dru is ten years older than Daddy, so he was a baby if he was even born when this was taken."

"Now, tell me your stories. They don't include delivering a baby since I last saw you, I trust."

I laughed softly. "No, thank goodness." Between mouthfuls, I filled him in on my morning. I hadn't realized how hungry I was. "The part about my aunt being seen on the water with someone else in her boat and returning alone worries me."

"The detective can't in all seriousness believe Miss Tilly killed her ward, can he?" he asked.

"I'm afraid he's considering the scenario as one of the possibilities. I've had a little time to think about it." I sipped my water. "Tilly has always been stern and judgmental. Aunt Dru hinted at some mystery when she said only Tilly should tell me about the circumstances of her taking in Frannie." I frowned and tapped the table as I thought.

"A kiss for your thoughts," David murmured.

I shook off my reverie to present my face for the promised item. Once bestowed, I went on. "I am spinning a tale from my imagination, of course, but what if Tilly had become impregnated long ago by someone who did not stand by her. Perhaps she gave up a child for adoption and the child was one of Frannie's parents?"

My husband tilted his head. "A bit far-fetched but not impossible in the least. Do go on, wife."

"Tilly might have been furious with Frannie about letting herself get in the same condition, and they could have argued. I cannot for a moment believe my aunt would purposely kill the girl. But if some kind of accident happened? Tilly's grief right now could be from causing the death of not only the girl she adored but a girl who was her own granddaughter."

"Most certainly. You told me Frannie was orphaned when both of her parents died, didn't you?"

"Yes."

"If your imaginings are correct, Tilly could have been keeping track of her child all along." David drummed his fingers on the table. "Have Tilly and Dru always lived here in West Falmouth?"

"They grew up in Lawrence with my father, of course," I said. "I think it was when my grandmother was failing that her sister passed away and left her nieces this house in her will. My great-aunt had married a man from West Falmouth, a boat builder, who predeceased her. They never had children."

"If Tilly bore a child in this area, the birth would have to have been registered with the county. I could check around, if you'd like."

I squeezed his hand. "Asking would be a help, my dear. But she might well have gone away for the last months to hide her condition, even back to Lawrence. I sent a telegraph to Daddy asking how Tilly came to take in a ward. Perhaps he'll know the answer, and more. Or all our conjecturing could be sheer fantasy, and Tilly was simply being charitable."

"Indeed, although I wonder about Frannie's parents. They must have had parents and sisters. Why wouldn't one of them have taken in the girl when her parents died?"

"Thee has brought up another mystery, my dear. I'll try to remember to ask my aunts. Going back to Edwin's suspicions, if Tilly had learned Frannie was pregnant, she might have been beyond angry with the girl. Except . . . now that I think about it, if they argued and somehow Frannie hit her head and fell overboard, surely Tilly would have gotten her back into the boat and brought her to shore."

"Maybe the man who impregnated her was the angry one." David raised a finger. "Whether Reuben or someone else, he might have been unhappy at becoming a father. Or the girl might have been demanding marriage, and he was having none of it. It doesn't explain what someone claimed they saw regarding Tilly and the boat. On the other hand, this so-called witness could be the guilty party and be lying."

I stared at him. "Good heavens, of course. I should have thought of that."

He threw his head back and laughed, but then winced.

"What's wrong, darling husband?"

"I thought getting some food into me would fix my head." He leaned back in his chair and closed his eyes. "It didn't," he murmured.

The outer door opened and banged against the wall as a flushed-cheek Aunt Drusilla bustled in. Her bonnet sat askew and she dabbed at sweat on her neck with a dainty embroidered handkerchief. David's eyes flew open as he straightened.

"Aunt Dru," I said. "We were finishing up a spot of lunch. Please sit and eat."

"Oh, no, I can't possibly." She shook her head fast, which only made her loose bonnet slide to an even crazier angle. "Rose, thee must come, and quickly."

I stood in a flash. "What's happened? Is Tilly all right?"

"Yes, but the detective wants to interrogate her. He's very serious

70

and won't take no for an answer." She stood rubbing her fingers against her thumbs as if it was the only action available to her.

I'd never seen her so flustered. I glanced at David, then back at Dru.

Dru grabbed my hand. "She says she won't say a word unless thee is at her side."

"Well, then, I'm on my way. David?"

He gave me a single nod. "Yes, you are. I plan to lie down with my eyes closed until this blasted head returns to normal." He blew me a kiss.

"A cold compress on thy brow might help, too." I hurried to the sink to rinse my hands, then grabbed my bonnet and my reticule with the tin of candy. "Aunt, shall we?"

SEVENTEEN

AFTER DRU AND I ARRIVED, she hovered nervously until Edwin asked her to leave him alone with Tilly and me. Sadie persuaded Dru to go out to the garden at the back.

"Miss Carroll, please let me begin by offering my sincere condolences," Edwin said.

"I thank thee." Her voice was barely above a whisper.

"I must warn you, Mrs. Dodge, to keep your silence." The detective gave me a stern look.

"I shall remain mum," I said from my seat next to Tilly in the same parlor where I'd talked with Zerviah yesterday. Tilly reached for my hand. I gave hers a light squeeze.

"I am ready," she said, her spine straight, her voice firm.

"Miss Carroll, when did you last take your fishing boat out?"

The slightest tremor passed through my aunt. I wouldn't have noticed if I hadn't been holding her hand in mine.

"Seventh Day morning early," she said.

"Seventh Day being Saturday, am I correct?" he asked.

"Yes," I said.

Edwin glared at me.

Oh, dear. I was supposed to keep quiet.

"Early," Edwin said. "What time, Miss Carroll?"

"It was a little after dawn, so about six thirty."

"Was anyone with you in the boat?"

She waited long enough for me to hear the clock. *Tick, tick, tick.*

"No."

My shoulders slumped in relief. Tilly had been alone. The so-called witness had lied. But . . . was my aunt telling the truth?

"Are you quite sure?" he asked.

"Yes."

"Where do you moor the craft?"

"At the town dock."

"What time did you return to the wharf?"

"By ten."

He gazed at his notebook, then up at her. "Did you know your ward was carrying a child?" He glanced at me.

Tilly's breath rasped as she sucked it in.

What an unfair blow. Surely Zerviah's conjecture hadn't been confirmed yet.

"I will not have thee maligning Frannie's character," Tilly said, chin raised. "She was a girl of sixteen."

"I maligned no one, Miss Carroll." He kept his voice quiet, calm. "I asked a simple question. Please answer it."

"I will not stoop to such a thing."

As instructed, I kept my silence, but I wondered at why Tilly had kept hers, in a way. She hadn't answered him.

"What do you know of a Miss Hazel Bowman?"

Tilly relaxed almost imperceptibly. "She's a girl in town. Frannie and she both worked at stringing tags and were friendly. She lives on Main Street."

"Was Miss Isley in the habit of spending the night at Miss Bowman's home?" he asked.

"On occasion."

"Your sister told us you both thought your ward was with Miss Bowman last Friday night. Was that what you thought?"

She lifted a shoulder. "I suppose."

"How much time did your ward spend with Reuben Baxter? Did she ever spend the night with him?"

Edwin was a skilled interviewer, clearly trying to throw Tilly off her guard.

"Young man, I will stand for no more of thy insolence." She began to rise.

I gently tugged on her sleeve. "Tilly, it's his job. Please sit down. He's not trying to be rude, but he has to ask these questions." I kept my voice as soft as I could while maintaining a touch of firmness. "All thee needs to do is tell him the truth."

She turned and studied my visage before settling back onto the settee.

Edwin shot me a quick look of thanks.

"Very well." Tilly faced the detective again. "No, she would not have spent nights with Reuben Baxter. They enjoyed each other's company, however."

"Did he come to your house to see Miss Isley?"

"My sister and I are often occupied with our duties at the library. I could not account for every minute of Frannie's time." She pressed her thin lips together.

"So you don't know if they'd had an argument recently?"

"I do not, but I also do not trust the boy."

He watched Tilly, but didn't ask her the reason for her distrust. I tilted my head. Why didn't he inquire?

Edwin went on. "Was there anyone else with whom your ward frequently associated outside of her work?"

Tilly finally smiled. It was wan, but it was a smile. "She very much liked Brigid McChesney, the Irish girl. They got along famously and could make each other laugh for hours with their stories."

"Did Joseph Baxter go to your home recently?"

Edwin had asked Dru the same question yesterday. I didn't know why.

"I don't think Joseph has ever been to call, no," Tilly said.

He studied his notes. "That will be all for the moment. Thank you for your time, Miss Carroll. I might need to speak with you again, and I request you make yourself available should that need arise."

Tilly stood and smoothed down her dress, her head held high. I rose, as well.

Edwin also rose. "Mrs. Dodge, could you please ask your other aunt to come in?"

"Of course." I escorted Tilly into the hall.

Tilly paused after a few steps, speaking so low and soft I could barely hear her. "Does thee believe me, Rose?"

Did I? I took my aunt's hand. "I feel thee might have held something back from the detective. Thee need not tell me, but if it has any relation at all to Frannie's death, thee must inform him."

"I know. Pray for me, dear." She opened the door next to her. "I do believe I need a rest now. Please tell Sadie," she said before disappearing into a darkened bedroom. The door shut with a soft click.

I closed my eyes and prayed, right there in the hall. Edwin could wait. I held my grieving aunt in God's Light until I heard a rustle from the back of the house. I opened my eyes to see Aunt Dru peering at me.

"What is thee doing?" she asked in a loud whisper. "Is Tilly still with Edwin?"

I beckoned for her to join me. "No, but he would like to speak with thee now." I pointed to the parlor door. I didn't deem it wise to say anything more about the questioning. "Tilly's resting. Go on in. I want to let Sadie know."

A moment later I resumed my place on the settee, now with an excited Drusilla next to me.

"Miss Carroll." The detective proceeded to ask her the same questions about Reuben and Joseph he had inquired of Tilly. He hadn't gotten far with Dru yesterday when he'd tried to query her during his mealtime visit. Now Dru gave him the same answer as Tilly had about Joseph, but her story differed when it came to Reuben.

"Has Reuben been around the house?" she echoed. "Well, I didn't see him, but I found an empty ale bottle behind the shed. It must be one he left."

"Was it there on Thursday?" he asked.

"How should I know? I didn't go behind the shed on Fifth Day."

"When did you discover the bottle?" Edwin spoke slowly, either out of an abundance of patience or to restrain himself from throttling the old lady for her meandering responses. I didn't blame him. He had to be frustrated.

"I found it on Seventh Day afternoon when I always tidy up the garden, small though it is," she said.

It seemed to me Reuben—or anyone else—could have left the bottle any time between the previous Seventh Day and the one in question.

"Where were you Saturday morning between six and ten thirty in the morning?" Edwin kept his eyes on his notebook.

"Why, I was at home, of course, making breakfast and baking the pies. I always bake pies on Seventh Day morning. It's so relaxing."

"Was your sister at home with you?"

"No. She went out fishing."

"Did she go alone?" Edwin asked.

Dru blinked. "She left the house alone, if that's what thee is asking. She wasn't in the habit of taking others out on the water with her, except for Frannie, of course. And the girl had started tiring of fishing with her old guardian. Those in their teen years discard the company of their elders as if we have not a thing to teach them." Her voice rose in indignation.

True. But I found it interesting to learn Frannie had formerly gone out fishing with Tilly. Maybe it had been a way for the two to share each other's company.

"What time did Miss Tilly return?" he asked.

"Let's see, it must have been about nine thirty. I'd gotten the bottom crusts rolled out for four pies and was cutting up apples and pears."

"How did Miss Tilly seem?"

"Seem?" Dru asked. "What does thee mean?"

"Her demeanor—was it normal? Did she appear to be in disarray at all?"

"Now, why would thee ask such a thing, young man?" She frowned at him.

"Dru," I murmured. "Thee needs to answer his questions." I again received a gratitude-filled glance from the detective.

"Very well. She always looks a bit disheveled when she returns from fishing, what with the sun and the wind and all. I didn't notice any difference this time."

"Did thee know Frannie was pregnant?" Edwin asked.

She gaped. "She never!"

"I take it your answer is no?"

"It most certainly is." She folded her arms. "Frannie Isley was a good girl, Edwin Merritt, and let thee not forget it. Are we quite finished?"

Edwin hoisted himself to standing with a tired sound. "I believe we are." He rubbed his forehead with his hand but he couldn't erase the lines of exhaustion etched on it. "I thank you both for your time. I shall let myself out."

EIGHTEEN

"THEE SHOULD HAVE SEEN Tilly's face when the detective asked her if she knew Frannie had been with child." David and I strolled down the main street of Falmouth in the late afternoon that day, his headache blessedly vanquished. "But she never actually answered his question, nor did Dru."

"Has the autopsy confirmed her gravid state?"

"Not that I know of. The medical examiner was only to arrive at midday."

"You imagine perhaps Tilly or Dru knew, after all?" he asked.

"I think when one lives in close proximity with another, it's hard to miss the signs." I walked a few more paces, passing the wide front porch of a mansard-roofed Walker's Pharmacy. Beyond it was Malchman's Clothing Store and Hewins Dry Goods. "That said, maybe my aunts didn't see what Zerviah saw. Neither Tilly nor Dru bore children themselves."

"Unless they did, or at least Tilly."

"True enough, dear husband. Nearly everything about the case is as yet unresolved, alas."

The oppressive weather had lifted. With the sun two hours from setting, it was a pleasant time of day to take in the sights of the town, which featured a lovely green anchored by a white Congregational church. Falmouth was a far more bustling town than its sleepy neighbor to the north.

I laughed softly. "Why in the world do they call it West Falmouth when it is due north from where we stand?"

"By George, you're right. I hadn't considered that. The answer will have to come from the historians or geographers, not us."

We came to Falmouth Town Hall, a two-story wood-frame structure that looked recently built. Contrasting trim framed multiple sections of tall windows, and a tower rose up from the front. Pausing in front of a bakery, I peered at a poster for a burlesque show pasted to the window. The advertisement for the Bon-Ton Burlesquers showed a shapely woman in a fringed costume covering only her torso. With feathers in her hair and heeled shoes, an oversized fan was her only contribution to modesty.

"Is this what is known as a variety show?" I pointed to the poster.

"I believe so, yes."

"It doesn't leave much variety for the imagination about her physique, does it?"

Two well-dressed matrons approached us on the sidewalk. One looked from me to the poster and back and muttered something in her friend's ear. The other glared, and both gave us a wide berth as they passed.

David winked at me. "I can see the headline now. Wicked Quaker Lures New Husband to Showgirls."

I snorted. "I don't care what they think, but I am exceedingly famished. Shall we hie ourselves to our supper?" We were to dine at the Tower House Hotel restaurant in Falmouth Heights, where we would have been staying if Frannie were still alive.

His smile disappeared faster than sea spume after a wave crashes on a rock.

"What is it?" I asked. I looked where he was looking. *Oh!* Currie sauntered toward us. "He's already back?"

"Looks like he followed us down here, after all," David murmured. "He obviously didn't stay and make things right with Mother. Rose, I don't have a good feeling about this."

All I could do was tuck my arm snugly through his.

"If it isn't my newly wed brother and my dear newly acquired sister," Currie said when he reached us, all bonhomie and bluster. "How fortuitous to encounter you on the streets of this fine town." He tipped his bowler at me, then extended a gloved hand to each of us. "I didn't know where to reach the happy couple in the wilds of West Falmouth, but here I find you."

"Hello, Currie," David said. "You decided not to tarry with our parents, I see."

Currie's smile dimmed. "I had, ah, business to attend to." When he caught sight of the poster, his beam returned. "The very business depicted on the advertisement in front of which you stand, as a matter of fact."

He'd said he was in the entertainment business. I now knew what he'd meant.

I dropped his hand. "What is your role in the variety show, Currie?"

"A little of this, a bit of that, you might say." He didn't meet my gaze. "I'm what one might call a talent scout for young female performers, always looking for new and accomplished girls. And of course we seek to scare up bigger audiences. I do all the above and much more. Things of a miscellaneous nature, you understand."

I most certainly did not understand what these miscellaneous things might be. And what kind of talent? I didn't care to ask.

"You'll have to invite us to your home some evening this week," David said. "I'd like to see where my brother has landed."

Currie cleared his throat. "I don't know about that, my dear Davey. It would be far more gay to take you two out on the town, as it were. Why, this very show is on tomorrow night at the theater right here in Falmouth. I can offer excellent seats to you both."

"We thank thee kindly for the offer, Currie," I said before David could respond. "We'll have to talk it over. Where can we reach thee?"

"You can write to me care of the theater. I'm there every day, aren't I?"

"Very well," David said. "Now, if you'll excuse us, we're on our way to our first dinner out as a married couple. I'd ask you to join us, but we've reserved the last available table, and it seats only two."

"Of course, of course. I already had plans, anyway." His laugh sounded hollow to my ears.

"Good evening, Currie," I said. "We'll see thee again soon."

He tipped his hat anew and strolled away from us, whistling "A Rollicking Band of Pirates We."

I waited to speak until we were well along in the opposite direction. "What does thee think he meant by talent scout, my dear?"

"First, I hope you'll forgive me for not inviting him to dinner with us and for lying to him. I have no idea how many tables are still available at the place, but I didn't want Currie to eat with us." He let out a sigh. "You saw how overjoyed I was to see him appear at our reception, but in truth he and I have not always gotten along."

"I understand. Families can be difficult. I would like to get to know Currie better in some setting, but our intimate dinner for two isn't the venue." In some setting where liquor and boasting were not included, with any luck.

"Thank you for understanding, dear Rose. About the talent, I expect he's looking for fresh young girls who can sing and dance and don't mind performing in a burlesque costume — or lack thereof." He held up a hand to hail a passing conveyance for hire.

My heart chilled despite the warm afternoon. Dru had said Frannie, who had a pretty voice, was a genius at picking up songs. She'd told us the girl was graceful and loved to move. I'd formed an instinctive distrust of David's brother. If Currie had somehow convinced Frannie to try out for the role of showgirl, what else might have happened?

NINETEEN

THE SEA BEYOND THE WINDOWS at the Tower House Hotel restaurant sparkled as much as the glassware on the table in front of us. The array of silverware shone on a white damask tablecloth. Small plates of chicken croquettes had been laid in front of us a moment ago by a genteel and unassuming man with a quiet voice. I was glad I'd donned my new wedding garment for the occasion, as every other diner was dressed in their Second Day finest, many of which were styled in the latest fashion.

My glass contained a refreshing mix of carbonated lemonade and cranberry juice over cubes of ice, a drink well suited to this region of cranberry farms. David had indulged in the British favorite of gin with tonic water. But my husband's drink didn't appear to be bringing him joy, judging from his serious expression.

"I'll extract a kiss from thee later for a glimpse into thy thoughts now, husband," I said gently. "Is it the encounter with thy brother which troubles thee?"

"It is. For one thing, I prayed he would truly reconcile with my mother. His speedy return here tells me he didn't. In addition, searching for talented girls for a burlesque show does not sound like a respectable occupation. Nay, simply imagine the trouble my brother could get himself into with the fathers of said young ladies. Currie has always been a bit of a rake, consorting with all manner of women and settling with none."

"I wonder how he carries out his scouting. I certainly hope he doesn't lurk at schools or other places girls congregate."

"One might very well ask. As for the shows themselves, some say they are in effect intelligent satires of the upper classes. They're often creative adaptations of plays by Shakespeare and other greats. Still, the performances are bawdy and often in poor taste."

"Has thee attended in the past?"

"Yes, when I was a student at Harvard Medical School. My cronies convinced me to go into Boston with them to take in a burlesque show. Once was enough for me."

"I'm also troubled by Currie's occupation." I spoke slowly. "Remember when Aunt Dru told us Frannie was good at picking up songs, and that she was graceful? Being paid to perform on stage could have seemed exciting to the girl. I'm concerned Currie might have somehow encountered Frannie in his search."

"As much as I hate to admit it, what you suggest is in fact quite probable. I just hope it isn't true."

We supped and didn't mention Currie for some minutes, talking instead about David's meeting with his colleague, about a lovely passing sailboat, about what President Harrison was up to recently. The waiter arrived to remove our plates.

"Excuse me, my good man," David said to him. "We earlier spied a handbill for a burlesque show in town. Is it good, respectable entertainment? Worth our while?"

The man shot me a quick look. "I might not call it entirely respectable, no, sir. An attraction for the general populace, it is. But the female performers are, shall we say, rather rudely dressed. Most ladies don't care to witness such a spectacle." He stressed the word "ladies."

"Are local young ladies the performers?" I asked.

The serving man gave a little start. Why? Did he not expect me to speak to him?

He cleared his throat. "Indeed they are. Much to the chagrin of their fathers, I must say. A rather unscrupulous gentleman is the recruiter of late and has been given the boot from more than one household."

Currie. David and I exchanged a glance.

"If that will be all, I'll bring out the next course," the waiter said.

"We thank thee." I smiled at him.

"It's as I thought." David waited until the man had left to speak. "How my brother ever landed in such a disreputable occupation is beyond me."

I laid my hand on his. "He might still find his way out of it, darling. Consider the possibility, if thee will."

It took him a moment, but he finally smiled gently. "Have I told you I loved you lately?"

"Not in the last hour, no." I returned his fond gaze.

"I love you, wife."

"I love thee, husband." I straightened my fork. "David, how did Currie end up on the Cape, anyway?"

"I don't know. It was during the time he wasn't communicating with us. My father has friends and business associates here, though, which is why he has the *Flying Dude* subscription. Maybe Currie thought he could find employment with one of them."

"Speaking of Herbert, it's curious that Clarinda was able to prevail in causing a family rift with Currie. Did thy father not defend him? Stand up to his wife in the matter?" Currie could have felt abandoned by the very man he'd surely always looked up to.

David spoke slowly. "He tried. But, as you must know, we can never really see into the inner workings of married couples."

I nodded.

"Father has always doted on my mother. I know she seems cold and imperious at times, but they have had a close partnership for many years. Herbert Dodge is no milquetoast. In the case of Currie, perhaps my father felt he could not push Mother too far."

Our man delivered our main courses. David had opted for fillet of beef with mushroom sauce, while I'd chosen the sole. I'd ordered it at the Grand Hotel in Amesbury last year and had loved the light treatment of the thin fillets.

After we'd eaten several bites, David asked, "Is yours good?"

"Very. It's mildly lemony and the cured capers scattered about add a perfect piquant spark. And thy beef?"

"Excellent. Very well prepared, with wine and thyme in the sauce, if I'm not mistaken." He'd switched to a glass of hearty red wine to accompany his meal and now sipped from it. "Our discussion of Tilly's interview with the detective was cut short by meeting my brother. Is there more to tell?"

"Edwin is a skilled interrogator. I sensed she was holding something back, not telling him the entire story of her morning fishing. He questioned Aunt Dru, too, separately, of course. They both appeared upset at Edwin's suggestion that Frannie was pregnant, but neither actually answered his question about what they knew of her condition."

"It seems both Miss Tilly and Miss Dru are quite busy with their own lives, what with their library duties and Tilly's fishing. I wonder how much time Frannie spent at tag tying. Not being in school, she must have had plentiful free time in which to do as she wished."

"Yes." I took another sip of my sweet, tangy drink. "Dru also mentioned to the detective that she'd found an ale bottle behind their shed on Seventh Day and seemed think it proved Reuben Baxter had been at the house."

"Their shed is quite near the train tracks, is it not? Any vagrant could have tossed the bottle there and no one the wiser."

"I expect the detective immediately thought the same." I let out a noisy breath. "Oh, David. Talking about murder and wicked shenanigans is not what I imagined we'd be discussing during our first week of marriage."

"Then let's speak no more of it this evening. I could talk until the cows come home about your beautiful brown eyes, the roses in your cheeks, and your perfect shape."

I laughed lightly. "That won't be necessary."

We did manage to avoid touching on anything the least bit unpleasant for the rest of our dinner and our short ride home on the train. It didn't mean the unpleasantness had gone away.

TWENTY

ONCE AGAIN I WAS ROSY-CHEEKED from the marital bed and smiling to myself the next morning as I strolled to the Giffords' home at around ten thirty. David had opted to stay home and read an article in a medical journal he'd been meaning to get to instead of accompanying me on my detecting rounds, as long as I promised to return by midday so we could sally forth on an excursion to Wood's Holl.

Sadie greeted me at the door. "Come in, Rose. Dru isn't here, but Tilly is busy penning notes to various friends and relatives about Frannie's passing." She glanced behind her, then whispered, "She's doing better, at least for now."

"I'm glad to hear it. I can't come in at the moment, but please tell her I'll back later in the day. David and I have an excursion to Wood's Holl planned."

"Of course. Thee will enjoy thy afternoon. Come for supper after thee both return."

"We will and I thank thee. Can thee tell me where to find Zerviah? I'd like to talk midwifery with her."

"Of course. The Baxters live in the caretaker's cottage on the Latting property. Thee knows the two big mansions on either side of the Meetinghouse?"

"Yes. Belonging to the Swift brothers, someone said."

"Precisely. Abial Latting's home—estate would be a better description—is beyond the one to the left as thee faces the Meetinghouse."

"I thank thee kindly."

She glanced over my shoulder. "Greetings, Marie."

I turned.

"Hello, Mrs. Gifford, Mrs. Dodge." She held up a canvas bag. "I bring more tomatoes, and a few squash, too. My mother was overambitious in her plantings this year." She smiled.

"What a lovely gift," I said. "How is thee, Marie, and thy mother?"

85

She tilted her head. "She's not recovering at the rate she or I would wish, alas. Frankly, I doubt she will, at seventy-nine."

"From what is she ailing, if I might inquire?" I asked.

"It's a wasting disease of some kind, probably cancer. She has a strong spirit and will to live, but there is no medicine to cure her. I'm truly only trying to keep her comfortable at this point. Part of the effort is assuring her that her garden produce is not rotting on the vine."

"Thee is a caring daughter," Sadie said.

"Very," I agreed.

"You know, someone will do it for me when my time comes. Perhaps my children, perhaps someone from my church, maybe a friend. I feel no good deed is wasted in God's eyes."

I smiled. "Has thee been out fishing for a moment of respite?"

Marie ceased smiling. "Yes, once, but I wish I hadn't."

"Why, pray tell?" I asked.

"I was in the inlet at high tide on Saturday morning."

Ah. Another possible witness to the murder?

"From a distance I spied two people in a boat," she went on. "It seemed they were arguing, perhaps struggling."

"Could thee see who they were?" Sadie asked, her eyes wide.

"No. A fish bit my line and the boat had turned when I heard a rather loud splash. By the time I looked again the other boat was gone. Now I wonder if I witnessed the poor girl's death."

"Thee might have," I said. "I think thee should tell the detective what thee saw. It could be important to his investigation. He's encamped at Huldah's office." I was surprised sensible Marie hadn't already thought of going to the police with what she'd seen. Her mother was ill, though. That likely absorbed most of her attention.

"I suppose I should. I shall go right now." She extended the bag to Sadie.

Sadie thanked her and told her where to find the office.

"I'll see you ladies later. I can pick up my bag after I return." Marie walked off with a brisk step.

I watched her go. "Many are reluctant to speak with the authorities. I'm glad she wasn't."

"Does thee think she really heard Frannie go into the water?" Sadie whispered.

"I don't know, but it certainly seems possible."

"I do believe such a memory would haunt me, if it had been I who was there."

TWENTY-ONE

I MADE MY WAY to the Union Store after checking at the telegram office. No message from my father had awaited. Perhaps he was busy, or maybe it was simply too soon for a reply to my inquiry. I surveyed the store but didn't see Brigid anywhere. What a pity. I wanted to ask her if she knew anything about Frannie going to Falmouth.

"Can I help you, ma'am?" a barrel-chested man in a long apron called out from behind the store's counter, where Brigid had been the day before.

I approached him, thinking quickly if there was anything David and I could use at the house. "Good morning. I am in need of a bottle of milk and a half dozen eggs, if thee has them."

"We surely do, ma'am. You're one of them Quakers, I see. New to town?"

"I am." I smiled at him. "My name is Rose Dodge. My husband and I are in West Falmouth for a few days visiting my aunts Tilly and Drusilla Carroll."

"Those are two fine ladies. I'm Gilbert Boyce, and I manage the store. Quite the pity about Miss Tilly's ward, may she rest in everlasting peace."

"It's very much a pity."

"Well, let me get those supplies for you." He disappeared into the back.

He'd said "manage." Did he also own the store? And was he the one Abial had been peeved not to find?

Gilbert emerged holding a quart of cold milk, with moisture already forming on the glass, and a small metal box with a lid. He flipped open the top, revealing six eggs nestled in individual stiff paper sleeves. "How do you like this? I invented it myself."

"It's a grand improvement over loose eggs in a basket, I'd say. Thee must have a tinkerer's mind."

"Yes, I do, Mrs. Dodge. I do, indeed." He stroked one of his long bushy sideburns. "Matter of fact, young Miss Isley used to come in

88

and pester me with questions about my inventions. She was a tinkerer, too."

A tiny lady with a wicker basket over her arm piped up. "May she rest in peace, young Frannie." A widow's hump misshaped her upper back.

"Did thee know her, ma'am?" I asked.

"Not to speak with, but everyone knew who the girl was, and I'd see her in here from time to time conversing." She pointed with a tanned and wizened finger at the shopkeeper, a smile splitting her face under a faded man's derby. "He's quite the inventor, is our Mr. Boyce."

"Why, thank you, Mrs. Bugos," Gilbert said. "Let me know what I can help you with."

"You know I will. I can wait until you're done with this nice lady." She fixed a keen gaze on me for a moment, then made her way with an uneven gait down an aisle.

"Can I help you find something else, ma'am?" Gilbert asked me.

"Nothing material, but I thank thee. Thee is the manager here. Does thee also own the store? An Abial Latting was in yesterday quite peeved with not finding the owner at hand."

"Oh, him. No, ma'am, I'm not the owner. I just run the place for him. And Latting? What isn't he peeved about?" His laugh was a hearty one. "I'm glad not to tangle with the man, though."

Interesting. "I had occasion to meet Brigid McChesney here yesterday. Might she be here today, as well?"

"Yes. The girl's a good worker, and I'm lucky to have her in my employ. I think she's around the side sweeping up." When a woman bustled in with three children, the shopkeeper greeted them, then said to me, "It'll be sixteen cents, Mrs. Dodge."

I paid him and drew out the cloth bag I'd remembered to bring on my peregrinations. "I thank thee, Gilbert," I said. "I'll return these containers before I depart for the north."

"I'd appreciate you doing so."

Making my way outside, I indeed discovered an aproned Brigid sweeping the perimeter of the store. "Hello, Brigid."

Startled, she looked up. "Mrs. Dodge, I didn't hear you." She paused in her work, holding the broom with one hand.

"Please call me Rose, Brigid."

"Oh, no. I couldn't do that, ma'am. Can I be helping you with something, then?"

I decided to come out with it. "Did thee know anything about Frannie seeking employment in Falmouth? Did she venture down there on occasion?"

Her expression turned stony. "You're after asking about that man, aren't you?" She nearly spat the word "man."

Currie. "What man?"

"The one looking for girls for his nasty show. Girls willing to take off their clothes and parade around on a stage. It's filthy stuff, Mrs. Dodge, make no mistake about it. He's a corrupter of innocent souls, that one."

"Does thee happen to know his name?"

"Nah, I don't. Frannie wasn't after telling me. But she was falling under his spell. She'd come back on the train with right stars in her eyes." Her own eyes filled. "I miss the girl, plain and simple." She sniffed and straightened her back. "If that despicable man was involved in her death, I'll be wanting to harpoon him straight through the heart."

She and I both.

"Brigid?" Gilbert's voice rang out from the back door.

"That would be me. Good day, Mrs. Dodge." She hurried toward the back, broom in hand.

"Thank thee, Brigid," I called after her. The man had to be Currie, didn't it? If it was, I still didn't know how he'd found Frannie. Maybe she'd gone to Falmouth on a lark and seen a handbill. Or maybe he journeyed up to this hamlet to find innocent girls. I hated that it was my own David's brother I was suspecting, my own brother-in-law. But what I'd learned was pointing in Currie's direction, at least in terms of luring girls to his show.

A dray piled high with pumpkins pulled up next to where I stood, the workhorse pulling it plodding under the load. I finally dislodged myself from my reverie. It was time to pay Edwin another call.

Five minutes later I trudged out of Huldah's office. The detective had not been in. Larkin didn't seem to know where he was, or maybe he knew but didn't want to tell me. He was at least polite today. I had one more stop to make, and then I was resolved to return to my new husband and forget about murder for the rest of the day.

TWENTY-TWO

I RAPPED ON THE DOOR of a modest cottage set well behind the Latting mansion. Late tea roses bloomed in tidy beds under the windows. Over the door wound the vine of a sweet autumn clematis in bloom, with thousands of tiny white starbursts smelling of jasmine. An extensive medicinal herb garden befitting someone of Zerviah's — and my — occupation flourished in full sun. I spied many of the same plants I grew and used, including pennyroyal, tansy, black cohosh, mallow, and more.

"Hello, Rose." Zerviah greeted me in her deep-toned quiet voice as she came around the side of the house. "I was expecting you." She held a flat-bottomed basket full of tomatoes and green beans.

"Thee was?" Did she have a sixth sense? I certainly hadn't sent word I was coming.

"I was. Would you like to sit in my garden or come inside?"

"Sitting in the garden sounds lovely."

She turned without speaking and I followed her around the back to a shady bower. Ripening apples and pears hung from branches. Two stumps had been placed under the trees. Zerviah set her trug on the ground and perched on one stump, so I took the other. I spied a good-sized vegetable garden beyond the small orchard.

"Please tell me if you've made any progress in the matter of Frannie's murder," she began.

"I've learned a number of interesting things, but right now it isn't clear what's important and what isn't."

She regarded me in silence for a moment. "I expect you don't want to share those interesting things."

"I'm not really at liberty to do so."

"Do any of them pertain to my son?" She kept her voice low, shooting a glance at a shed to the rear of the property.

"Barely. One of my aunts found an ale bottle by an outbuilding behind their house and claimed it was proof Reuben had been at their home when Frannie was there alone."

"Proof? It is true Reuben sometimes indulges in alcohol when he should not. But the railroad tracks are right next to their house. This is a ridiculous claim."

"I agree with thee," I said. "As yet I'm not aware of any real evidence. Was thy son out clamming on Seventh Day morning?"

"No. It was high tide. He goes out only when the waters ebb."

"Was he at home, then?"

"I believe so," Zerviah said, but she didn't meet my gaze, instead looking somewhere over my shoulder. "I was out for a day and a half at a long labor and birth."

"Has thy husband vouched for Reuben's whereabouts to the authorities?" I held my breath. I hoped she wouldn't take offense at my questions.

"Mr. Baxter was away and still is. Mr. Latting sent him to the western region of the state to inspect one of his businesses there."

Which meant Reuben could have come and gone at will for the period during which Frannie was killed: Sixth Day evening stretching into Seventh Day morning. No one would have marked his whereabouts, at least not his parents. The big house next door had plentiful windows but was set back from the road a bit. Possibly a lane or a path ran behind these properties. Anyway, a lad sneaking out at night might not be noticed by anyone.

"*Nitka!*" A young man burst out of the back door of the house. "Have you seen my cap?" He stopped short when he saw me. "Pardon me. I didn't realize you had a visitor." Looking to be still in his teens, he had straight black hair like his mother's, but his locks were neatly cropped above his collar, not worn in a long plait.

"Reuben, come and meet Mrs. Dodge." To me she said, "This is my son, Reuben."

Reuben approached. "Pleased to meet you, ma'am." His tone was polite but perfunctory.

I didn't blame him. Why would he take an interest in a lady calling on his mother? "And I thee, Reuben. I am very sorry for the loss of thy friend, Frannie." I held out my hand.

Eyes the color of dark chocolate flew wide open. Now he truly looked at me, his mouth turned down in sadness. "Did you know Frannie?" He stared at my hand and finally shook it for a brief moment. He had a stockier build than his mother but shared her long hands and fingers, although his were work-calloused. He wore work trousers and a sweater that were well-mended, but clean and tidy.

"Not well, but we were cousins of sorts," I said.

"Mrs. Dodge is Miss Tilly and Miss Dru's niece, son," Zerviah explained.

"Ah." He blinked. "You'd be Rose Carroll, the midwife, then. Frannie spoke of you."

"I am." I had no idea she'd known of my occupation. Tilly or Dru must have told her. "I recently was married, so now my name is Rose Dodge."

He swallowed. "And you're some kind of detective, too." His gaze was over my shoulder, not at my face.

"Not exactly." I smiled at him. He must have known he was under suspicion. I wasn't surprised he wouldn't look me in the eyes.

The bell at the church down the road chimed twelve times. Sadie had said the building was newly constructed by those in the Methodist faith.

"Crikey, it's noon already." Reuben said. "I've got to get out on the flats. Mama, you haven't seen my cap?"

"Did you lose it, son?"

"I guess. I can't find it anywhere."

"Wear your father's old one."

The boy grimaced. "The one that looks like a rat ate it? I guess I'll have to. Good day, Mrs. Dodge." He touched his mother's shoulder.

Zerviah held his hand and gazed at him with a somber look. "Stay safe and come home promptly, *peissesit*."

"Yes, Mama, but please stop calling me 'Baby.'" He freed his hand and hurried back into the cottage.

"He's still my baby," she murmured, gazing after him.

I stood. "I'd best be going, too. I told my husband I would be back by midday. I'm glad I got to meet Reuben. He's a polite young man, Zerviah. Thee has trained him well."

She bobbed her head once. "Among my people, good manners are important, as is showing respect for your elders."

"I should say those things are important for all people. Does thee have other children, as well?"

"Three, but they are older and off on their own."

My surprise must have registered on my face. She laughed and stood.

"I was only eighteen when I had my first child and I've now passed forty-five winters. Reuben is the baby of the brood."

Forty-five? She didn't look her age at all, with her smooth, nearly unlined skin.

Reuben hurried out of the cottage wearing a flat cap that indeed had seen better days atop his head. He rode off on an old bicycle fitted out with large woven baskets hanging down from either side of the rear wheel.

"You see, don't you?" Zerviah kept her voice low. "My son is not a murderer."

He'd shown only a little grief for Frannie, when I'd offered my sympathies, and had become evasive when he heard who I was. I bade Zerviah farewell and walked briskly back to my aunts' home and my husband, but my brain was aroil with thoughts.

TWENTY-THREE

DAVID AND I ALIT from the railroad's terminus at Wood's Holl by two o'clock. After I'd arrived back at Dru's and Tilly's, stashed my purchases in the ice box, and had a bite to eat with my husband, we'd caught the one thirty local. The depot here, which went right up to the water, was bustling. Passengers descended the train with us, sightseers waited to board, and cargo was unloaded, with more waiting to go on. When the island-bound *Monohansett* sounded its airhorn, travelers carrying parcels and satchels pushed toward the large side-wheel steamer, including a number of well-dressed colored people.

David saw me watching the latter. "Martha's Vineyard has a sizeable community of former slaves. The area is called Cottage City."

"Is that so? I had no idea."

"Yes. The cottages are well-appointed and almost fancifully decorated."

"It must be a comfort for them to relax apart from prejudicial attitudes," I said. "I wonder if my colored friends from Amesbury ever journey down here. I'm aware of the many Friends who reside on the smaller island of Nantucket, of course, but I confess I know little of Martha's Vineyard. Who was Martha, anyway?"

David laughed, tucking my arm through his. "I am not a compendium of general facts, my dear, much though you might believe otherwise. I'm sure someone in this lovely hamlet will know the answer to your question, though. Let's stroll, shall we?"

Stroll we did. Yesterday's oppressive weather had not returned, leaving us another sunny, breezy afternoon. We meandered along Water Street past shops and men mending nets. Two strong young women cleaned fish and shooed away screeching gulls looking for a treat. A man in the front window of a sweets shop pulled taffy.

"Look, David." I pointed at a wall plastered with handbills. They featured the same picture of the burlesque show we'd seen in Falmouth, but the words read, "Performers Wanted! Apply at the

Cape Cod Burlesque Theater weekdays between noon and five o'clock."

"My brother's recruitment efforts, no doubt," David muttered. "I hope my mother doesn't get it in her head to travel here and see what he's up to."

"She won't, will she?"

"I doubt it, but you know Clarinda. When she resolves to act, good luck trying to dissuade her. Let's move on. I don't want to let thoughts of Currie spoil an afternoon with my beautiful bride."

I gazed up at an imposing square building built from massive blocks of pink granite.

"I believe it's the old candle factory," David said. "I read about it once. When whaling was in its heyday and before we had the convenience of gas lighting, they manufactured candles in this building from the crude whale oil. I doubt the business is in operation now, and I don't know what the building currently houses."

"I hope it's not sitting empty. It's so sturdily built, it's clearly not going anywhere. It should house a thriving business, which could feel safe from any damage from hurricanes and the like."

We paused at the new marine research laboratory at the corner of Albatross.

"It seems there is water everywhere here," I said. "What an excellent place to study all the types of life thriving in the ocean."

"This sign says it's open to the public," David said. "I'd like to see what they have on display."

"I would, too."

Inside were educational placards about seals and pelagic birds, barnacles and codfish, plankton and mussels. A pretty girl in a shirtwaist sat at a table full of information pamphlets. A sign reading *Science Aquarium* was posted over another door.

"Welcome," the girl greeted us. "The pools are through yonder door if you'd like to see them. Our harbor seals are still here, but we'll be releasing them back to the wild next week." She gestured toward the door.

"My goodness," I murmured once outside. Two large granite-lined pools were surrounded by a waist-high iron fence. A seal basked on the paving stones between the basins, and fish swam silently beneath the surface.

We leaned on the fence to watch.

"See the ray?" David asked, pointing.

"It looks like an underwater bird," I exclaimed. "Wouldn't it be marvelous to move about so smoothly?"

He laid his arm over my shoulders. "We can go back into the ocean tomorrow if you'd like."

After some minutes we resolved to move on. David pulled open the door to go back inside but stopped all of a sudden, making me bump into him. From the room with the displays I heard, "Why, if it isn't my doctor brother and his lovely new wife." *Currie*.

I gave David a gentle push. Inside, Currie leaned against the girl's desk with his arms folded.

"Good afternoon, Currie," I said. David hadn't spoken.

"I'm here conversing with one of our future performers, if I have my way." Currie grinned at the girl, who blushed.

"I'd be careful around this fellow, miss," David said to her. "His business is not an honorable one, and I daresay your father would be ill-pleased to know you were associating with Currie Dodge."

The girl gaped, then slid her chair back and away from Currie. As for Currie, he narrowed his eyes at David and pressed his lips into a line.

"We were just on our way, brother," David added. "Good day."

I opened my mouth to speak, but shut it again. Out on the street I could barely keep up with his brisk stride. I grabbed his elbow.

"David, stop a minute."

He halted and passed a hand over his face before turning to me. "I'm sorry, Rose. It irks me that my brother is completely cavalier about making his living in such a disreputable—and possibly harmful—way."

"I understand. The poor girl was entirely taken with him, too, wasn't she?"

"I hope my warning has some effect on the creature." He blew out a breath. "Currie has disappointed me more than once. When he appeared at our reception, I prayed he'd reformed his wayward habits. It seems he hasn't."

I spoke softly. "And thee is both angry and saddened." I'd wanted to linger and learn about the marine life. David had clearly needed to leave. I threaded my arm through his.

He gazed out at the harbor for a moment, then touched my cheek. "I am, but there's nothing to be done about it. Can I rescue our afternoon together? I hear Prescott House offers a sumptuous afternoon tea."

"Show me the way, kind sir."

TWENTY-FOUR

WE MADE IT BACK to Sadie's by six forty-five, admiring the setting sun we glimpsed from the train as we rode. I hoped it wasn't too late for supper. Sadie hadn't given me a time this morning when she'd extended the invitation. Not that I was very hungry. The Prescott House tea had indeed been laden with delicious small sandwiches, sweets, and fruits. David and I hadn't spoken further of Currie. It didn't mean my thoughts weren't on him.

Sadie pulled open the door. "Do come in, Rose and David. We sat down to eat not a moment ago."

I thanked her and we followed her through to where my aunts sat at the table. I kissed them both and sat. "Where is Huldah?"

"He's off at some meeting and dining out as part of it," Sadie said. "Here, let me dish up the chicken stew."

"Only a small portion for me, please," I said.

"I lured her into tea at the Prescott House," David explained with a smile.

"A lovely hotel with an excellent chef," Sadie said.

After we observed our silent grace, I was glad to see Tilly at least dipping into her stew even if she didn't look particularly animated. A pang of guilt stabbed me. This was a painful time for my aunt, and she wasn't even in her own home. Perhaps she didn't want to be, though, with all the reminders of Frannie and no one but Dru to be with. Here at least Sadie was taking care of her physical needs. It was up to Edwin and me to resolve the mystery.

I dug into my stew, savoring the fresh herbs Sadie had used. The dish tasted of basil and rosemary, perhaps parsley. She'd chopped up fresh green beans and must have thrown them in at the last minute, because they added a welcome crunch and brightness.

"How are my aunts today?" I asked.

"Has thee made any headway, Rose?" Tilly asked instead of answering me. "In finding Frannie's killer?"

"Now, Till." Dru patted her sister's hand. "Rose and David don't want to be talking about anything so distasteful at the dinner table."

Distasteful? Homicide was indeed that, and so much more. "It's all right, Aunt Dru. No, Aunt Tilly. I haven't heard of the sheriff making an arrest yet."

"But thee has been making inquiries, I'm sure," Tilly pressed. "Thee passes along what thee learns to Edwin. I don't understand why they haven't yet put Reuben Baxter behind bars."

"I've learned a great deal about the criminal justice system during the course of courting Rose," David said. "The authorities can't make an arrest unless they have firm evidence a crime was committed by a particular person."

"This is true," I said. "Why does thee think Reuben is the guilty one?" I asked Tilly.

She straightened her spine and spoke in measured words. "Because he is a young man. Because he was smitten with Frannie. Because, despite being a cheerful girl, she was willful and sometimes acted in a hurtful way."

Dru nodded as she spooned in more stew.

"And because men are generally not to be trusted, present company excluded, of course." Tilly locked her eyes with mine as if willing me to agree.

"I see." What I saw was that, in fact, she had no good reason to suspect Reuben. That said, she seemed stable enough for me to ask the question I'd telegraphed to my father. She wouldn't answer if she didn't want to.

"Aunt Tilly, it might help me understand the situation better if I knew how Frannie came to be thy ward."

She halted the progression of her spoon to her mouth and returned it to her bowl. Dru frowned at me. Sadie blinked, looking from Tilly to me and back.

"I thought thee knew Frannie's parents died in an accident," Tilly said softly. "She was orphaned. Someone needed to take her in. So I did."

"With my blessing," Dru added.

"But thee was already advanced in years by then," I said to Tilly. "Why thee and not a younger family?"

"And didn't Frannie have grandparents, aunts and uncles?" David asked.

Dru shot Tilly a look. "Frannie's father was an orphan. Her mother—"

"Let me, Dru." My angular aunt bowed her head for a moment and then looked up. "I shall tell thee, and Sadie and David, as well. Dru already knows my sad story. Rose, when I was a young woman about thy own age, I still had not married. Dru and I were already living here in West Falmouth, and I fell in love. The man was a charmer. He said we would be wed. I let myself be swept away by his ardor. Soon enough I was left both alone and carrying a child."

No. My heart broke for her.

"I went away for my confinement and gave up the baby girl to be adopted. It was the hardest thing I have ever done." She raised her chin. "But I was able to keep track of her even though she knew nothing of me. She married and had a baby girl of her own. The baby was Frannie. My granddaughter."

Sadie's breath rushed in. David made a sound of sympathy in his throat. I rose and went around the table to put my arms around Tilly. I could barely see for the tears welling in my eyes.

"I never knew," I murmured. "I am so, so sorry, Aunt Tilly." At least now my earlier musing made sense. I knew something had looked familiar about Tilly's childhood picture. The connection I hadn't made was with Frannie's picture at the same age. The dark curly hair, identical dark eyes. The tragedy was almost too much to bear. Tilly's daughter, lost in an accident. And her granddaughter, murdered.

"My daughter and I never had a chance to know each other," Tilly continued.

I straightened but kept my hand on her shoulder.

"The couple who adopted her were, shall we say, less than ideal parents. They had no other children, so Frannie didn't have aunts and uncles to take her in. When I learned of Frannie's parents' death, I contacted the grandparents. They weren't interested in caring for a toddling orphan, and the baby's father's parents were deceased."

David made a sympathetic sound in his throat.

"Now thee understands why I took in the girl, Rose," Tilly continued. "Thy father knows this story, but I made him swear not to tell a soul, not even thy mother." She swallowed. "It's why I was so upset at Frannie gallivanting around and associating with the likes of Reuben Baxter. There was an older man she spoke of once, too, who showered her with affection."

Currie? Or someone else?

"I did not in any way want her to become mired in the same predicament as me," Tilly went on. "I failed, Rose. I failed our Frannie. And she was taken from us."

TWENTY-FIVE

DAVID AND I STROLLED HOME from Sadie's arm in arm. A wind shushed through the needles of the pine trees and set the swamp oak leaves to whispering with the reddening sugar maple leaves.

I sniffed the air. "I do believe it's going to rain."

"Mmm."

"Is thee thinking about what dear Tilly said? I know I am."

"The poor woman. What scoundrel would impregnate a young woman and then abandon her?"

"Husband, surely thee knows a great many men have done precisely that. He might have left before she knew she was carrying a child."

"But to promise her marriage?" He shook his head. "I'm afraid too many of my sex think with their manly parts instead of their brains."

"This is true, alas." The very same thing as Tilly underwent had happened to me in my teen years, minus the promise of marriage. A wild boy I'd liked had forced himself on me. I'd been fortunate my body had miscarried the fetus early on. I hadn't had to carry a child to term whose father was a despicable and irresponsible man. "Tilly's history must have been why she was so strict with Frannie."

"Not strict enough, as it turned out."

"Or too strict. Frannie might have felt pent in. Some man took advantage of that." Dare I again raise the possibility with him about Currie being the culprit not just in enlisting Frannie for the theater — which was distasteful but legal — but perhaps being the father of her baby? No, I would wait and see what else I could learn. With any luck, I would be completely wrong.

We walked in silence for a couple of minutes, each in our thoughts.

"Rosie, have you wondered if my brother might have been too zealous in his courting of young ladies for his employment? Of Frannie, in particular?"

Aha. What did they say? Great minds think alike? "I confess the thought had crossed my mind, but I didn't want to speak of it."

He pulled me closer to his side. "Wife, you can tell me all your thoughts. I want to know them."

"I am of a like mind. Currie's rakish ways are a bit, shall we say, unseemly."

David let out a long sigh. "He has always been a rascal, but I would hope he wouldn't cross the line into having intimate relations with young girls."

"I would hope the same. But some man did. I pray it does not turn out to be Reuben Baxter, either."

"He would seem to be the most likely culprit, being of the same age and enamored of Frannie."

"And she with him, from all reports," I said. "This morning, when he learned I knew Frannie, he looked somewhat evasive. I couldn't figure out why."

"I'm sure you will, with your talent for detecting. But please promise me you won't attempt anything risky, dear Rose. I don't know what I would do if something happened to you." His voice rasped with emotion.

"I promise, dear David. I shall keep myself safe and preferably at thy side." With any luck, for the rest of our days together.

TWENTY-SIX

I'D BEGUN TO AWAKEN the next morning when a loud rapping came at the door. I nudged David's shoulder.

"Huh?" His eyes fluttered open. He smiled, reaching his arms toward me.

"Someone's at the door," I said over the sound of rain pattering on the roof.

More knocking was followed by a voice calling, "Telegram for Dodge."

"Oh!" David pushed aside the covers and hurried to the window.

It was probably Daddy's return telegram, but why so early? Regardless of the telegram's contents, I couldn't help but admire my husband's naked backside.

"Just a moment," he called down. He hurriedly pulled on his trousers without the benefit of underdrawers, fastened the pants, and grabbed his shirt before trotting down the stairs in his bare feet.

I pulled on my dressing gown, donned my glasses, and peered out the window as David took the missive and gave the boy, wearing a slicker against the rain, a coin. I waited a moment, but when David didn't return to bed I padded down the stairs. I found him sitting at the kitchen table staring at the yellow paper, the raindrop-spotted envelope abandoned on the table. He looked stricken. I laid my hand on his shoulder.

"What is it?" I asked in a soft voice.

"It's Mother. She's fallen gravely ill, Rose. Father thinks it might be her heart."

I brought my other hand to my mouth, eyes wide. "I'm so sorry." Clarinda was a trim woman who took care of herself. She wasn't the kind of overindulgent and sedentary person sometimes prone to ill health. "Has she had heart incidents before?"

"She's had a few troubling attacks previously, yes."

"It might be a condition she was born with. Either way, we must go to Clarinda." And pray for her. His mother and I had come into conflict many times, but I did not wish her harm, nor want David to lose his mother so soon.

He stood and took me in his arms. I embraced him tightly. His heart beat against mine and I breathed in the scent on his neck, so much a part of him.

After a long minute, he pushed back and took my hand. "No, I must go to her. I'm so sorry to interrupt our stay in West Falmouth, my darling Rose. But you're needed here. Tilly needs you."

"But thee is my husband." I tilted my head to the side. "I should be at thy side as thy helpmate."

He put a finger under my chin, his face full of love. "You will be with me in spirit, and you'll be home before long. Who knows, this could be a ploy by Mother to ruin our first week as a married couple."

The same unkind thought had skipped through my mind. Unfortunately, it was a possibility. And David, as wonderful as he was, still seemed to be at Clarinda's beck and call.

"I know you, Rose. Stay and resolve this mystery, or you won't be able to rest easy. Also, I have a task for you."

"A task?"

"Yes. Please find Currie and tell him Mother is possibly on her deathbed." His voice caught on the last word. "Ask him to travel home to see her, to be by her side. Tell my brother his mother needs him."

I opened my mouth, but closed it. What if Currie was the guilty party in Frannie's pregnancy—or even her death? He should not be leaving Barnstable County.

Finally I spoke. "Very well. But I will be home as soon as I ever can be."

"To our new house."

"To our home and to thee."

"Oh!"

"Oh, what?" I asked.

"I never searched for Miss Tilly's birth record for you. I said I would."

"It doesn't matter, David. I can, or Edwin might already have."

A frown creased my husband's handsome brow. "But you will be careful, won't you? Do your detecting, but please, please, pass along anything you learn to Detective Merritt and be content with doing only that."

"Of course."

"I'm serious, Rosie." He set his hands on my arms and peered into my face. "Will you promise me not to put your lovely self in harm's way?"

"Yes, my dear." I smiled to reassure him. "I promise. Now run along and get thyself washed and properly dressed. I'll put together some bread and cheese for thee. It's nearly seven, and thee should be able to catch the morning express to Boston."

"Have I told you I love you lately?" he growled.

"Not today, thee hasn't."

"I love you, Rose Carroll Dodge." He swept me into a long and passionate kiss.

I pulled away, laughing. "Go!"

TWENTY-SEVEN

I TRUDGED UP THE WIDE STEPS to the well-appointed Bowman home on Main Street later that morning. I was grateful today I'd brought my oilskin cloak on the trip, because a chilly wind drove the rain sideways. I felt I needed to speak with Hazel again. Maybe she knew something about the father of Frannie's baby. The man's identity had to be part of the key to solving her murder. She and Hazel had been close friends. She surely had some knowledge of whom Frannie spent time with, if anyone, apart from Reuben. I would go in search of Currie soon. I also prayed Clarinda would recover before David even arrived

A moment later I trudged back down. A uniformed maid had told me Hazel was at work at Mrs. Boyce's tag factory, which was situated near the train station. It would be interesting to see a thriving business owned and run by a woman, and if I could have a short conversation with Hazel, so much the better. I had only a short walk down Chappaquoit Street to the factory, a two-story building adjacent to the tracks.

I entered a busy office, with a boy loading boxes onto a handcart and a woman at a counter addressing a stack of labels. Others packed fat bundles, presumably of tied tags, into boxes. One employee secured sturdy string around full boxes, readying them for shipping. Rain dripped off my cloak as I pushed back the hood. I removed my spectacles, drying them with a clean handkerchief.

The woman at the counter glanced up. "Can I help you, ma'am?"

"I'm Rose Dodge, Tilly Carroll's niece."

"We all miss our dear Miss Isley. Poor Miss Tilly." She wagged her head in sorrow. "What a grievous loss she's had. How is she coping?"

"As best she can, I thank thee. I'm here because I'd like to have a brief word with Hazel Bowman, if I may."

"Miss Bowman is working upstairs." She frowned. "But by rights you should ask Mrs. Boyce if she approves. That's her office there." She gestured to an open door with her chin.

I turned toward the office.

"The thing is, Mrs. Boyce stepped out to the post office a little bit ago," the woman said. "What's it in regard to, anyway, your word with Miss Bowman?"

"I'd like to talk with her for only a minute or two about Frannie's death."

The woman's eyes widened. "Are you a Pinkerton girl?" she whispered.

"No, not at all. But she was my aunt's ward." Given Tilly's revelation, I now knew I was Frannie's blood cousin, a first cousin once removed. This woman didn't need to know that, though. "And I know Hazel and Frannie were friends."

"Well, that'll be fine, then. You go on up. Have you met Miss Bowman before?"

"Yes."

"Then I don't need to introduce you. The stairs are around the back, but you can leave your rain garment down here first, if you like."

I hung my cloak on the coat tree and made my way up. Two dozen women, both young and older, sat around long tables deftly threading strings through holes in the ends of thin cardboard tags in various colors and sizes. Their fingers moved like flashes of light. Another operated a metal winding machine, and yet another cut winds of cotton string. I spied Hazel using a machine that perforated a stack of tags with one press of a lever. I approached.

She started when she saw me. "Hello, there. Mrs. Dodge, isn't it? Frannie's relation?" She'd tied a kerchief on her light hair today, and wore an apron over a summery dress.

"Yes. Good morning, Hazel. This is quite the enterprise."

"You could say so. Might I ask what you're doing here? You didn't come to the factory to study how we string tags, surely."

I laughed. "No, but it's quite fascinating now I see what's involved. Do the tags come already cut?"

"Yes, except for the holes."

"That's an ingenious machine." I gestured toward the winding device.

"Different-sized tags need different lengths of string," Hazel explained. "You can change the setting so the strings will be the correct size once they're cut." She folded her arms and narrowed her eyes. "Let me guess. You want to talk about Frannie."

"I do. I'm curious about any suitors Frannie might have had. Boys or men she spent time with?"

"She never wanted for attention from the opposite sex, I can tell you. She was pretty and shapely and saucy."

Hazel's tone contained a touch of envy. She herself was not unattractive, but she wasn't particularly striking. Her observation concurred with what Dru had told me about Frannie. Not the saucy part, but the beauty.

"Can thee help me with details, please, about with whom she might have been consorting?" I asked.

She twisted her mouth. "You mean like Reuben Baxter? He pretends to be a nice boy, but he can be pushy. And he's an Indian. I don't know what Frannie saw in him."

"How did they meet?"

"Around town, how else?" Hazel raised a single eyebrow.

"Was there anyone else?"

"Yes." She glanced around the room and turned her back on the bustle. "Mr. Latting was, shall we say, overly solicitous to Frannie."

Abial Latting? The Quaker businessman? This was not the suitor I'd expected her to speak of. Although Tilly had also mentioned an older gentleman.

"Thee means Abial Latting?"

"Yes. I saw the two of them together not too long ago," she continued. "They were behind a stone wall and I'm sure they thought no one could see them. She was giggling, and he was not acting like a proper gentleman, I'll tell you. Kissing her hand and playing with her hair and all. Disgusting, that's what it was. He was near old enough to be her grandfather." Her whisper was harsh.

An older woman at the table cleared her throat, looking pointedly at Hazel.

"Sorry, Mrs. Dodge," Hazel said. "I'm here to work. I don't want yon biddy to report me to Mrs. Boyce."

"I thank thee for thy time, Hazel. I'll be at my aunts' for a few more days, at least. If thee thinks of anything else, please send me a note."

"Very well." She straightened the stack of tags on her machine and slammed down the perforating handle. With a *thunk*, a sharp rod sliced through the cards.

TWENTY-EIGHT

AFTER TALKING WITH HAZEL, I felt compelled to tell the detective what she'd shared with me. I retraced my steps through the rain toward Main Street and Huldah's law office. The sky was lightening a bit and the wind had eased up, but a steady salt-scented rain still fell. A covered buggy pulled by a spirited mare sped through a wide puddle in the road, wetting the hem of my dress and even spattering my face. I cried out to no avail. The vehicle was gone. Drivers needed to be far more careful not to splash pedestrians.

As I picked my way along, I mused about Hazel mentioning Abial's behavior. He had been alone at Meeting for Worship. Was he married? Was his wife ill, or away? Did he have children? They would be adults, unless he'd been married later in life to a younger woman, as many men were.

I also thought about why a girl of sixteen would have enjoyed the attentions of an older man like him. Hazel had said Frannie was giggling and seeming to enjoy Abial's behavior. Was it because she'd grown up fatherless? Liking to flirt was one thing. Having intimate relations was another entirely. I prayed Abial hadn't forced himself on Frannie. And if Reuben knew about Abial—his father's employer—how had he felt? He would have been powerless to react.

This time when I called on Edwin Merritt, he was in. Today Larkin was extra solicitous of me, deferential and polite as he led me back to Edwin's office. The young fellow took my wet cloak and said he'd hang it for me, then nearly bowed before he hurried back to the front. I smothered a laugh, glad the lesson on respect had taken. Or perhaps it was because Larkin knew I'd report him to Edwin if he didn't treat me well.

I sat in the wooden chair opposite Edwin's desk, which was marginally neater today than the last time I was here on Second Day. I once again had to dry my glasses. They didn't do much good speckled with raindrops.

After the niceties were out of the way, the detective said, "I hope you've dug up some useful information for me, Mrs. Dodge. This is a tough case, and the sheriff isn't appreciating our lack of progress."

"Thee isn't any closer to making an arrest, I gather?"

"Alas, no."

"On First Day thee seemed to believe one of the Baxter men might be the culprit. Clearly thee isn't in possession of pertinent or sufficient evidence to accuse either Joseph or Reuben." And why would Joseph be suspected at all? I would hate for it to be merely because he was an Indian.

"I don't mean to say our inquiries have gotten us nowhere, but it's hard when a witness or two is obviously lying."

"Who might that be?"

He gave me the same kind of look Kevin often did. "You must know I can't tell you."

"Very well. I assume thee and thy men are attempting to track Frannie's movement in the time before her death."

"Yes, of course we are." Edwin spoke as if that was obvious.

"What did thee think of Marie Deorocki's observation? She came and told thee, didn't she?"

"She did. I'm afraid what she says she saw was rather too vague to be of use."

"That's a pity. Well, I came here because Hazel Bowman told me something interesting not half an hour earlier."

"She did, did she?" He folded his hands on his desk.

"She said she'd seen Abial Latting alone with Frannie, and he was behaving with her in a manner unseemly for a gentleman."

"Mr. Latting?" His voice rose. "The Quaker businessman? Curiouser and curiouser, as thy namesake author put it."

I was impressed he'd read *Alice's Adventures in Wonderland* closely enough to remember the coined phrase. "Lewis Carroll was a pseudonym, thee must know."

"That's as it may be. I believe we were discussing an equally fanciful thought, that an upstanding member of our community — and your own faith — might have been dallying with a girl of sixteen."

"Edwin," I began. I straightened my spine and wiped any trace of amusement off my face. "Surely this is an avenue of investigation thee must pursue, regardless of Abial's position in thy regard. If Frannie was carrying a child when she died, some man was responsible for her condition, whether he participated in her death or not."

The detective harrumphed as he tidied the papers on his desk. "Of course, of course. Tell me more."

"Hazel saw Frannie and Abial somewhere in town. I expect others might have spotted them, too. The topic is worth pursuing, including Abial's alibi — or lack thereof — during the period in which Frannie's whereabouts are unaccounted for. Also, Brigid McChesney told me Abial Latting was not a man one wishes to tangle with. I suspect, Quaker or not, he might be manipulative in his business dealings. And if this is true, such behavior could easily extend into his private life."

"I'll grant you that, Mrs. Dodge." Edwin jotted down a note, then selected a piece of paper with an official-looking stamp on it. "I have the autopsy report. Miss Isley was definitely with child. Her condition was advanced about fourteen weeks."

I bobbed my head. "Still early enough for a girl to be able to hide her condition from all but a midwife's knowing eyes. Thee had mentioned a laceration on her head. Was she already deceased when she drowned, or did drowning cause her death?"

"The medical examiner believes cause of death was drowning."

"So she might have been unconscious from the blow." I prayed she had been. Drowning was a terrifying way to die, I'd heard. "Where on her head was the laceration?"

He touched the back of his head. "A little bit down from the crown. Her skull had been hit crosswise."

I drummed my fingers for a moment, thinking. "Doesn't this seem like an odd finding? If you were to hit someone on the back of the head, it would be a downward blow, wouldn't it?" I raised my hands over my head as if holding a heavy object.

Edwin laughed. "Now the Quaker lady is practicing assault?"

"I'm serious, Edwin. If she hit her head horizontally, it could have been on the gunwale of a boat, couldn't it?"

"It could. But she could have been struck laterally, too. Think of how a bat is used in the game of baseball." He pushed aside the report. "Now, Mrs. Dodge. I have heard a rumor. I don't like to indulge in idle gossip, but when an item comes to my attention which might be pertinent to a case, I must needs follow up on it.

What do you know about Miss Isley being a blood relative of your aunt? I mean, of Miss Tilly?"

Perhaps Tilly and Frannie's relationship wasn't as secret as Tilly believed. "Who did thee hear this from?"

"It doesn't matter. Is it a fact?"

"I learned only yesterday it is true, a result of Tilly's having been the victim of an unscrupulous man when she was about the age I am now."

"She bore a bastard child and gave it up for adoption," he said softly.

"Yes. But she was able to follow her daughter's upbringing from a distance. When the daughter and her husband died, leaving two-year-old Frannie, Tilly took her in."

"This is likely irrelevant, but do you know why she didn't adopt the girl?"

"No." Had I even asked Aunt Tilly? "She didn't offer the information, and I've not asked."

"Do you have anything else for me?" Edwin glanced at the clock.

"Actually, I might. I stopped in yesterday but thee wasn't about." I hated to have to tell him about Currie, but I had to. "My husband's brother, Currie Dodge, is currently residing in Wood's Holl, or so he told us. He apparently works for the burlesque theater in Falmouth, and, among other responsibilities, he recruits young woman to perform in the variety shows they put on."

The eyebrow over Edwin's green eye went up. "You don't say."

"I do. I am unhappy at having to relay this, but he might be a possibility for the father of Frannie's child. He's quite the charmer. David and I saw him in action at the aquarium in Wood's Holl yesterday. He was trying to worm his way into the affections of a pretty young lady who works there."

Edwin didn't quite rub his hands together, but his eyes sparkled. "And 'the plot thickens,' as George Villiers wrote."

"Who was he?" I tilted my head.

"The author of a play called *The Rehearsal* from late-seventeenth-century England."

"My, thee is quite well read, Detective."

"Does this surprise you?" He sat back in his chair.

"I might have ascribed the phrase to Arthur Conan Doyle,

instead. I'm glad to know its origins. And that the Barnstable County Sheriff's Office hires well-educated detectives." I smiled as I stood. "I can't think of any other avenues for thee to pursue at the moment, but I shall return should something else occur to me."

He rose, as well. "Please feel free to leave a message for me if I'm not in."

We said our goodbyes. I retrieved my cloak and made my way down the steps, the rain having reduced itself to a light drizzle. My feet slowed as my inner small voice told me I'd forgotten to convey some critical piece of information. But what?

TWENTY-NINE

"MISS CARROLL?" Brigid hailed me as I walked past the market on my way to Sadie's. She stood in the doorway with an envelope in her hand.

In those few minutes since I'd left Edwin, the precipitation had completely ceased to fall. I pushed back the cloak's hood and let it flap open.

"Yes, Brigid?" I looked both ways and crossed the road ahead of a spirited team of stallions pulling a large closed carriage.

"A Special Delivery letter for you came in earlier. I spied you through the screen." She handed me the missive.

"I thank thee." Could I bear any more bad news this morning? Whether I could or not, I needed to read the contents. I opened the envelope and blew out a breath. It was from Daddy, and the only news was what I had learned from Tilly yesterday about Frannie's origins. He ended the message by writing, *Shall I come to West Falmouth?*

The idea stopped me. My husband was gone. Did I want my father here as support? Or maybe he meant to provide solace to his sister. I flapped the paper in my hand. I needed to send a reply.

"I hope it's not after being bad news." Brigid clasped her hands and looked worried.

"No, no. Please don't concern thyself. But I do need to send a note in return. Can thee sell me a single sheet of paper and an envelope?"

"Of course. Come with me."

"Wait a moment," I said. "I heard something troubling this morning, and I wondered if thee had witnessed it, too."

"If I can help you, ma'am, I'd be honored."

In the moment, I decided not to tell her Hazel was my informant. "When I was here two days ago, Abial Latting came by the market. Does thee remember?"

"That man is hard to forget, he is."

"At the time thee mentioned one wouldn't want to get in his way, correct?"

116

"By the blessed Mary, yes. It's a fact, Mrs. Dodge." She nodded vigorously.

"Did thee ever see him, ah, dallying with Frannie around town? Possibly in a clandestine manner?"

She squinted at me. "I'm not knowing this word, dallying."

"I mean, he might have acted overly affectionate toward Frannie, a young unmarried girl."

"Oh, ho. So dallying means trying to, you know, get into her knickers, does it? Hoping to get her alone so he can shag her?"

Shag must connote the sexual act. I hemmed and hawed for a moment. "Dally doesn't signify exactly that, but yes, that's what *I* meant."

"Sure, and I saw them more than once. Out behind the Quaker carriage sheds one time, and down beyond the wharf building. But he wasn't the only gent hoping to get too close to Frannie."

"Oh?"

"There was that other lad. No, he's too old to be a lad, and a slick chap, he is. Looked for all the world like he thought he was in London town instead of this sleepy fishing village." She snapped her fingers. "Oh, that's right. I mentioned him to you, the one looking for the girls."

Currie.

"Once he came into the market and tried to get a little too friendly with me. Mr. Boyce, he didn't like that. He sent me back to the storeroom, and I heard him give the gentleman what for. The chap didn't come back, then, did he?"

I was glad Gilbert Boyce hadn't blamed Brigid for Currie's behavior, as sometimes happened. I followed her inside. Maybe the shopkeeper could verify the man had been Currie.

"Is Gilbert in?" I asked Brigid.

"No, he's off at the bank. Let me get you those letter supplies."

I paid her and made my way over to the postmaster. What should I tell my father? Come or not come? I stared at the piece of paper. I made up my mind and picked up the pencil.

Thee would be welcome here, Daddy. Love, Rose

THIRTY

I ARRIVED AT SADIE'S at a little after noon to find the ladies—including Marie—sitting around the dining table eating chicken salad sandwiches.

"Come and eat, Rose," Sadie urged me. "Take a plate from the sideboard there and sit with us."

"I thank thee." My breakfast of a poached egg on toast had been hours ago. "How fares thy mother, Marie?"

"She is a shadow of herself and spends a great deal of time sleeping, I'm afraid, but I thank you for inquiring." Her smile was a sad one. "My sister has arrived to help me take care of her."

"I am glad thee has assistance and solace," I said.

"Where is thy husband?" Drusilla asked me.

"He had to return home in a hurry," I replied. "He received a telegram early this morning saying his mother Clarinda had taken gravely ill."

Sadie placed her hand on her heart. "My goodness. Shall we pray for her?"

Marie drew out a rosary and began fingering the beads, praying silently. We Quakers closed our eyes and also prayed without speaking. I held David's mother in God's Light, that she might heal quickly and easily. I'd also held Clarinda in the Light for some minutes this morning after David had departed. I opened my eyes when I heard the rustling of movement and a clink of silverware.

"Here, Rose." Sadie passed me the plate of sandwiches.

"I thank thee." I helped myself and took a bite. "My, this is good," I told my hostess. "Thy mayonnaise is extra creamy, and the bits of celery add a nice crunch."

She smiled. "What has thee been up to today?"

I gazed around at the curious faces of these womenfolk. What a blessing their company was. "One thing I did this morning was stop by the tag factory. It's an interesting industry."

"Indeed," Dru said. "Annie Boyce is quite the businesswoman."

"Was the call part of thy investigation?" Sadie asked me.

"Possibly."

"That Hazel girl works there," Dru said. "She's a shifty one."

Shifty? "What does thee mean, Aunt Dru?"

"She's like a spider," Dru said. "Excellent at spinning stories and webs."

"My sister means the girl is a habitual liar." Tilly's voice was so subdued as to be barely audible. She'd only nibbled at the edges of her sandwich. "She has fibbed to our faces about losing library books."

Dru nodded her head so energetically her hairpins nearly flew out. "Yes, while we know full well she set the novels on her bookshelf and never gave a thought to returning them."

I was pretty sure Hazel had lied to me when she'd said Brigid might have done Frannie harm. What other untruths was she telling? And if she was constantly on laudanum, as Brigid had claimed, would she even realize she was lying?

Tilly turned her plate clockwise a quarter turn but didn't eat.

I peered at her. "Aunt Tilly, is thee all right?"

She lifted her face, her eyes as haunted as they'd been on First Day. "We need to bury our girl, Rose. They only now told me I could have her back."

My throat thickened. Interring a granddaughter wasn't the way life was supposed to go. The younger generation should be tending to their elders' deaths, not the reverse. Tilly had already lost her daughter and wouldn't have been able to mourn for her in public.

"I'm helping arrange the Memorial Meeting for Worship for Sixth Day," Sadie said. "But the grave will be dug later this afternoon. We'll gather at sunset to bid Frannie farewell."

Marie frowned. "Aren't you doing things in reverse? Don't you usually have the funeral and then the burial?"

"No," I began. "As we don't believe in embalming, we need to bury the . . ." I caught myself before saying "body," which would be too harsh a word for Tilly to hear. "To bury the deceased as soon as possible. And the Memorial Meeting is much like our regular Meeting for Worship, except it focuses on the person who has gone on ahead. Typically a coffin is not present."

"I see," Marie murmured. "It's a different way of proceeding than I'm accustomed to, but I suppose it doesn't really matter."

I opened my mouth to ask Marie how her talk with Edwin had gone when she went to tell him about the splash. I shut it again. We didn't need to bring up the topic during a meal in front of Tilly. She was in enough pain as it was.

"Thy interlude with David has been interrupted, Rose," Sadie said. "Will thee return to Amesbury soon, as well?"

"I'm not sure. I offered to go with him to provide wifely support, but he wanted me to stay here and continue my investigations. And now, with Frannie's Memorial Meeting on Sixth Day, I certainly won't leave before that happens."

"Good," Dru said. "Thee is a comfort to us here."

"My father asked if he should make his way to West Falmouth. I sent him a reply he would be welcome, and that was before I knew about the service."

Dru batted a hand. "I mailed him a note not an hour ago, too. We received a lovely letter of condolence from him this morning, in which he asked if we'd appreciate his presence."

"Rose, rest assured I'll continue to watch over these ladies here at the house, and thy father, too, whenever he arrives," Sadie said. "Thee doesn't need to worry about them. Concentrate instead on discovering the truth. But do know thee is always welcome to sup with us."

"I appreciate the offer, Sadie, and I thank thee for the repast." What a jewel Sadie was. I patted my mouth with the napkin. "Now I need to go to Falmouth to find David's brother. My husband commissioned me to let Currie know their mother is ill." I surveyed the caring faces around the table. "Currie and his mother had been estranged until immediately after David and I married last Seventh Day, when Currie appeared at our reception. David had urged him to stay in Newburyport and mend fences, but we saw him in Falmouth on Second Day. He didn't remain long with his parents."

"And Mr. Dodge isn't sure his brother will go to their mother?" Marie asked.

"Precisely," I said. "I'm to do my best to convince him."

"Every family has its black sheep as well as skeletons in the closet." Dru shook her head but sneaked a glance at her sister. Tilly didn't seem to notice.

"Sadie, does thee have the train timetable at hand?" I asked.

"Why don't I drive thee in my carriage?" Sadie asked. "The rain has stopped, and having a conveyance will make it easier and faster to search for the man."

"It certainly will," I said. "I thank thee, Sadie."

"Our Miss Brooks could use an outing, too," she added.

"Miss Brooks?" I asked. "Who's that?"

Dru chortled. "She's Sadie's mare. Has thee heard of a sillier name for a horse?"

Sadie rolled her eyes with a fond expression on her face. "Miss Mary Brooks was Huldah's nursemaid when he was young. He wasn't raised as a Friend, you see, but enthusiastically became convinced in our faith before we married."

I only smiled. Miss Brooks was a silly name, but not so different from Peaches, the dun-colored gelding David had insisted I use last winter, along with a loaned buggy.

"I'll come along for the ride, if I may, now that my sister is here to spell me," Marie said. She stood and began to collect the dishes.

"Of course," Sadie said. "Our wagon buggy seats four comfortably, and I love to drive. Dru, will thee join us?"

"No, I'm back to the library for the afternoon," Dru said.

"Very well. I'll have my boy ready the horse now." Sadie bustled away.

I went around to Tilly and laid my hand on her bony shoulder. "We'll be back well before the burial, Aunt Tilly. Why doesn't thee rest for the afternoon? It's likely to be a difficult evening for thee."

"I believe I shall, Rose. No period in my life has been harder to bear than the events of this week."

THIRTY-ONE

WE THREE LADIES clopped along on the route south to Falmouth, with Sadie in the driver's seat of her Rockaway wagon buggy. The dark blue vehicle had a roof but open sides and was trimmed with a wide stripe of light blue edged in gold. It had been manufactured in Amesbury, a fact about which I—someone with no direct connection to my town's internationally famous carriage industry—felt unreasonably proud.

Sadie sat tall and appeared to be a competent horsewoman. I held on to the side of the carriage with one hand and my bonnet with the other so as not to lose it. The wind that had blown the rain clouds away now gusted briskly enough for a record-breaking sailboat race, or so it felt to me. Marie had insisted on sitting in back.

"Where to first, Rose?" Sadie asked.

"I suppose the theater in Falmouth, since I don't know where Currie's abode is." When we drove through a sheltered spot, I ran a finger over the fine blue broadcloth upholstery. "He told David and me he works for the theater."

Sadie glanced over at me, raising a genteel eyebrow. "The Falmouth Opera House or the rather disreputable one presenting the burlesque shows?"

"I'm afraid it's the latter." I pulled my mouth to the side. "As distasteful as it sounds."

Marie leaned forward. "My cousin danced in some of those shows up in Lowell. Certainly the ladies are scandalously clad, but the entertainment can be quite amusing. It's not all distasteful, Mrs. Dodge, and it is at times quite intelligent."

"Marie, please call me Rose. I insist."

She laughed. "Very well. But I meant what I said. This fellow you're searching for shouldn't automatically be assigned a place in hell simply because he's employed by a burlesque show."

I twisted to look at her. I thought of myself as a forward-looking person, but in this case perhaps I'd been too quick to judge burlesque as low and worthless entertainment. "I think thee is

122

correct, Marie." Still, simply working for the show might not have been all Currie had been up to.

"I know the owner of the Opera House," Sadie said. "He might be acquainted with the people who run the other theater. We can pay him a call."

"I like the way thee thinks, Sadie," I said. I contented myself for the next twenty bumpy minutes with holding on and watching the scenery pass.

As we went, we passed a field with a team of oxen pulling a mowing device, the farmer trudging behind. We crested a rocky hill clad in nothing more than scrubby plants and stone walls. Sadie steered the horse around a slow-moving span buggy. It featured extra-wide axles, which Sadie explained made it easier to traverse the sandy roads of this terrain.

The uneven road jogged my brain's thoughts, too. Sometime soon I should interview Reuben more closely. He could have been responsible for the pregnancy. Had anyone asked him outright if he was? Having little means to care for a family, he could have argued with Frannie. I also wondered if Joseph was back from his trip. I thought Zerviah had said he had left before Frannie died. Was she telling the truth?

And then there was Hazel. According to Brigid, Hazel was a laudanum addict, a girl angry about her friend taking up with a boy, someone who had lied about more than one thing. Could she be involved? From what I'd learned talking with David about the soporific effects of laudanum, I doubted the drug alone would push Hazel to kill, unless she was agitated from a lack of it.

I had to discount Tilly as the cause of Frannie's death, despite Edwin's suspicion she might be. After learning Frannie's heritage, I knew in my heart my aunt could not possibly have killed her own granddaughter, not for any reason under the sun, not even accidentally.

When we found Currie today — if we did — would he speak truth or lie to me in self-protection? If he had impregnated Frannie, he might have thought it would ruin his life for her to bear his child and make the father's name public. It would change his life, certainly, but if he'd killed to prevent such a change, David would be devastated. I knew that as well as I knew myself.

The stakes would be higher, in a way, if the guilty party was Abial Latting, who had far more to lose than Currie. I supposed being a Friend didn't make men immune from acting irresponsibly, but our faith had a strong belief in comporting oneself peaceably without violence. Every person had that of God in him or her and was equal in God's eyes. We learned from a young age that to harm a child of God was to also harm God. Being a Friend should have prevented Abial from committing a violent act. And yet, people violated the tenets of their faith regularly, no matter which religion they practiced.

A double jolt jostled me back to the present. I looked around. In my reverie I hadn't even noticed we'd entered Falmouth proper, where we'd just crossed the railroad tracks. The town here was thickly settled, with a mixture of houses, shops, and journeymen. We passed the open door of a blacksmith's forge. A little farther along a woman sat outside mending a sail, its white canvas spread out around her like a giant skirt.

"Sadie, what does thee know about Abial Latting's family?" I inquired.

"Why does thee ask?" She slowed the horse to a walk.

"I have learned a few curious things about him. Is he married? Does he have children, and if so, how old are they? He appeared to be unaccompanied at Meeting for Worship."

"He was married. It's not a pretty story, Rose." She gave a quick turn of her head toward the back, then focused on the road again, lowering her voice to a near whisper. "Marie's asleep, so I'll tell thee in confidence. Abial's wife died five years ago. The circumstances were a bit murky. After that, his son argued constantly with his father when he reached maturity and then left abruptly to attend Haverford College. He has not been seen in town since. The daughter was younger."

Was? A chill overtook me, one unrelated to the weather. "How old is the girl?" I prayed Abial hadn't been preying on his own daughter, old enough to have become a woman.

"She was sixteen when her brother left. None of us quite knew what went on in the household, except a sister of the late mother came to town one day and swept the girl away with her."

At least the daughter hadn't also died under murky circumstances.

But had the aunt fetched her to hide a pregnancy, as had happened with Tilly? Or to rescue her from her own father's advances? "So Abial now lives alone?"

"Well, he has a housekeeper, of course. A man like him doing for himself? I can't fathom it. A nice local woman." She snorted. "He apparently asked the Indian midwife if she would take care of the house and the cooking, and she refused."

"I can understand why. And Joseph Baxter is his handyman," I said, picturing Zerviah and her family in the cottage behind the mansion.

"He is."

What if Joseph hadn't actually been out of town, but had been doing Abial's dirty work for him, instead? If Abial had wanted Frannie killed but didn't want to sully his own hands, would Joseph have carried out his order?

"Whoa, Miss Brooks," Sadie said, pulling up in front of an ornate four-story brick structure.

The opera house stood at the end of the main thoroughfare. David and I must have missed it during our stroll two days ago. It was every bit as beautiful an edifice as the one in Amesbury, which hosted all kinds of public events not restricted to opera. Political parties had even held rallies in it shortly before the presidential election last fall.

"Are we here?" Marie asked, startled. "I think I dozed off. I was up late with Mother last night."

"We have arrived," Sadie said. "Let us see what we shall see. Yes, ladies?"

"Yes." If I were one to indulge in superstitions, I might have crossed my fingers and done whatever else people do to ensure a good outcome. As it was, I took a deep breath, straightened my spine, and climbed down out of the carriage.

THIRTY-TWO

WE WAITED IN THE LOBBY of the opera house while a deferential young fellow went in search of the owner. The walls were ornately decorated, with gilt edging various curlicues on the trim. The ceiling was painted a deep cerulean blue, evoking the color of twilight. Marie seemed awestruck by the richly elaborate designs, but to me they were too fancy to enjoy. The walls also bore large posters in frames advertising coming performances, including *Much Ado About Nothing* next month, a rousing Shakespeare play I had viewed in Newburyport last year. No burlesque dancers here, that was clear.

"Marie," I began, "I haven't had a chance to ask thee how thy conversation with the detective went."

She looked startled at my words and blinked for a moment before she answered. "It was fine. He asked why I didn't speak up sooner, and he seemed frustrated I couldn't identify either person in the boat."

"I'm sure he was," I said. "No more details have come to thee since? Were the occupants of the boat male or female? Did thee see the color of a garment or the shape of a hat, say?"

"I really couldn't tell if I saw men or women." She narrowed her eyes, peering into the distance, as if it helped her picture the scene on the water. "Perhaps there was a flat hat on one and maybe dark hair on the other?"

Frannie had had dark hair, and if Reuben's hat was like his father's it was a flat cap.

"But I could be wrong," she added. "I was not at all close to the boat."

"Sadie," I said, "did Frannie wear a bonnet like other Friends?"

"Of course she had one, but the girl was forever going around with the bonnet hanging down her back by the strings. It drove Tilly to distraction." Sadie's own bonnet today was of a fine midnight blue lawn matching her dress.

"Mrs. Gifford, how splendid to see you again." A silver-haired gentleman approached Sadie with both hands outstretched. "You are looking lovely, as always. She and her husband are longtime benefactors of the opera house," he told Marie and me. The man was dressed as elegantly as his theater, wearing an impeccably tailored suit, gold cufflinks, and a crimson brocade bow tie.

"Wesley, thank thee for seeing us with not a word of forewarning." Sadie clasped his hands for a moment, then released them. "May I present my friends Rose Dodge and Marie Deorocki? Rose, Marie, this is Wesley Stewart, owner of this beautiful theater."

He gave a little bow. "Please come with me to my office, ladies."

We followed him, his heels clicking on the polished marble floor, through a hallway wallpapered in red brocade. He ushered us into a sumptuously appointed room with a wide desk at one end next to a sitting area. Armchairs upholstered in red leather clustered about a low table. This was definitely not a burlesque theater, although I did spy a cabinet with decanters of amber-colored liquids and several stemmed glasses out at the ready. The room smelled faintly of tobacco and a masculine eau de cologne.

"Please sit. Shall I ring for tea, or perhaps you'd prefer something stronger. I have sherry, cognac, and whiskey." Wesley laughed. "I know you'll refuse me, Mrs. Gifford, but maybe these ladies will keep me company in an afternoon tipple?"

Or maybe this wasn't so removed from the other theater, if the man was eager to drink in the middle of the afternoon. I was sure if Currie was here, he'd readily take Wesley up on his offer.

"I don't mind if I do, Mr. Stewart," Marie said.

Sadie glanced at her in surprise. "I would love a cup of tea, please."

"Of course. Would sherry suit, Mrs. Deorocki?" he asked.

"Thank you, yes."

"Something for you, Mrs. Dodge?" Wesley asked.

"I thank thee," I said. "I would like a simple glass of water, if thee has it."

"Another Quaker, are you?"

"Yes, Wesley." I folded my hands in my lap. He might have been able to discern my faith from my plain dress and bonnet, but apparently didn't. Women who were not Friends also dressed in this fashion, of course.

He pulled a small lever in the wall, which summoned the young man from before. Wesley gave him the tea and water order before pouring himself and Marie a full glass each from one of the decanters.

Once we were all settled with our drinks, Wesley crossed his legs, clasped his hands atop his knee in a dainty gesture, and beamed. "What can I help you ladies with today? Were you wanting a tour of the opera house, or do we have more pressing business?"

"Rose here is trying to find her brother-in-law, whom she recently met," Sadie began. "Rose, thee should explain."

I thought for a moment how to approach the topic. "My new husband, David, and I came to West Falmouth a few days ago to console my aunts, whose ward is recently deceased."

"Oh, my." Our host fanned himself, brown eyes wide. "Do you mean the girl who was murdered?" His voice was hushed.

"Yes," I said. "Thee has heard."

"Well, who hasn't? But what has this to do with the Falmouth Opera House, if you don't mind my asking?"

I cleared my throat. "My husband's brother is Herbert Dodge, but he goes by the sobriquet Currie. My husband was called home suddenly this morning, and he tasked me with finding Currie. We hadn't yet learned the location of Currie's residence in Wood's Holl, but he'd told us he worked for the, ah, other theater here in Falmouth."

At this Wesley blinked and lifted his chin slightly, gazing away from us at the corner of the room, an odd reaction to a simple statement.

"Wesley, does thee know the manager at the other theater, or anyone who might know how to reach Currie Dodge?" Sadie asked. "It would help Rose immensely."

He emptied his glass and let out a noisy breath before regarding us again. "As it turns out, I happen to also own the burlesque theater."

Sadie stared. I suppressed a smile at Wesley's discomfort. I didn't care what theaters the man owned, but Sadie was clearly shocked.

Marie lifted her glass, also now empty. "I told these ladies burlesque isn't so scandalous as some make it out to be," she said. "Could I trouble you for another drop, sir?" Her smile was already a bit sloppy.

"Of course, of course. Forgive me for not noticing." Wesley covered his unease by bustling over to the drinks cabinet and refilling both glasses. He faced Sadie. "I see you are displeased, Mrs. Gifford. It was a simple business decision to acquire the theater when it was about to go under. Running a respectable opera house and a somewhat-less-so burlesque theater require many of the same skills, equipment, and staff. It really wasn't as far-fetched a move as it might appear."

Sadie gave herself a little shake. "Please don't worry about my reaction, Wesley. I am not so prudish a Quaker as thee might imagine. Perhaps I'll take in a burlesque show myself one of these days." She gave a little smile.

He harrumphed. "Be that as it may. As for the question of Mr. Currie Dodge's whereabouts, I daresay he's over at the other theater now. We have a performance tonight. Shall I telephone for him to join us?"

I held up a hand. "I would prefer to proceed directly there and speak with him *in situ*, if it's all the same to thee, Wesley," I said in a rush. If summoned, who knew if Currie would actually appear? If he had anything to hide, he might evade a confrontation with us, or at least with me. Perhaps my logic was faulty, since ostensibly I simply wanted to convey the message about his mother. "Would this be possible?"

"Certainly. I shall escort you ladies over myself." He stood, pulling his suit coat straight. "Whenever you all are ready."

Marie gave a panicked look at her glass and drank the contents down in one gulp. She stood, grinning, but swayed a bit and grabbed the back of a chair. "What an adventure we're having, eh, girls?"

THIRTY-THREE

WE STROLLED WITH WESLEY the few blocks to the burlesque theater. He'd offered his arm to Marie, for which I was grateful. She wasn't a large woman, and two glasses of sherry downed quickly in succession had about done her in.

Sadie and I followed them as Wesley turned down a side road. Here the more genteel face of Falmouth's main street turned grittier. The buildings in this neighborhood clearly either housed people hard at work for little pay, those down on their luck, or both. Garbage littered the street, while grimy urchins kicked a ball made of rags tied into a rough sphere. Two women wearing low-cut gowns stood in suggestive poses on the other side of the street, faces caked with powder, eyes lined with kohl.

"Three new ones, Mr. Stewart?" one called, setting her hand on a cocked hip. "You trying to make me jealous, honey?"

Marie shrank behind Wesley as if afraid the woman would snatch her off the street. Sadie shot me an amused glance.

Wesley's face reddened as he cleared his throat. "Please ignore her," he muttered to us, then pointed to a sign. "I know the street isn't much, ladies, but it's quite a reputable theater, for its type."

The sign, in garish red and black letters, proclaimed *Cape Cod Burlesque Theater*, with "Finest in New England" etched below. Wesley tried the door but found it locked. He beat his fist on it as we waited. He grumbled under his breath, and I thought I heard a muttered expletive slip out.

Finally he shouted, "Mr. Dodge. Open the door!"

A window upstairs flew open and a coatless Currie leaned out. His face paled when he saw us. I smiled and waved at him.

"Hey, Currie baby, you got fancy lady callers," one of the prostitutes called.

"And the big cheese, too," the other added.

"Perhaps I won't be taking in one of these shows, after all," Sadie murmured to me.

"One moment, Mr. Stewart," Currie said in a panicked voice before slamming down the window.

It wasn't long before Currie unlocked the door and pulled it open. He'd slid into a coat, but his tie was as askew as his hair, and his feet were shod only in stockings.

"What the devil are you up to in here?" Wesley demanded. "The door is to be unlocked and the ticket office open and doing business the afternoon before a show. You were supposed to be working, Mr. Dodge." He detached from Marie, pushed Currie aside, and strode into the theater.

This was a different side to Wesley than the genteel theater owner we'd met. He was obviously also a manager one would not wish to cross. I followed him in.

"Hello, Currie," I said.

Sadie took Marie's arm. Currie shut the door once we were all in the lobby. The light was dim from several weak electrical bulbs in sconces but provided enough illumination to show walls plastered with posters, a shabby carpet, and dingy woodwork. Double doors likely led to the theater proper. Wesley, Sadie, and Marie faced away from a staircase, which ended next to another door labeled *Exit*.

A young woman in a respectable dress crept down the stairs with eyes wide and shoes in her hands. I glanced at Currie, who clearly saw her, but jammed his hands in his pockets and looked determinedly only at his employer. The tiptoer eased opened the Exit door. If it creaked, both she and Currie were done for. I held my breath. But the hinges were silent, and she slipped away. Maybe Currie had oiled the door on purpose.

"This lady wishes to speak with you," Wesley addressed Currie, gesturing at me. "And then I plan to have a word or a dozen with you myself." His scowl could have scoured a dirty pan, it was that rough. "Let me show you other ladies where the performances take place." He led Sadie and Marie through one of the double doors.

I stepped next to Currie and waited until the door shut before speaking. "Thee took quite a risk, having thy girl slip out under Wesley's nose."

"Don't I know it?" He shook his head. "I really need to mend my ways. But how was I to know he'd descend on the place like he did?" He focused on me. "Why are you here anyway?"

"I'm afraid I have some bad news, Currie." I touched his arm.

"David received a telegram from thy father early this morning. It seems thy mother has fallen gravely ill."

Currie's mouth turned down but he didn't speak.

"David left on the first train to Boston. He asked me to find thee. He prays thee will join Herbert and him at Clarinda's side."

"Knowing my mother, I wouldn't be surprised if she's only pretending to be ill, in a pathetic attempt to lure me home." His expression turned sour. "You don't know her, Rose. She's capable of such a trick."

"I do know her a bit, actually." He didn't need to know Clarinda had lied to me once, trying to turn me against David. Between us we had discovered the true story, and her machinations had only brought us closer. "Will thee be going to her?"

"I can't. I need this job. I'm in a lot of debt, you see, and . . . and that's all I can say." His face hardened as he began to turn away.

"Wait." I stepped in front of him. "I must ask thee something else. Will thee promise to tell me the truth?"

"What's the question?"

"Does thee promise?" I gazed straight into his face, so much like David's and so different, too.

He stole a glance at the theater doors. "If I can."

I mentally rolled my eyes, but forged ahead. "Did thee have sexual relations with Frannie Isley?" I kept my voice low and firm.

"What?" He reared back. "Me? It's an outrage, Rose, to even suggest such a thing."

"Did thee?" I pressed.

"I'm offended you would even consider such a scandalous idea." He folded his arms across his chest, lifting his chin.

Both double doors opened. Wesley ushered Sadie and Marie through. I got a peek at red brocade swags and an abundance of gold paint before the door swung closed.

"We had quite the tour, Rose," Sadie said.

"It's lush in there," Marie said, seeming not quite as wobbly as before.

"Have you conducted your business, Mrs. Dodge?" Wesley asked.

In a way. Except for Currie not answering my question. "Yes, and I thank thee."

"I think we'd appreciate an escort back to our carriage, Wesley, if thee wouldn't mind." Sadie clasped her gloved hands.

"Of course, of course. My man Dodge here is going to get tidied up and open the ticket window without delay. Isn't he?" Wesley stared at Currie.

"Yes, sir," Currie said.

I looked back at him, now standing alone, before I stepped outside. I thought I saw a trace of panic remaining on his face. Was this alarm at having endangered his employment by tangling with his boss, or something worse?

THIRTY-FOUR

THE AFTERNOON HAD TURNED FINE by the time we were back in West Falmouth. I'd declined Sadie's offer to join my aunts indoors. Instead of going straight back to Tilly and Dru's to freshen up before the burial, I took a stroll past the Friends Meetinghouse. I doubted the building would be open for a spur-of-the-moment midweek worshipper, but being near such a quiet and deeply spiritual place might help me discern my path forward in the murky fog that was this investigation.

It didn't help that I'd come away from Falmouth no more the wiser, thanks to Currie. He'd been indignant when I'd asked if he'd had relations with Frannie. Or perhaps he'd had training as an actor. Either way, he hadn't answered me. A pity there was no way to ascertain who the father of a given baby was, or fetus in this case. A woman, of course, nearly always knew who the mother of her child was. I imagined some future in which a simple blood test or other means would show if a baby had been sired by this man or that. He could thus be forced to be responsible for the child's upbringing instead of leaving the mother destitute or having to rely on her family for support. As it was, we might never know who had impregnated poor Frannie.

I'd planned to think—even though praying might be more effective—as I perched on the low stone wall surrounding the burying ground behind the Meetinghouse. My plan, however, was thrown off course by a man with a shovel. A man with a salt-and-pepper braid who wore the same old cap Reuben had clapped on his head yesterday. This had to be Joseph Baxter. And he was digging Frannie's grave.

He worked in a back corner of the graveyard, throwing dirt onto a growing pile next to the long hole in which he stood. Only the top half of his body appeared aboveground. Grunts accompanied the *scritch* of dirt on metal.

I didn't think he'd seen me. Not wanting to startle him, I called, "Good afternoon, Friend." I doubted he'd become a Quaker, but of course it was a friendly greeting whether the word was capitalized or not.

He paused and turned to look at me but didn't speak. I approached him.

"Thee must be Joseph. I am Rose Carroll . . . I mean, Rose Dodge. I'm Frannie's cousin." Or was. I supposed one never ceased being a relation even when the relative was deceased.

"I'm Joseph Baxter. I'm digging the poor girl's grave now." He looked to be older than Zerviah, with a face more lined than his wife's, but he had the same nearly imperceptible accent as hers.

It was interesting, I mused, that Reuben didn't speak with any accent at all. Perhaps he didn't speak much of the Wampanoag language, although he had used a few words in it with Zerviah. "Was thee close to Frannie, then?"

"Not close. But she grew up here, didn't she? We all knew her. She would come to talk with me sometimes as I worked." His brief smile was a sad one. "She was always full of questions about us being Indians. Wanted to learn some words in our language. Wanted to know how to use a saw and how to prune the fruit trees. The world's missing a bright light since she's gone." Joseph took off the cap, swiped his forehead with the back of his hand, then donned the hat anew. "Burial's at six, so forgive me if I keep working, ma'am."

"Please don't let me stop thee. I have met thy wife and thy youngest son. I am also a midwife, so Zerviah and I have much in common. May I fetch thee a cup of water?"

He paused mid-dig and regarded me. "I'd be much obliged, and I thank you kindly."

As I headed for the pump near the building, which had a tin cup hanging from a hook, I heard him murmur, "Quakers. Some of those people take kindness a step too far."

I expected he wasn't the recipient of such kindnesses from Abial Latting, his employer. When I returned, Joseph paused long enough to drain the cup and hand it back to me.

"How was thy business trip?" I asked.

He peered up at me sideways. "Mrs. Baxter told you?"

"Yes."

"Hmph. It was long. Had to journey out to Springfield. Got back on the last train last night."

"Abial seems to do well for himself." I supposed he did, given the size of his home. It seemed odd that a handyman would be sent to inspect a business, but perhaps Joseph was more of a right-hand man than a simple gardener and fix-it man. "What kind of business does he own out there?"

"You should ask him."

Interesting. Did Abial have something to hide about his business dealings? "He must greatly appreciate thy talents. How long has thee worked for him?"

He leaned on the shovel handle for a moment. "If you'll excuse me, Mrs. Dodge, I don't have time to be talking with you. I have a grave to dig for a poor lost soul."

"Of course. Please forgive my intrusion." He was right, of course. I was being nosy, and he had a job to do. I wandered to the far side of the cemetery, with the simple whitewashed Meetinghouse between us, its graceful eight-foot-tall windows looking out at the world. I didn't want Joseph to think I was watching him. I sat on the wall facing the imposing Swift mansion on this side, with Abial's visible beyond. I couldn't see the handyman, but the rhythmic scratch and thud of shovel and dirt kept my thoughts company.

In a village this size, of course everyone would have known Frannie. I hadn't thought of that. I so wished I'd known her, that our families had made the long journey to reunite more often, whether here or in Lawrence. When Daddy arrived, I'd have to ask him why we didn't. I know I would have liked my cousin, ten years younger than I, with her spunk and her curiosity.

What a tragedy Frannie's life had been cut short in such a cruel fashion. Had she known she was carrying a child? She was so young, she might not have. At sixteen some girls' monthly cycles were not yet completely regular, and Frannie might not have noticed she'd missed one or two. My musings circled back to Currie. Had he been having intimate relations with the young lady upstairs in the theater or simply canoodling? If he wasn't the father of Frannie's baby, was Reuben?

Or . . . I fixed my gaze on the turrets of Abial's large abode. Brigid didn't trust him. Sadie had described the son turning against his father, and the daughter being rescued. From a powerful man who preyed on newly matured girls, possibly including his own daughter? It was a horrifying thought, but I knew full well it went on in the world. Hazel and Brigid both had seen Abial be overly affectionate to Frannie in public, canoodling as it were, even if he thought he wasn't being observed.

The shadows stretched out like skinny reflections as the sound of digging ceased. I shook loose my thoughts. I needed to hie myself to my aunts' cottage so I could arrive back here in time to help Tilly inter her granddaughter and Drusilla her great-niece, an event entirely out of order in the way people's lives were supposed to proceed. Before I left my perch, I closed my eyes and held Frannie's released soul and my aunts in the Light, and Detective Edwin Merritt, as well. He could use all the help he could get.

THIRTY-FIVE

WAGON WHEELS CREAKED with the arrival of Frannie's simple pine coffin at the Friends' graveyard. The bell at the Methodist church tolled six times in the distance. We womenfolk—Tilly, Dru, Sadie, and Brigid—waited at graveside. I didn't know how Brigid had learned of the solemn occasion, but I wasn't surprised and was glad to see her. I half expected Hazel to appear, too. Brigid was already sniffling, and Dru patted her own eyes with a black-edged handkerchief. Tilly stood stony-faced and still, a monolith in her high-necked mourning gown. I hadn't brought a black dress on the trip, but I knew no one cared what I wore. At least the Friends present didn't.

Huldah, Abial, Joseph, and Edwin slid the coffin off the wagon and carried it to the gaping hole Joseph had dug. After Edwin had appeared near the wall a few minutes earlier, Huldah had enlisted him as pallbearer when Joseph scowled and said his helper was missing. Did he mean Reuben? I was surprised to see Abial here. Perhaps he acted as an elder of the Meeting, or maybe he simply got word of the burial and came to . . . what? Pay his respects or thank his lucky stars he hadn't been caught *in flagrante delicto* with Frannie? I didn't know.

Joseph had laid out two long ropes next to the grave. The men set the coffin atop them, then stepped back. Joseph retreated to the periphery of the burying ground, as did Edwin, but separately. Huldah joined Sadie. I'd thought perhaps Zerviah might be here, but she wasn't, nor was Reuben. Tilly clasped her hands in front of her and bowed her head while the others murmured in soft conversation.

I moved over to stand next to Abial, who today wore a long cloth coat that flapped in the breeze. "It's a sad day," I said in a soft voice.

"It most certainly is." He wagged his head in sorrow. "A young girl taken before her time."

I glanced at him. It seemed a rote response and didn't sound heartfelt in the least. "I hope the detective soon finds the person who caused her death. It can't be easy for my aunt to have such a person free to go about his life instead of being brought to justice."

"No one is safe in our fair town until the wretched killer is apprehended." Abial stared at the coffin. He cleared his throat, raising his voice as he addressed the gathering. "I shall offer a few words."

"No." Tilly spoke with force. She raised her head, glowering at him. "Thee shall not. Friend Sadie knew Frannie and loved her, unlike thee, Abial Latting. Sadie will speak of our girl."

Abial blinked, with a look of displeasure passing fleetingly over his face. He folded his hands in front of his waist and pressed his lips together. He had no choice, and for this I was glad. Did Tilly say that because she knew of his association with Frannie? I was also grateful Tilly had found the strength to speak her wishes, a strength no doubt enabled by our faith, which recognized women's role in life as equal to that of men. Why shouldn't a female longtime member of the Meeting—a clerk of the women's business meeting, no less—offer the burial message?

Sadie, more somber than I'd yet seen her, stepped forward, her blue dress matching the color of the shadows.

"Frannie Isley was dearly beloved by all who met her. Her lively interest in the workings of this world cheered us, and her energy invigorated so many of those whose nature is more sedate. May her bright soul, now released to God, find its peace with ease. May we each retain a portion of her sweet essence. May her love of music and joyful expression live on in our memories. And may our dear Frannie—" Sadie's voice broke. She pressed her eyes shut and breathed deeply in and out, composing herself. She raised her voice, looking around the circle, and spoke slowly, somberly. "May our dear Frannie rest in God's loving arms."

Brigid murmured, "Amen," and crossed herself.

I joined her, also saying "Amen." To do so was not the custom of Friends. Still, the word echoed around the small group. I sneaked a glance at Abial, his face a pious mask.

"Let us hold Frannie in God's Light." Sadie closed her eyes again. We Friends followed suit. The silence was broken only by the scratching cry of a crow in a distant tree and the clatter of a carriage passing on the road. I cracked open my eyes and peeked at Brigid, who clutched a rosary, and at Edwin, who was regarding a bowed-head Joseph with keen interest.

After some minutes, Sadie spoke. "I thank each of thee for joining us. Gentlemen?" She moved to Tilly's side and wrapped an arm around her.

I was next to Dru, and did the same to her. She whispered her thanks.

Joseph stepped forward, gesturing to Edwin to join him. Huldah and Abial also approached the coffin. Each took an end of rope. Slowly they lowered Frannie and her coffin into her final resting place.

Dru stooped and grabbed a handful of dirt from the mound. "From dust do we come and to dust do we return." She tossed the dirt onto the coffin.

The other mourners slowly added their bit of God's dust, with the exception of Edwin and Joseph, who stayed apart. Abial maintained his fake sorrowful expression, but after he tossed in a bit of dirt he immediately dusted off his hands and hurried away. When it was Brigid's turn, she recited a prayer quietly. She slipped off the small cross she wore and kissed it before tossing it onto the coffin. I was next to last, and held Frannie in silent prayer for a moment while I listened to my contribution patter lightly onto the wood below. I glanced at Tilly.

She shook her head. "I shall not. Only when her murderer is behind bars shall I consider Frannie Isley decently buried." She turned toward the gate but stopped stock-still. "Thee!" She pointed with a shaking finger. "Thee does not belong here."

The object of her ire was Reuben. Hat in hand, he stood at the front entrance to the burying ground, tears streaming down his face. Zerviah stepped up beside him. Edwin edged nearer.

I hoped we wouldn't have an altercation to ruin the somber moment.

Joseph glanced from Edwin to Reuben. "Son—"

"I only wanted to bid her farewell," Reuben choked out. "Frannie was my light."

Zerviah laid a hand on his shoulder, murmuring something only he could hear. Tilly glared at Edwin, but he shook his head slowly in response. Dru looked at me with panic in her eyes.

"What should we do?" she whispered.

"It's time to go home, Tilly." Quiet, competent Sadie took Tilly's arm, nudging her toward the opening in the wall at the back of the graveyard. "Dru, come along with us. Rose, join us if thee wishes."

I watched the three make their way down the path. Thank goodness for Sadie's strong presence. At a touch to my arm, I turned back.

"Mrs. Dodge, will you Quakers be holding a funeral, too?" Brigid asked. "I didn't miss it today, did I?"

"No, you didn't, and yes, we are holding a Memorial Meeting for Worship on Sixth Day at two o'clock in the afternoon." At her look of puzzlement, I added, "What thee calls Friday. Thee is welcome to join us here." I gestured toward the dark-windowed Meetinghouse, which silently observed the doings of the humans beyond it.

"I will come. My da won't be pleased, and neither will the priest. We're not supposed to be entering pagan houses of worship, are we, then? But I'm not after caring. Thank you, Mrs. Dodge. Frannie was a fine girl, and that good of a friend to me." She trudged toward the gate with bowed head, but paused to greet Reuben and pat his grieving shoulder.

Brigid was Frannie's closest friend, and she bore no ill will toward Reuben. A vote in favor of his innocence.

Edwin had slipped away, leaving only the Baxter family and me. Reuben must have been the helper Joseph mentioned earlier. Father and son now began the sad job of shoveling the pile of dirt into the burying hole, with Reuben pausing to blow his nose on a dirt-stained handkerchief. I joined Zerviah.

"I told my son he should wait until the mourners had left to join his father in this sad task, but he refused."

I waited, listening to the thuds of shovelfuls of dirt as they covered the coffin.

"My boy is innocent, but he should not have disturbed the somber act." She shook her head. "He is my most willful child, and I confess my most beloved, too." She regarded me with those deep brown eyes. "Rose, I saw Mr. Latting leave as we arrived. What was he doing here? It seems an act of disrespect, nearly."

"He's a member of this Meeting. Why does thee say it was disrespectful for him to be present?"

141

She turned her gaze to the men, clasping her hands in front of her. "Everyone knows of his immoral behavior, Rose. Toward Frannie, even toward his own daughter. He should be in prison, but that's unlikely in this world of men and their influence. The rest of us would be better off if he happened to meet with an unfortunate accident."

I could only stare at her.

THIRTY-SIX

I LIT SEVERAL LAMPS after I arrived back at my aunts' home, but the windows pressed in with darkness. I hurried around pulling all the curtains shut and made sure the doors were locked, too. Maybe Dru and Tilly didn't lock their doors, but I certainly did. I hadn't been alone here at night before, and with an unapprehended murderer out there? Caution was only prudent. I sank into an armchair. Had it been only this morning when David received the bad news about Clarinda? It seemed like a week ago. I'd halfway hoped for a telegram from him to be stuck in the door, informing me of good news or bad. I'd have to wait for the morrow. I supposed I should write and tell him Currie wasn't on his way.

Sighing, I untied my shoes and slipped them off, and removed my bonnet, too. I had stopped by Sadie's on my way to say I wouldn't be spending the evening with them. I felt a need for quiet and contemplation tonight, and I knew Sadie would take good care of Tilly and Dru. She'd insisted on sending me home with a meat pie and an apple tart, so my supper awaited on the table at my elbow. I was hungry enough to gobble it down right now, but I needed to wash up first. All I wanted to do was put up my feet and think. Instead I dragged myself to the necessary, then loosened my collar and scrubbed my face and hands. I grabbed a glass of water from the kitchen pump. Now I could relax.

Feet on an ottoman, I removed the pins from my hair and let it fall loose on my shoulders. After I spread a cloth in my lap, I nibbled away at the pie. I was still struck by what Tilly had said to Abial. What was it? That Sadie had known and loved Frannie, unlike him. My aunt had been vehement in her insistence that Abial not speak in Frannie's honor. Had she known of his possible abuse of girls? And if so, other Friends would have, too. I could ask Sadie if Abial had been eldered. And if a Meeting elder had chastised him with no effect, why hadn't he been expelled from the congregation?

Zerviah certainly seemed to be aware of it, judging from her remarks to me after everyone but her family had left. Had anyone spoken of Abial's behavior to the authorities, to Edwin? I added doing so to my mental list for tomorrow.

Poor Reuben. To have come to the burial in such grief and be greeted instead by Tilly's harsh accusation. Clearly Edwin wasn't as convinced as my aunt of Reuben's guilt, or the boy would be in jail. I felt for my aunt, too, to have the object of her suspicions interrupt her sorrow.

Brigid had certainly been mourning. I wondered at her leaving her cross in Frannie's grave. Often the symbol of Christ that Catholics wore had been a present from a family member, as my apprentice back home had told me. Brigid's must not have held such a connection. If it had, it was an even more meaningful last gift to her friend.

What else had I learned today — or been confounded by? Hazel had also spoken of Abial Latting's misdeeds. Yes, that was certainly something to bring to Edwin's attention.

How I wished David were still here to explore these facts with, and to be my comfort. I missed him already and we hadn't been apart even a full twenty-four hours. I hoped Clarinda was improving and had not expired before he arrived or even while he was at her side. I would hate for him to be mourning.

Maybe I would journey home on Seventh Day, whether the murder was solved or not. I was doing my best to assist Edwin in uncovering information, but after a certain point such cases had to be left entirely to the professionals.

I glanced at my lap to discover I'd demolished the entire pie. I laughed. I might as well do the same to the hand-sized tart. When I finished, I sipped the cold well water, still thinking. I stood abruptly. Here I was alone in the house, and I'd never even looked into Frannie's bedroom. Maybe the key to the case was getting to know her better. Her room was a good place to start.

The last door on the left upstairs was the one I'd peeked into earlier. It was a small room, perhaps divided out of a larger one when the aunts had brought the girl to live with them. A neatly made narrow bed lined one wall, with a patchwork quilt splashed with spots of color. A desk, which for a girl studying at the academy would be piled with books and papers, instead was scattered with small tools, a couple of metal contraptions made of wire and tin, and a notebook. A diary, perhaps? I would come back to the book.

A shallow closet was tucked under the eaves. Inside I found several green and blue dresses in plain style, one nicer than the rest but still without flounces or frippery. A worn pair of black shoes was lined up tidily underneath, and a bonnet in a muted green hung from a hook next to a long flannel nightdress.

Back in the room, in a low bureau I found a drawer full of folded undergarments, both lightweight and woolen, and another holding darned stockings, lawn handkerchiefs, and two pairs of gloves. I was about to close it when I spied a bright color beneath. Digging, I pulled out a pink ribbon and one of Currie's recruitment posters. So that part of the story was correct. She'd at least known about the theater and the chance to audition for a part in the show. How much further had her relationship with Currie gone, though, if in fact she'd met him?

I fingered the ribbon, an adornment very much out of keeping with the Quaker value of simplicity. I didn't fault Frannie for it. My niece Faith had also admired her Catholic friend's colorful ribbons a few years ago when she was Frannie's age. What girl or boy in their teen years didn't rebel against the ways of their parents?

I returned the ribbon and poster to their hiding place and slid the drawer shut. So far, unless Dru or Tilly had come in here tidying up, it was apparent Frannie liked her possessions to be orderly, neatly arranged. She'd probably been good at the tag-tying work, which would require meticulous care in the knots and stacking.

The desk, where she obviously did her tinkering, was the only messy spot in the room. I sat and picked up one of the contraptions. The body, made of flattened pieces from a tin of tomatoes, was affixed with wire legs and three tiny wheels. An angular head was stuck on top and painted with big black eyes. Underneath the body was a tiny mechanism, maybe purloined from a discarded music box, which had a wind-up key. I wound it up and set the object on the desk. I clapped my hands as it started wheeling across the surface. It hit a pair of narrowly pointed pliers and veered off the edge of the desk into my lap. What a clever girl Frannie had been to invent a mechanical toy like this.

My smile of delight sagged into sadness at the loss of Frannie, to her family and to the world. I shook it off and opened the book. I'd hoped for confidences, secrets jotted down, a window into why she was killed. All I got were sketches for inventions. In a neat small hand she'd included measurements. Arrows and question marks annotated the drawings, which proceeded in increasing detail as I flipped through to the middle of the book. My heart pattered faster when I saw a page of words.

I shut off the gas lamp and headed downstairs, book in hand.

THIRTY-SEVEN

AT THE TOP OF THE PAGE was written *19 Ninth Month*. Two days before Frannie had been found dead. Under it she'd drawn a heart, with FI + RB written inside it. Frannie Isley and Reuben Baxter. I read on.

> *I do love Reuben. But is that it for my life? What about dancing, singing? I want to experience things. I want to be a famous inventor. I want to see the world (AL promised me that).*

Abial Latting? AL could be no one else, which chilled me.

> *I want to find my grandparents, my mama's parents. If I stay with Reuben, can I do any of those things? And I grow worried about missing my monthly.*

The ink on the next word was smudged. From a tear falling on the page? My heart broke for Frannie.

> *ask Brigid. She'll know what I should do.*

I turned the page but there were no more confessions, no more soul searching. The following pages were blank. I shut the book and set it aside. Frannie had grown up without a father. Was she somehow looking for that in Abial? And she clearly knew something was amiss with her body. The poor dear girl.

I yawned and removed my spectacles. *Tomorrow,* I mused, as the clock on the mantel chimed eight times. I'd pay the detective another call tomorrow and bring him the book.

A foot-tall mouse scratched at the baseboard, searching up and down the room for its hole. *It's futile, mouse,* I told it. *The hole is too hard to find. It's hidden. It's—*

My eyes flew open. A giant mouse? I'd fallen asleep. There was no giant mouse. In my dream it had been searching in vain for something. What had been hidden? The clock read nine twenty-nine.

It clicked over to nine thirty and chimed once. But . . . I froze. I was wide awake and still heard the scratching noises.

No! Was a murderer trying to get in? Had Frannie's killer come to get me, knowing I was in the house alone, without a telephone or means of escape? Because I'd been asking questions, talking to anyone who would share information with me?

I listened closely, my fingers icy. Now the house grew quiet. Too quiet. Only the gentle ticking of the clock sounded. What if I had to get away? The building certainly had a back door as well as a front, but did I know the path well enough not to give myself away? The moon should have risen an hour ago. I peered out the eastern-facing window above the half curtain but saw no silvery orb. It would be my luck that clouds had covered it while I dozed. Still, maybe all I'd heard had been wind brushing a branch against the house.

A barely discernible tapping started up, alternating with the scratching sound. Someone could be trying to pick the lock or find a way in. My throat thickened. Why hadn't I taken Sadie up on her offer for me to stay at her home with my aunts? I quickly donned my glasses. I should put my shoes on and be ready for—

The tapping turned into a knocking on the front door. It was followed by, "Mrs. Dodge?"

My eyes flew wide. Who was it? This could be a ruse.

"Rose? It's Zerviah. My lady is in labor. Are you there?"

I took in a deep breath of relief and, standing, blew it out. If this was a ruse to convince me to open the door, someone was using Zerviah. I'd most certainly heard her voice. I hurried to the door but paused with my hand on the lock.

"Zerviah, is thee alone?" I asked. Which was silly to ask, because if she was at gunpoint or someone was holding a knife to her throat, she would be forced to say she was by herself. I swallowed and turned the key.

"Good. I didn't want to knock too loudly for fear of awakening you if you'd already retired." Zerviah stood unaccompanied. "Can you accompany me?"

"Yes. Please come in. It will take me only a minute to be ready and find my birthing satchel."

She passed through but I glanced around the yard before shutting the door. One couldn't be too careful.

THIRTY-EIGHT

DAWN GLIMMERED ABOVE THE RIDGE in the east as Zerviah and I let ourselves out of her client's cottage tucked halfway up the hill behind town. I smothered a yawn from my sleepless night.

"Thank you for coming with me, Rose. It was a difficult breech, but we can thank the Great Mother for helping us guide the little boy out safely."

The last few hours of labor had indeed been difficult, with the baby's posterior positioned to be born before its head. It was the young Wampanoag Indian mother's first child, and she'd clearly been frightened. Her nervous mother and older sister didn't help, flapping about like helpless hens. Zerviah had finally shooed them out of the room and shut the door.

"I admired thy calm in the face of those womenfolk, Zerviah."

"There's no other way to be, truly. You, yourself, are a calm presence. It's the best approach to birth."

After she'd banned the nervous ones from the room, the Indian midwife had perched on a low stool at the end of the bed and waited as the girl labored, assisted only by my offering a cool cloth for her forehead and gentle encouragements. Zerviah had also murmured the occasional suggestions, some of which wouldn't have occurred to me.

"Thy birthing stool is a clever innovation, too," I added.

After the young woman tired of squatting, Zerviah had produced an ingeniously designed low folding stool with a C-shaped seat. It kept the mother-to-be in an upright position, which is often best for allowing the baby to come down, and also allowed space to avoid pressure on the opening to the birth canal.

"Thank you," Zerviah said. "I designed it myself and had Joseph construct it."

When it had come time for the mother-to-be to push, I had stepped away and watched, learning from Zerviah when she asked the woman to squat on the bed holding the headboard, saying it was the best position for bringing out a breech baby. Zerviah knelt behind the birthing woman. I observed her technique for extracting a leg that seemed to be hung up on the shoulder and for bringing the head out promptly after the torso. We all smiled when the dark-haired little fellow gave a vigorous cry. Zerviah had originally asked me to assist in case I knew methods she didn't. As it happened, she was the teacher at this birth, and I was happily the student. After we'd gotten mother and baby cleaned up and settled, the formerly nervous new grandmother turned out to be an excellent tutor in infant suckling, instructing her daughter how best to position her newborn for feeding, and we had slipped out.

"Zerviah, tell me where thee trained to be a midwife," I asked while we walked.

"From my auntie. She was a healer and a wise woman."

"I learned by apprenticing myself to a wise woman midwife, as well, one Orpha Perkins."

"We can't really learn without being there, watching and doing. I also have a friend in Falmouth who is a nurse, and she gave me a copy of the Leishman textbook."

"*A System of Midwifery.* I have it too, and consult it often." No wonder she knew the terminology and techniques.

"It's quite comprehensive."

"Indeed." As we passed the market, I added, "I didn't see the new baby's father anywhere."

"No, he's out at sea, trying to earn enough money to support his new family. He's a responsible fellow, but working on a ship is a dangerous occupation, as I'm sure you're aware. We lose too many of our best young men. Between that and our losses in the recent War for the Union, the males of our tribe are in short supply."

"I'm sorry to hear it." I'd never thought about Indians fighting in the war, but of course they had, and bravely, I expected. "Thee must value Reuben and Joseph being close at hand even more."

"I do, very much. It was before I was married, but my husband had insisted on enlisting to fight in the conflict between the states. He very much wanted to serve his country. He's blind in one eye, though, and they wouldn't allow it. Being an Indian sealed the rejection."

"Thee and thy tribe must encounter a great deal of prejudicial treatment."

"As you've seen, almost none of us uses our traditional names or ways of dressing. Most of us make our way in the world with outsiders none the wiser about our origins. People think some of us might be Portuguese, Greek, or of other swarthy descent. When we celebrate our heritage, we do so in private in neighboring Mashpee, where we own land in common and have built traditional *wetus*, our round houses."

"Does thee long to return to the Wampanoag ways?"

"That would be a different world, Rose." Her smile was as wistful a wisp as the cloud overhead. "I live in this one. I do my best today, and that is all I can do." Her expression hardened. "But we do face severe judgment, and for what? For the vicious defense certain other native groups mounted in the past against white people taking their lands, making them sick, enslaving them? For the color of our skin? It's unconscionable. Your own aunt seems to think my son is a killer because he's an Indian. I wish you could convince her otherwise."

"I wish I could, as well."

We walked in silence for a few moments. It was odd that Friend Tilly would turn against Reuben so vehemently. Unless she knew something she wasn't yet saying.

"At least the detective doesn't think thy son is guilty," I said, "or he would have arrested him by now."

"At least there's that," she agreed.

"Zerviah, thee mentioned Abial Latting's immoral behavior. Did thee ever see any other adult man paying untoward attention to Frannie or other young women of West Falmouth?"

She paused and gazed southward along the main thoroughfare running from Falmouth to Bourne. "Yes, there has been another. A rather dandyish man who seems to have a high opinion of his own charms."

Currie. "Brown hair, thin face?"

"Yes. You know of him?"

"I do." I let out a sigh. Here was where the lane to my aunts' home diverged from the way to Zerviah's. I was too tired to go into the fact that Currie was my brother-in-law. "I'm going to sleep for a bit. I thank thee for inviting me to the birth."

"And I thank you, in turn. I have a young apprentice, but she's white. Her mother lets her train with me but doesn't allow her to assist me in births when the birthing mother is one of my people."

"That seems like a peculiar form of ignorance." I shook my head.

"One of many we encounter along this path of life, Rose. Rest well. I shall see you about town, no doubt. Please don't depart without bidding me farewell."

"I promise." And I meant it. I held out my hand to my new friend and colleague. While the color of our skin was different, our hands did the same work, caring for mothers-to-be and bringing new life into this world. Her firm smooth grasp was like holding my own hand.

THIRTY-NINE

I AWOKE, FULLY DRESSED, when the clock downstairs chimed ten times. I'd barely had time to unpin my hair and remove my shoes before sleep overtook me like an opiate stupor, or so I imagined. I had never experienced even a single dose of laudanum, but I'd seen the effect the potent poppy had on those who ingested it by whatever means. Yawning and stretching, I caressed the other side of the empty bed. I would be home soon enough to share marital joys with my David.

For now, a little more than three hours of sleep would have to suffice. I had things to do and places to go today, starting with a good wash downstairs, some breakfast, and penning a letter to my husband.

With a clean self garbed in a fresh day dress and freshly washed hair in a plait down my back, coffee and two eggs happily in my belly, I found paper and pen on the small desk in Tilly's room. It was sparsely decorated, smelling faintly of rosewater. A small vase filled with dried wildflowers sat on a doily on the dresser, and a bookmark marked her place in the novel *Middlemarch* on the stand next to the bed.

I wondered again if Tilly felt bad not to be in her own home during her time of mourning, and concluded again it might be easier for her to not be surrounded by reminders of Frannie, at least for these first few days.

I sat at the writing desk to compose a missive to my husband. A dictionary, a volume of Emily Dickinson's poetry, Whittier's *Snowbound*, and a copy of *The Journal of John Woolman* were lined up between bookends on the shallow shelf above the desk. A small brass letter holder next to the books contained envelopes that had been slit open and restuffed with their contents.

Instead of writing, I took down the itinerant Quaker minister's journal, penned over a hundred years earlier, and read about his occasional employment as a scribe. When a Quaker slave owner hired Woolman to write his will, Friend John refused to include the part about deeding the slaves to the man's son, thereby convincing him to grant them emancipation upon his death. John Woolman was a man who lived by the values of his faith.

I sat back. Did I do the same? I tried, certainly. I did not kowtow to power. I treated all as equal children of God, and I attempted to conduct myself peaceably. I had to admit I had occasionally blurred the lines of integrity, telling a small lie here and there, but only in the pursuit of a murderer. My mother had once remarked that if we were all perfect, God would get jealous. I didn't think there was much danger of that happening in my case.

Peering more closely at the letter file, I spied a corner of paper sticking up at an odd angle behind the envelopes. I could see only the letters *Fra*. It had to be about Frannie, or maybe a note to her that hadn't been delivered in time. But why would Tilly write a message to a girl who lived in her household?

I was dying to look, but this was Tilly's private correspondence. In light of Quakerly integrity, I had no business poking into her personal files. On the other hand, she had requested my help in finding the person who ended her ward's—her granddaughter's—life. What if the slip of paper held a clue? My hand crept toward it, but I pulled it back. I could simply ask Tilly. She might not tell me, though. I sensed she still held back a secret beyond the one of Frannie's identity, which she'd already revealed.

No matter how much I wanted to see what else was written, I had to let integrity rule. I tore my gaze away from the siren call of that "Fra" and began my letter to David.

> *How I miss thee, my dearest David. I am apprehensive to receive news of Clarinda's condition and pray she is already much improved.*

But had I prayed enough for her? I laid down the pen and closed my eyes, holding my mother-in-law in God's Light. I pictured her in fine form, tending her gardens, hosting her lady friends, and attending services at her beloved St. Paul's Episcopal Church. I exiled all negative thoughts about her less-than-pleasant side.

I resumed writing.

I am well, although a bit fatigued from being up all night assisting at a birth with Zerviah, the Indian midwife. She's a wise woman, and we are fast becoming friends.

We had the sorrow of burying Frannie last evening and will remember her with a Memorial Meeting for Worship tomorrow afternoon. Daddy arrives tonight, for which I am grateful.

I lifted the pen for a moment. While Sadie and Huldah had been more than welcoming, they weren't family, and I'd never been close to my aunts. I was truly looking forward to my father's support and comfort. Both he and Mother had always offered the kind of love that had no conditions set upon it. Even when my sister and I had been firmly disciplined as children—with words, not corporally—it was with the understanding it was about our behavior. We knew we were still loved for ourselves. I hoped to be such a parent myself.

I regret to write that, although I was able to locate thy brother at his place of employment yesterday, he was not eager to journey home and rally around thy mother in her time of need. He seemed to think she might have been claiming to be ill as a ruse to lure him home. I was unable to convince him otherwise. We met the owner of the opera house, who also is the proprietor of the burlesque theater. It's located in, shall we say, an interesting neighborhood. I'll tell you all about it when we are joyfully reunited.

I've been working diligently—and safely, I assure thee—to uncover the truth about Frannie's death, but I plan to travel back to Amesbury on Seventh Day, whether the case is solved or not.

David didn't need to know about my scare last night, which had turned out not to be a threat at all.

I expect I'll go as far as Boston with Daddy, and perhaps he'll decide to accompany me all the way to

Amesbury so he can enjoy a few days with his Bailey grandchildren. Won't it be a delight when we can also invite him to come and play with a few Dodge grandchildren?

I hope thee and thy father are both well, and that Clarinda's health is rapidly improving. Please convey my best wishes to her.

Adding a few endearments, I signed the letter and set it aside while I addressed the envelope. I looked up, startled, at a loud knocking. I peeked out the curtain at the front, still drawn from last night, to see Edwin Merritt raising his hand to knock again. I hurried to open the door.

"Good morning, Edwin."

"Hello, Mrs. Dodge. I wondered if I could trouble you for a few minutes of your time."

I gazed out at the day, which was sunny and mild. "Let's sit out here." I led him to two chairs at a small ironwork table in the shade of a young maple tree, its leaves beginning to transform themselves into fall's unQuakerly bright palette of reds and golds.

I folded my hands and waited.

"More and more troubling details seem to be drifting into my case, Mrs. Dodge. I don't mind telling you I'm stumped. Donovan up there in Amesbury wrote again urging me to avail myself of your keen investigator's brain, so here I am. Might you have discovered anything new for me?"

"Let's see. We last spoke yesterday morning, I think." What had I learned since then? Not much, really, except possible confirmation of Currie's involvement with young women. No, Sadie had told me the bit about Abial's daughter. "I did hear about the unfortunate circumstance regarding the departure of Abial Latting's children, particularly his daughter. Thee must be aware of what happened."

He tilted his head, regarding me. "When his late wife's sister removed the girl from the house? Yes. Is there more than that?"

"I'm not sure. But if he was beginning to accost his own daughter, surely that would be reason for her to want to flee."

Edwin's expression turned to that of a man who had tasted spoiled milk. Still, he jotted down something in his small notebook.

"Thee thyself heard what Tilly said to Abial yesterday as we were burying Frannie. She had harsh words for him."

He looked thoughtful. "Yes, I did."

"And thee also witnessed the extent of Reuben's grief?"

"Yes, indeed." The detective sighed. "I'm no more the wiser."

"Thee hasn't had luck discovering any more facts about the actual death on the water?"

"Alas and alack, nothing specific. But we might have a lead on it."

"And what about Hazel Bowman?" I asked. "Is she on the list of suspects? We spoke of her on Second Day, as I recall."

"Miss Bowman is certainly a person we've been watching carefully. This line of inquiry might prove fruitful yet, Mrs. Dodge."

"Both Tilly and Dru say she is prone to telling mistruths, that she makes a habit of it."

"Duly noted." He stood. "I must be off. I thank you for your time."

I rose, too. "Thee is welcome to join us at Frannie's Memorial Meeting tomorrow afternoon at two o'clock," I said. "I should inform thee I plan to leave for home the following day."

"Let's hope we get a break in this conundrum today."

"I shall pray for a swift resolution." I watched him trudge away. I would do more than pray, if I could.

FORTY

AT A FEW MINUTES PAST NOON I once again sat at Sadie's table with her, Marie, and my aunts. We partook today of a lettuce salad topped with late tomatoes, steamed green beans, bits of ham, and sliced boiled eggs, with fresh bread as accompaniment. I savored the creamy topping.

"Sadie, thee could be a chef in a restaurant. What is this delicious sauce?"

"It's my own mayonnaise dressing. I'm glad thee likes it. It's lighter than the usual recipe."

Dru nodded her approval, her mouth full of bread topped with thickly slathered butter.

"And the tomatoes must again be from thy mother's garden," I said to Marie.

"Indeed they are." She smiled.

"Marie brought over many more yesterday," Sadie said. "I did a spot of canning this morning and have several jars to return to her as thanks."

"What has thee been up to, Rose?" Tilly asked. She was looking a bit less haggard today, more herself.

"I attended a birth during the night with Zerviah Baxter, and I learned a trick or two from observing her. She's a talented midwife."

"I expect she is," Tilly said. "Was the newly delivered mother Indian or white?"

"In this case she was a member of the Wampanoag tribe, but Zerviah assists any birthing woman."

Tilly tapped her fork on her plate. "When I asked, I meant what has thee been up to with regard to the investigation."

"Doesn't thee think we should leave investigating to Edwin and his men?" Dru asked her sister.

"Drusilla, I'll thank thee to mind thy own business." Tilly glared at Dru.

Dru lifted a shoulder and dropped it. "I think it could be dangerous for our dear Rose to toy with a killer."

"Of course it is ultimately up to the county sheriff." I hurried to placate Dru, who today seemed more clear-minded than in past days. I knew senility could wax and wane for a time as it developed. "In fact, I had a chat with the detective this morning. He hinted he might have a couple of leads." Well, only one, but they didn't need to know that. And I didn't want to go into the sordid details of Abial's or Currie's consorting with girls too young for them.

"Good." Tilly resumed nibbling at her salad.

"Did thee find the errant brother-in-law in Falmouth yesterday?" Dru asked.

Sadie must not have told them. "Yes," I replied. "Thanks to Sadie's friend who owns the opera house. Wesley was most helpful."

"I partook rather too generously of Mr. Stewart's libations, I'm afraid," Marie said in a rueful tone.

"Wesley Stewart?" Dru asked, her voice rising. She glanced at Tilly, who stared at her plate. "Thee knows him, Sadie?"

"Yes, we have become friendly due to Huldah's and my support of the opera house. I took Rose to meet him, thinking he might be able to locate David's brother, and he did. Why does thee ask?"

Dru kept her gaze on her sister, who did not return it. "Oh, the name sounds familiar from long ago, that's all."

We ladies ate in silence for the next minute or two, absorbed in our thoughts, accompanied only by a show-off mockingbird's wildly varying songs floating in through the open window. Something was clearly up between my aunts at the mention of Wesley Stewart, but I hadn't a clue what.

I sipped from the glass of lemonade Sadie had served, then addressed Tilly. "I took the liberty of borrowing thy writing desk and supplies this morning, Tilly, to pen a note to my husband. I hope thee doesn't mind."

My aunt's fork froze halfway to her mouth. *Why?* I wished there was some way to ask her about the corner of paper. Try as I might, I couldn't devise one.

Tilly set down the implement. "Using my desk is fine, of course. I'm afraid thee might have glimpsed a piece of correspondence I'd begun but not finished. I can't remember if I left it out on the desk or if I'd put it away."

The letters. "There was nothing on the desk, but I did see the

corner of a piece of paper sticking out from thy correspondence file."
I took a chance, speaking gently. "All I saw were the letters *F-r-a.*
Had thee been composing a letter to Frannie?"

She stared at the wall above my head. "Yes, Rose." She stood. "If
thee will excuse me, Sadie, I am indisposed." She kept her shoulders
straight and her chin high as she moved out of the room. A door
shut quietly in the hall beyond.

"I've upset her. I feel terrible at mentioning the letter." I gazed
after my aunt. "Should I go to her?" I looked from Sadie to Dru.

"No." Sadie patted my hand. "Our Tilly is troubled at present. I
think we should let her rest."

"She'll be fine," Dru said with a little roll of her eyes. "My sister
keeps her feelings to herself."

"Tilly has had a hard week," Marie said. "I think she can be
excused from her reaction. Whatever she'd been writing, she took it
to heart."

I jiggled my heel on the floor, thinking. "Dru, tell me how thee
knows the name Wesley Stewart?"

She chewed a bite of egg and swallowed before speaking. "Once
again, I think thee should ask Tilly for the details. But I'll tell thee
this. Long ago Wesley was a dashing and charming young man who
stole my sister's heart." She rapped the table once.

Sadie's eyebrows nearly hit her hairline, and mine did the same.
Was silver-haired Wesley the man who had left Tilly pregnant all
those years ago? He was certainly still charming. Had Frannie been
his granddaughter?

"My, my," Marie murmured.

"I had no idea," Sadie whispered.

"Well, he did," Dru said in a firm tone. "He broke her heart, too.
He spoke to her of marriage. When he had the nerve to disappear,
Tilly's heart shattered into a million pieces. She never heard from
him again."

So much for letting Tilly tell her own story.

"And thee hadn't heard Wesley's name bandied about?" Sadie
asked.

"No. As we don't frequent the opera, we didn't know the man
was sitting right down the road there in Falmouth."

"Hearing his name must have been like conjuring a ghost for

her," I said softly. My thoughts then took a darker turn as a clock chimed once somewhere in the house. What if Frannie had discovered her grandfather? Was there any way exposure of his past would have threatened him in his comfortable, successful life? My brain spun at the idea. Could he be the murderous culprit we'd been searching for?

FORTY-ONE

I MEANDERED BACK toward my temporary lodgings half an hour later. How could I find out if Wesley knew about Frannie? If he did, it clearly wouldn't be from Tilly or Dru telling him. They'd both been surprised to hear he was living not ten miles distant. Didn't they read the newspaper? Surely his name would have appeared in conjunction with owning the opera house. Or perhaps not.

It occurred to me that I'd talked with Wesley about Frannie's death but I'd referred to Tilly not by name but as my aunt. I was pretty sure he hadn't reacted about my connection with Tilly. If he knew about Frannie's death, he must have read Tilly's name in the paper. Had he forgotten her, or had his lack of reaction been an act?

But I didn't want to take the time to make the trip to Falmouth once again, this time on a train for which I didn't know the schedule. Anyway, the smooth-talking owner of the opera house might not take kindly to my questioning him about his amorous activities of many decades past. I had no idea why he'd disappeared so long ago, nor where to. Should I inform Edwin what I had discovered? I wasn't sure it was pertinent to the case, so I wouldn't, not yet, anyway. So far nothing but my imagination pointed to Wesley Stewart as a killer.

Also, in lieu of a confession from the guilty party, the most important aspect of the investigation into Frannie's death was finding evidence to convict the killer. Edwin and his team had to have already questioned the wharfmaster about the comings and goings of local boats. Perhaps I could pose my queries differently. How, I hadn't a clue, but I'd found in the past I had a certain knack for improvising on the spot. I prayed as I changed my route that Way would open for me again this time. I pushed my spectacles back up the bridge of my nose and quickened my pace. I was always happier when I had a goal in mind, a purpose to achieve.

A train's whistle shrieked as its cars clacked southward several blocks away. Wagons must have been awaiting the delivery of goods, evidenced by the heavy commerce on Chappaquoit Road. Horses clopped along hauling ponderous loads. A woman trudged pulling a cart laden with small boxes. When I reached the station, a man stood outside directing the movement of bundles and bales.

I crossed the tracks and kept up my brisk pace until I reached the inlet and the small wharf. This, in contrast to the train station, was calm, bordering on sleepy. Here was not the busy fishing town of Falmouth. There ships dropped anchor offshore and plied their wares on land. Seamen came into town for fresh food and fresh entertainment, possibly in the neighborhood of the burlesque theater. New goods were rowed out to the larger vessels.

In contrast, West Falmouth supported only the locals: boaters, clam-diggers, and those who enjoyed a quieter life. I approached the wharf, which was merely a long dock with a building barely more than a shed erected on it. A man sat in a chair tilted back against the wall, hat over his eyes, having his postprandial snooze, perhaps.

A dory was tied to the wharf, its oars neatly stashed in the bottom. I peered at the company name painted in small letters on the side. As I'd thought, it was a Lowell Boat Shop dory, a sturdy and well-built open craft constructed in Amesbury's own boatmaking shop. A skiff floated next to it, and a larger fishing vessel was the last, full of nets and traps and ropes. The nearly high tide slapped gently against the sides of the vessels.

I was about to speak to the man when the sound of girls' voices made me turn. Hazel and another girl her age sauntered toward the wharf, arm in arm. Hazel tucked a curl behind the other girl's ear, making her blush.

Curious. Hazel's touch and the other girl's reaction looked more like the acts of lovers than of platonic friends. They clearly hadn't noticed me watching.

When Hazel pointed at the dory, the other girl's smile disappeared and she pulled back. She shook her head. Hazel faced her and seemed to be trying to convince her.

The wharfmaster snorted in his sleep, which must have aroused him. The front feet of his chair hit the planking, and he moved his hat back to the top of his head, then jumped to his feet.

"Oh, hullo, ma'am. Apologies. I didn't see you there." His face was weather-beaten but his smile was a warm one.

"It's not a problem." I glanced over at the girls. Why wasn't Hazel at work at the tag factory?

Hazel looked up and saw me. She glared for an instant from under a straw boater. She composed her expression back to neutral just as quickly, and took her friend's elbow, nearly marching her the last few yards.

"Good afternoon, Mrs. Dodge," she said when the two neared us. "Greetings, Mr. C. We're going to take my dory out for a ride."

"I don't really want to," the other one said plaintively.

"I know what I'm doing, don't I, Mr. C?" Hazel asked.

"That you do, Miss Bowman. You're in good hands, miss."

Hazel whispered in the other girl's ear, who nodded.

"Enjoy the water, ladies." He tipped his hat to the girls.

Hazel handed her friend into the boat, then lifted her skirts and climbed in opposite her. The wharfmaster untied the rope and tossed it in after them.

"You be careful with the tide going out, Miss Bowman. Could be hard to row back in."

"Yes, Mr. C." She rolled up the sleeves of her shirtwaist, revealing strong, tanned arms, and fitted the oars in the oarlocks. "This isn't my first time out on the water, you know."

The other girl let out a high-pitched laugh as Hazel rowed them away.

"The Bowman girl." Mr. C shook his head. "She's going to come to no good one of these days."

"What does thee mean?"

"I've known Hazel Bowman pretty much her whole life. She's always been a headstrong thing and won't take no for an answer, not even from her papa. Not that he says no very often, he dotes on her that much."

Goodness, he was revealing a lot to a stranger like me. Maybe he was simply a gossip.

He tore his gaze away from the water. "Can I help you with a boat or something, ma'am?"

"No, but I thank thee. I'm out for a stroll. I'm visiting West Falmouth for several days. A pity about the girl who drowned last week, isn't it?"

He removed his hat and held it over his heart. "Young Frannie Isley, may she rest in peace. She was another spirited girl, but there was nothing mean about her, not like . . ." His voice trailed off as he watched Hazel's boat get smaller and smaller in the distance.

"Hazel can be a bit nasty, can she?" I murmured.

"Yes, she can, and no mistake."

"Were she and Frannie friends?"

"Used to be. Lately their friendship had seemed to go sour." He redonned his hat. "Indeed it had."

"I suppose thee works here every day."

"Yes, ma'am, I do, every day but the blessed Lord's of course. You'll find me right here from dawn 'til five, leastwise until the cold weather comes. When it's dark and chilly, folks needing help don't go out on the water, only those who make their living from the sea."

So he would have been here the morning Frannie was killed. But what if she'd gone out before the sun came up? It couldn't hurt to ask.

"Did thee happen to see Frannie go out on a boat the morning she died?"

He squinted at me. "So you knew her, then. Calling her Frannie and not Miss Isley, as you did."

"She was my aunt's ward. Unfortunately, because of distance, I didn't know her well."

"I see. Well, that detective fellow already asked me the very same question as you posed. And the sad truth is I did not see her go. I wish I had. Who knows, I might have had a premonition and been able to warn her. I have a bit of a sixth sense, don't you know?" He shoved his hands in his pockets and rolled back on his heels. "Miss Bowman, though, she took her dory onto the water that same morning."

"You saw her go out?" I tried not to sound too eager for the answer and wondered if he'd told the detective this bit.

"No, but I was here when she came back. Told you she was headstrong. Going rowing alone before it's light? It's a foolhardy thing to do, make no mistake about it."

FORTY-TWO

AN OAR COULD EASILY HAVE MADE the kind of injury to Frannie's head that Edwin had reported. Trudging away from the dock after I thanked Mr. C, I caught sight of a stooped-over old woman tending the blooms flourishing in front of a small cottage. The house had a direct line of sight to the wharf. I hoped Edwin or one of his men had already queried her in case she had witnessed Frannie going out on a boat. It wouldn't hurt for me to ask a few questions, too.

I waited until a large carriage passed, then I crossed the road and approached the woman. "Good afternoon, ma'am. Thee has a splendid garden." When I reached her, I saw she was the little old woman I'd spied in the market a few days ago.

She set a hand on the small of her back and straightened. The top of her kerchiefed head came barely to my shoulder.

"Why, thank you, dearie. It's my primary joy, producing beauty." She plucked off a faded zinnia bloom surrounded by a riot of color. She squinted up at me. "Move over here, will you, so you don't have the sun behind you." She ushered me toward a bench under an ancient dogwood, its boughs bending with grace to provide a corner of shade. She sat, dusting her hands off on her apron.

I perched next to her.

"You're not from these parts, am I right?" she asked.

"Thee is correct, ma'am. My name is Rose Dodge."

"And I'm Effie Bugos." Her eyes were a faded golden brown a shade dimmer than the goldenrod blooming behind her. "I'm pleased to meet you, Mrs. Dodge."

"And I thee, Effie. I hail from up north near the New Hampshire border, but I'm down here seeing my aunts for a few days."

"Which would be Miss Tilly and Miss Drusilla. I offer my condolences on the loss of their plucky girl."

"I thank thee. We buried her yesterday and we'll be holding her Memorial Meeting for Worship tomorrow afternoon, if thee wishes to attend." A honeybee buzzed to a jasmine bloom and made its way inside, while a showy golden butterfly alit on a yellow aster. "Thee has an excellent view of the harbor from here." Mr. C had resumed

166

his snooze. Coots and terns bobbed on the sparkling water near a fisherman standing and casting from a skiff, while a cormorant balancing on the gunwale of a rowboat extended its mountain-shaped wings to dry.

"Yes, I do," Effie said. "My father was wharfmaster before that lazy bum over there. You never would have caught my daddy sleeping on the job. Anyway, the man who owned this tract of land deeded the cottage to my father. I was born here, and I expect I'll die here."

"Did thee marry?"

"Oh, yes, and I had quite a happy life. My boys are grown and gone, though, and my dear husband slipped off this earthly coil twenty years ago. It's only me and my flowers now. Well, that and keeping track of what goes on around here."

Keeping track. This could prove useful. "What does thee mean?"

"I don't sleep much, you see. I spend a great deal of time in my chair at the window just there." She gestured over her shoulder with her thumb at the window to the left of the front door. "I see the dalliances between the young, and between the young and the old, too. I watch industrious fishermen set out before dawn, and the laggards who drag themselves out on the water later than they should. You name it, I've witnessed it. And my hearing is as sharp as it ever was."

"Then perhaps I might ask what thee saw last Seventh Day before dawn."

She raised a single pale eyebrow. "I thought you might ask me that. Your reputation precedes you, Mrs. Dodge."

"It does?"

"My, my, yes. It most certainly does." Her laugh was a gentle wave of tiny bells ringing. "Mrs. Gifford and I are friends. She told me all about you."

"Sadie's a lovely and caring person. She's been watching over Tilly this week." Better than Dru or I had, in truth.

"Yes, I know."

"I would be happy for thee to call me Rose."

"Pshaw." She batted the air. "I won't be taking such a liberty, Mrs. Dodge. Mrs. Gifford is always after me to address her as Sadie. I tell her every time, I'm having none of it. I might be an old lady gardener, but society has its strict code of conduct for a reason. What would come of us if no one showed proper respect?" She blinked and held up a lined hand. "Excepting you Quakers, of course. Even with your Christian-name ways, I've barely met a one of your lot who acts with disrespect."

Barely. I wondered who the exception was. I'd opened my mouth to ask when Effie beat me to it.

"That Mr. Latting, now. I'm surprised you all still let him come around to your meetings of a Sunday." She wagged her head, her smile gone.

"I've heard more than one person mention certain of his proclivities," I murmured.

She snorted. "Proclivities is hardly the word for a man who diddles the girls. He's living alone now, though, isn't he?" She sounded satisfied.

I'd neglected to ask Sadie why Abial hadn't been at least eldered for his preying on girls. On the other hand, he was a widower, no longer married, and sixteen was of the age of consent. Perhaps, especially because of his standing in the community, West Falmouth Friends disapproved of how Abial conducted himself but didn't have grounds on which to expel him.

Effie gave herself a little shake. "But Abial Latting's disgusting activities isn't what you were asking about. I do declare there was a surprising amount of activity at the wharf on Saturday before the sun came up. The moonset should have provided more light, as it was full the very next night. But my eyesight in the dark isn't what it used to be, and clouds covered the moon, you see. Everything I tried to observe was murkier than it might have been."

Like this confounded case. *Murky* was the watchword of the week. "Did thee happen to see Frannie go out on a boat with anyone?" I was stabbed with an idea. No one had raised the possibility Frannie might have gone out alone, perhaps because the fish bit best at dawn. What if, like the man fishing in the skiff, she had stood to cast and slipped? Could she have fallen into the water, hitting her head on the gunwale on her way down? It might have caused the contusion and knocked her unconscious. Edwin had said the injury was crosswise on the back of her skull. Perhaps it was a suspicious death but not actually homicide.

Effie continued. "As I told the nice young policeman, Frannie might have gone out on a boat, with someone or alone, but I can't guarantee it was her I saw."

"But you saw someone wearing a skirt get into a boat?" I peered at the wharf as if I could see into the predawn five days ago.

"I believe so. Possibly more than one."

"Two girls?" I pressed.

"I really can't say, Mrs. Dodge. I'm terribly sorry. I will tell you I heard a female voice among male voices in boats. Sound carries so well on the water, don't you know?"

FORTY-THREE

AS I RETRACED MY STEPS away from the wharf, frowning, I barely
saw where I placed my feet. What a disappointment Effie hadn't
been able to see the comings and goings clearly. I knew two things
for sure. Effie, with her keen hearing, had detected a female voice.
And sometime after Mr. C was on duty, Hazel had come back alone
in her dory. What if she hadn't gone out alone but had convinced
Frannie to go for an early ride to watch the full moon set, clouds or
no clouds? Since Frannie had spurned her for Reuben's affections,
Hazel's rage could have led to murder on the water.

I'd neglected to ask Mr. C if he'd told the authorities about
Hazel. If he hadn't already, Edwin needed to check the boat for
blood, for evidence. Or maybe finding hard evidence was the lead
he'd mentioned to me this morning. I'd better go straight to his
temporary office and tell him what the wharfmaster had related.

But as I neared where the railroad tracks crossed the road, I
decided to first stop and inquire if any new telegrams had come for
me. One never knew, and if David had written and not marked it
Urgent, the office could be holding it for me.

In the station, the telegraph clerk handed me the yellow paper. I
thanked him and turned away, unfolding it.

> *Am delayed by sick horse. Arrive tomorrow noon.*
> Love, Daddy

My heart sank. I'd been so looking forward to seeing my father
tonight, talking with him, feeling his comfort. I'd have to accept the
delay. He wouldn't be here until the morrow. I was on my own until
then. I'd offered to switch places with Tilly and Dru and let them
have their house back, but they'd insisted on staying with Sadie
until Daddy and I went home. Dru had confirmed my thought that
it would still be too painful for Tilly to be at home with all the
reminders of Frannie.

Once outside again, I gained the road and resumed my mission
of seeking out Edwin. A train approached from the south. From the

platform, the station master blew his whistle, waving a red flag at the road, cautioning people on both sides to halt. The engine, which was pulling passenger cars, puffed slowly past then pulled to a stop. To my surprise, Currie was the first person to alight.

Settling his bowler on his head, he strolled whistling toward the road with one hand in his pocket, carrying a slim leather case in his other hand. I didn't think he'd seen me, so I stepped forward.

"Hello, Currie. What brings thee to West Falmouth?"

He stopped short. Did I glimpse panic on his face again? A clock in town chimed three times.

He shook off whatever reaction it had been. "Rose, my dear." His voice shook slightly, and a tic beat next to his lip, just like I'd seen on Clarinda's face at the reception. He pressed a finger to it, not answering my question.

"It's a fine afternoon," I said. "Does thee have business to conduct here in town?" I hoped he wasn't here to prey on more girls.

"Why, yes, I do." He glanced down at his case.

"I'll walk with thee."

"Very well." His smile was perfunctory, but he extended his elbow in a gentlemanly gesture.

"No, I'm fine, thank thee." We crossed the tracks and strolled toward Main Street. "Currie, thee might not have heard we are holding a Memorial Meeting for Worship for Frannie tomorrow afternoon at two o'clock. I can't remember if thee said thee knew the girl. Either way thee is welcome to attend." In fact, I'd never asked him if he knew her, only if he'd had intimate relations with her. A question he hadn't answered. I gazed at him, curious about his reply.

"Ah, thank you. I, ahem, might be tied up tomorrow afternoon." He didn't meet my eyes.

"I thought, as thee missed our Meeting for Marriage, thee might find it interesting to witness how Friends worship."

"I will check my schedule, Rose."

We reached the main thoroughfare, which was busy with vehicles of all sorts. A high-stepping stallion pulling a sleek buggy passed a plodding workhorse hauling a wagon full of freshly sawn boards whose perfume tickled my nose. The scent soon vanished when the workhorse deposited a load of manure as it went. Two men in knickers cycled by sitting atop the big-wheeled bicycles known as Columbia penny-farthings. They managed to avoid the steaming pile just in time. When a fringed surrey full of gaily clad young women in boaters passed, Currie's face lit up. He waved to them and doffed his hat, receiving a chorus of titters and waves in return.

"What is thy first destination?" I asked as we paused at the intersection.

"I shall stop by the Union Store."

Which was right beyond Gifford & Co. But why would Currie travel to West Falmouth to visit the store? Unless . . . "I'll accompany thee partway. Is thee planning to place handbills for thy show on their board?" I'd seen a board near the door of the market where various notices were pasted up.

"As a matter of fact, I am." He kept his chin high. "It's part of my employment, you see."

"Of course. Thee apparently decided against going to thy ailing mother?"

"I did, yes. I simply can't get away."

If he were in financial straits, of course he would need to stay and do the work he was paid to do. Also, it might be hard for him to readily forgive Clarinda for past hurts. As we neared the law office, I had one more question for him. I slowed my gait. "Currie, does thee know if Wesley Stewart ever met Frannie?"

Currie stopped short and turned to me, eyes wide and mouth downturned. "Mr. Stewart? Why in the world do you ask?"

What a curious response. "I thought perhaps thee could inform him about the Meeting tomorrow." I kept my tone mild. "In case he wanted to come and pay his respects."

"Oh." He blew out a breath, his relief as obvious as if the word was written on his forehead. "Well, the answer is, I don't know."

"Please pass along the message to him for me." I was glad I hadn't seen him tipsy even once since our initial meeting. Perhaps he'd been so nervous about seeing his mother again he had overindulged.

"I will gladly do so."

"This is my destination, the temporary office of the sheriff's detective." I gestured at the clapboarded building.

He looked in that direction. "The sheriff's detective?" His voice rose. "What business have you with him? Should a proper married woman even be talking with such a person?"

"Currie, I have called on more than one police detective in his office and come away with my reputation intact. It's simply a place of business no different than a haberdasher or a mercantile." This stretched the truth a bit, as the police were a public agency dealing with crime of all sorts, not a store selling wares. I expected he'd learned this attitude about the police from his mother, who wasn't at all pleased with my investigative activities.

"Does my brother know this?" He scowled.

"Of course he does. David respects his wife's mind and choices. He does not stand in my way." Currie had much to learn about me, it seemed.

"Well, I never." He gave his head a little shake. "Good day, Mrs. Dodge."

I watched him stride away, barely swerving to avoid a round old woman trudging with a heavy market basket. My brother-in-law was nervous about something, perhaps more than one something. The question was, what?

FORTY-FOUR

I FINISHED OUTLINING what I had seen and heard and sat back in my chair across from Edwin. "Was evidence on the dory the lead thee mentioned this morning? Traces of blood, perhaps?"

He tented his fingers. "No, Mrs. Dodge, it wasn't. You say Miss Bowman is out in her dory now?"

"I don't know if she has returned or not. She rowed away with her friend at about two o'clock."

Edwin pulled out a pocket watch. "And it's nearly half past three now. I'll get a man down there."

I thought for a moment. "It's a pity Effie Bugos doesn't have better vision."

"It is that and more."

"Has thee discounted the idea of Frannie dying alone from an accidental fall in a boat? She could have hit her head on the edge and fallen in."

"Boats are not so wide to allow the type of contusion she had. I can imagine her unbalancing and falling, but she would have hit her back or her torso, not the back of the head."

"I suppose so." So much for that idea.

Larkin stuck his head in the doorway. "You've got your meeting with the sheriff, sir."

Edwin thanked him and stood, then asked me, "Do you have anything else about the case?"

I rose, too. "Only that Effie mentioned Abial Latting's habit of diddling girls, as she put it." Pronouncing the word made me blush. "I know he is a prominent businessman in the community, but I think his activities bear looking into."

"And I shall." He whistled. "It won't be pretty, though."

Neither is what Abial has been up to. At least Edwin had heard me out about Hazel and the dory. I was grateful to have encountered a detective who listened with respect to my ideas about the case. Kevin's advice to him could be the reason. Many police officers would automatically discredit the word of a woman not yet thirty and refuse to give her opinions a second thought. Like young Larkin earlier this week, whom Edwin had set straight. Law enforcement departments rarely employed women, and when they did the matron's job was confined to care of women in the lockup. I could only imagine the day when uniformed men and women would serve side by side without prejudice or sex-restricted roles. I hoped one day to have the chance to meet one of the famous Pinkerton girls, who did valuable undercover investigative work for the agency. Some might call them infamous, but, oh, the stories we could share.

Once down the stairs, I aimed myself at the market. I hoped to have a missive from David. Who knew, maybe I could convince Brigid to talk more about Hazel or even Abial, if she were at work. I went in. A shelf of hurricane lamps near the door smelled of kerosene, but farther in a bin of unground wheat gave off an earthy, somewhat sweet scent.

"Good afternoon, Mrs. Dodge," Brigid called from behind the counter.

I waved in return. I wanted to speak with her but headed first for the post office counter. "Does thee have anything for Rose Dodge?"

The clerk wordlessly handed over an envelope addressed to me with David's and my new address as return. The envelope bore a blue Special Delivery stamp bearing the words, "Special Postal Delivery. Secures Immediate Delivery at Any Post Office." It featured a picture of a postman running, letter in hand, and cost ten cents.

I slid open the flap of the envelope from my husband. The note, dated this morning at seven o'clock, wasn't a long one.

> *Dearest Rose,*
>
> *I write to tell you Mother's health is out of the woods. Her condition has stabilized. She is clear of mind, is sitting up and taking soft nourishment, and breathes with ease. I still hear some disturbance when I listen to her heart, but for the moment her life is not threatened.*
>
> *I'm very sorry not to be there with you and trust*

you are well and staying safe. Please let me know when
you plan to return to my welcoming arms.
   With undying love,
   Your adoring husband

I smiled to read his affectionate words. Our letters had crossed in the mail. I found it remarkable his had traveled all this distance in a matter of hours. Special Delivery mail must come down on the *Flying Dude*. Tomorrow David should receive news of my planned return on Seventh Day. I read the letter over again. Clarinda's health had improved remarkably fast, making me wonder if Currie's claim she'd conjured her collapse was true, or perhaps she'd made a slight illness sound like a dire one. *Oh, well.* There was nothing any of us could do about Clarinda being Clarinda.

I made my way over to Brigid and waited while she sold a man a coil of thin wire and a sharpening stone. I scolded myself for not returning the egg container. The milk bottle, which I also owed the store, was still half full. I'd bring them both back tomorrow or before I left on Seventh Day.

"Hello, Brigid." I spied a rack holding rounds of bread behind her and inhaled their alluring aroma. "Are those loaves freshly baked?"

"Yes, they are. A local lady makes them. She usually delivers them in the morning but she was delayed today."

"I'd like one, please, and a wedge of cheddar cheese." I decided on the spot to dine alone at home and the larder was pretty bare by now. "Does thee have cured ham, as well?"

"Of course. A quarter pound of each?"

"Please." Ham, cheese, bread, and a sliced tomato would make a perfectly satisfactory supper, if a simple one. I never minded simple.

Brigid turned her back and busied herself cutting and wrapping my purchases. I glanced around but no one was nearby.

"I saw Hazel go out on a boat with another girl an hour or so ago," I began in a low voice. "I think thee told me she was mad when Frannie started keeping company with Reuben Baxter. Does thee think her anger might have stemmed from jealousy?"

She faced me again, setting the paper-wrapped meat and cheese on the counter. "I know it did. Miss Bowman wanted Frannie to herself and that's a fact." She cast her eyes upward with a toss of her head. "I can't fathom it myself, but I'm not after judging others. Live and let live, that's the way to go."

I smiled at her tolerance.

"Well, except for . . ." Her voice trailed off as she also surveyed the store. She leaned closer to me. "Except for Mr. Latting. He was in here trying to get a bit too friendly with me again, he was, trying to lure me out from behind the counter. I wasn't having it, Mrs. Dodge." She slapped the counter, her eyes ablaze. "No, I was not."

"I'm glad thee has not fallen prey to his advances." Speaking of making advances to girls, Currie's faced flashed in my mind. "Was a man in here a little while ago posting handbills? I think thee mentioned thee had seen him before, the slick fellow who was also overly friendly to thee."

"Oh, that gent. Yes, he was. He didn't pay me any mind this time, for which I was glad. He posted his notice out by the door and hurried off as if a banshee was at his heels."

"Did you ever see him with Frannie?"

"I don't think so, even though she told me she'd been going down to Falmouth town." She cocked her head and frowned. "Are you after thinking he killed the poor lass, then?"

"Not at all." I prayed he hadn't. "I'm simply assisting the detective on the case by asking a few questions here and there." Not that it was a simple task by any means, and possibly not a safe one.

"I see." She looked like she didn't quite believe me. "No, I would remember if I'd seen the gent with Frannie."

Gilbert Boyce bustled in from the back and looked from me to Brigid. "Afternoon, Mrs. Dodge. Has Brigid been finding you what you're looking for?" His tone indicated he might have overheard us talking about much more than my supper makings.

"Yes, Gilbert." I smiled to myself. In fact, she'd helped me find one piece of the puzzle. *Maybe*.

FORTY-FIVE

As I LEFT THE STORE with my bundles, I supposed I should get my supper makings home and in a cool spot. Only a little ice remained in the ice box, but I'd forgotten to ask Dru when the ice man came. Still, the weather was cooling with the shorter days and turn of the seasons. Cheese and cured ham should keep fine without having to be overchilled.

What I wanted to do was dig deeper into where Abial had been the night and morning of Frannie's demise. I couldn't quite picture the wealthy businessman rowing Frannie to her death, though. It didn't seem like something he would do.

I yawned. My lack of sleep from attending the birth last night was catching up to me. But instead of heading for my aunts' house, my feet steered me toward Zerviah's cottage. I felt drawn to her calm presence, so much like Orpah's. I could ask about the newborn. Perhaps I could also chat with her a bit about these thoughts roiling in my brain like a storm-disturbed surf, thoughts which had been equally turbulent the last time I'd called on the Indian midwife.

As I approached the Latting mansion, the front door burst open. Abial rushed out, barely closing it behind him. He clapped his hat on his head and trotted down the steps, his long coat flying out behind him. He stopped short when he saw me.

"Good afternoon, Abial." I smiled. "It looks like thee is in a hurry."

He smiled, patting his robust midsection, but his puffy eyes narrowed for the flash of a second. "Ah, hello, Rose. Where I'm off to isn't anything that can't wait. I suppose thee is up to thy detecting?"

How did he know about that? "No. I'm actually paying a call on Zerviah. I attended a birth with her last night and want to ask how the infant fares. Thee must know the first few days can be perilous to one so freshly of this world."

"Precisely so." Now he sounded relieved. "I raised puppies when I was a lad. The same applied to them."

Puppies? He must have a tender side to him I hadn't yet glimpsed. "Did thee sell the dogs?"

"Oh, yes. Mother and I had quite a breeding business. Irish setters. We belonged to the American Kennel Club, of course." His voice was wistful.

"Of course."

"After she passed on, my father wouldn't allow me to continue." He cleared his throat.

While I had his attention, I decided a quick question couldn't hurt. "It seems everyone in the village enjoys a spot of fishing. Does thee also take a boat out on the water from time to time?" I kept my tone mild.

He stared at me and waited a beat before speaking. "Me? Go fishing? Never. It's a disgusting pastime and a worse occupation. Catching a live being with a hook through its mouth?" He shuddered. "I never go near fish or any seafood. Hateful substance. Give me a nice joint of beef or a crisp roast chicken any day, with potatoes aplenty on the side. Now I must be off. Good day." He hurried down the road toward town.

My, my. Such a vehement reaction. Could it mean he protested too much, as Shakespeare had written of? I wondered. It would be hard to avoid eating seafood in a coastal town like this one. Shaking off my thoughts, I continued on to the Baxter cottage behind the big house. Hearing voices from the garden, I made my way around to the back.

Reuben sat on one of the stumps under the arbor with a bucket of water between his knees, scrubbing clams with a small stiff brush. His father stood with his back to me, fists on hips, glowering at his youngest.

"You have to," Joseph demanded. "I order it."

"And if I refuse?" Reuben spat out the words and glared back up at him, but closed his mouth when he saw me. He gestured with his head to Joseph, who whirled.

"Greetings, Reuben, Joseph," I said. "I don't mean to intrude, but I wanted to speak with Zerviah."

Joseph struggled to compose his face. "Good afternoon, Mrs. Dodge. My wife is not here."

"I see. I'm sorry to bother thee, then."

"It's no bother. I think she'll return soon. Please sit. May I offer you a drink of water?" Joseph asked.

My fatigue and the exertion of my perambulations hit me suddenly. "I should love some water. I thank thee." I lowered myself onto the other stump.

Joseph hurried into the house.

"Hello, Reuben." I sniffed the air. Grapes were ripening somewhere nearby, their winey fragrance scenting the breeze.

"Mrs. Dodge." Reuben kept his gaze on his work.

His father returned, handing me a tin cup full of cold water. "I'm afraid I'm late for an, ah, appointment, and must go, Mrs. Dodge."

"It's not a problem," I said. "I thank thee for the water."

"Reuben will gladly provide you with more refreshment, should you wish, while you wait." He stared pointedly at his son, waiting for his response.

"Yes, *Noeshow*," the boy mumbled, but he didn't look up. "I will."

"We will continue our conversation tonight, son. Good day, Mrs. Dodge." Joseph settled a derby on his head and hurried out of sight, maybe off to join Abial, wherever he'd rushed to a few minutes ago.

After a moment, I asked, "Thee dug these clams today, Reuben?"

"Yes, ma'am. I'm to deliver them to Falmouth, where they'll be served in a restaurant. They don't like to receive them dirty."

"Has thee heard of our service for Frannie tomorrow afternoon at the Friends Meetinghouse? I hope thee will attend."

He looked me in the face, his eyes full of sorrow. "Miss Tilly won't want me there, I know it."

"I expect thee is right," I said. "But it's a public service. Thee could sit in the back and bother no one. Frannie would want thee to share in remembering her." Did he know Frannie had been pregnant? If the baby was his, he could be doubly mourning his loss.

"I'll think about it." Reuben returned his attention to his task.

"Did thee ever find thy cap?" It occurred to me in a flash he might have lost it when Frannie went missing. Was there any way to find out?

"My cap?" He squinted at me. "I remember. You were here talking with my mother when I asked her about it. Alas, no. It hasn't turned up."

I sipped my drink, which went down cool and wet. Had water ever tasted so good? Finally I spoke.

"Does thee know Hazel Bowman?"

He spat in the dirt on the far side of his bucket. "I've had the misfortune of meeting her, yes, ma'am."

"I understand she and Frannie were friends."

"Miss Bowman does not know how to be friends with anyone. She preys on girls and twists the words of anyone who tries to stop her. She's as bad as . . ." His voice trailed off as his gaze strayed in the direction of the mansion at the front of the property.

As Abial Latting? I waited for the boy to go on.

Reuben resumed his scrubbing, this time with rather more force than was necessary. A bird of prey, perhaps a falcon, alit on a branch in the pine tree to our side. A snake writhed in its talons, but it was no match for its captor. I watched, both fascinated and horrified, as the attacker proceeded to hold the reptile with one foot while pecking at its skin with a sharp curved beak. The snake, its life extinguished, ceased its struggles. I cleared my throat.

"All I can say is, Hazel Bowman thinks she can twist life to suit herself," Reuben continued. "She hated me for wooing Frannie. In Hazel's mind, I robbed her of someone she thought she could control. But Frannie told me she had tired of Hazel's vindictive ways." He stood, stretching his back. "I do believe she was the one who claimed to the police I killed my Frannie. Me!" His voice broke during the exclamation and he turned away until he composed himself. He faced me again. "It's a complete falsehood. An outright lie. For all I know, Hazel Bowman killed my girl herself, just so I couldn't have her. I ask you, Mrs. Dodge. What kind of a friend is that?"

FORTY-SIX

I NEVER DID GET TO SPEAK with Zerviah during my visit. Reuben had to leave with his bundles of clams tucked into the bags on the back of his bicycle. He'd said I was welcome to wait for his mother, but I opted not to, instead making my way to my temporary home. Reuben's idea that Hazel had killed Frannie wouldn't get out of my brain. He and Frannie must have been stepping out for some months. Why would Hazel choose this moment to get rid of her former friend? It didn't make sense to me.

As I walked, I almost popped in to speak with Effie again but decided against it. I very much needed to rest up for tomorrow, which surely would be emotionally difficult. I felt bad I had neglected my aunts, especially Tilly.

After I dropped my parcels in the kitchen, I washed my face and hands and unpinned my hair. I hummed to myself as I sliced two pieces of bread and spread them with a bit of prepared mustard I found in my aunts' pantry. Food could improve any situation. Topping the crusty bread with a slice of cheese, one of ham, and a thick juicy slab of tomato made my mouth water and my stomach rumble.

I carried the plate out to the bricked area facing the garden. The railroad tracks ran beyond the back hedge, but unless a train clattered by, it was a peaceful place to sit and think. And think, I did.

Abial having a soft spot for puppies had surprised me greatly. I wondered why he hadn't taken up breeding again as an adult. And his reaction to my question about fishing had been extreme. Too extreme? Maybe he was covering up his own crime.

I also wondered what Joseph had been ordering his son to do. Reuben hadn't been happy about it, whatever the demand was. Of course, it needn't have anything to do with Frannie's death. Sons who were nearly men and their fathers often came into conflict, butting heads like stags, as Abial and his son apparently had also done. I was curious about what happened to Reuben's cap, and whether it could have gotten lost in a tussle on a boat. A tussle about what, I did not know. And whose boat? It was strange that Dru had said Reuben had a temper. The angriest I'd seen him was a little while ago as he argued with Joseph. Reuben's temper hadn't seemed out of control at all. It seemed Dru had been spreading gossip, not fact.

Currie. Could he possibly have killed Frannie? He'd said he was in debt. If he'd fathered her child, he might have been desperate to avoid having to support her and a baby, too. David had said his brother was terrified of the water, or at least of the ocean. It was hard to conceive of him going out in a boat. I supposed he—or someone else—could have whacked Frannie on the head and then pushed her boat into an outgoing tide. I shuddered at the thought. But tides, now. Those were a matter of record. I would check into the tides first thing in the morning. Perhaps Tilly even had a tide table here in the house somewhere.

Or maybe Hazel was the villain. She was clearly comfortable in a boat. She was a habitual liar, according to my aunts. She was manipulative, according to both Reuben and Brigid, and abused laudanum. According to Reuben, she was jealous of Frannie consorting with him.

And then there was my fanciful idea of Wesley Stewart being confronted by Frannie. It saddened me to imagine their meeting, Frannie perhaps both nervous and excited to meet a blood relative— her mother's father—and him shocked and threatened by his past coming back to meet him in an unexpected way. Currie had said he didn't know if Frannie had met his employer, but was he telling the truth? Now I wished I had relayed my thought about the theater owner to Edwin. I would do so tomorrow early. But . . . wait. Frannie hadn't known Tilly was her grandmother, had she? It seemed Tilly might have been about to tell her in her letter. How sad she never got the chance.

I popped in the last bite of my simple repast and leaned back in my chair. A blue jay called its metallic see-sawing song, bouncing my thoughts from suspect to suspect. Why did I feel so compelled to do the work of the detective? Was my need for justice so strong? Was it my Quaker upbringing or something in my nature that drove me? Perhaps I loved the intellectual exercise of solving the puzzle. I closed my eyes, the late afternoon sun warming my cheek.

At the scrape of metal on brick, my eyes flew open. Drusilla settled herself in the other chair.

"Thee was asleep," she observed. "I am sorry I woke thee."

"Goodness." I wiped a bit of drool from the corner of my mouth and sat up straight. "Good afternoon, Aunt Dru. I was helping Zerviah with a birth all last night and my lack of sleep caught up with me." The sun was lower but it wasn't yet dark out. I might have napped for half an hour.

"I came by because I needed to fetch a few things for my sister and myself. Will thee be joining us for supper?"

"No, I already dined here. How is Aunt Tilly doing? I think tomorrow might be very difficult for her, and for thee."

"I expect it will be. Tilly has reverted to her usual taciturn stolid self, Rose. Thee witnessed her emotions flowing out through the cracks of sorrow, but she's got them sealed up tight again."

We watched a busy chickadee flit from one branch to another.

"Aunt Dru," I ventured, "I know thee seemed shocked when the detective relayed the news to thee that Frannie was carrying a child. Was thee aware of her condition and simply didn't want to acknowledge that the girl might have strayed?"

"I truly didn't know, Rose. I never attained the blessed state of motherhood myself. I've always wished I had. I must have missed the signs in our girl."

I gazed at her. My aunt didn't seem a bit dotty at the moment. She was speaking clearly and making sense. How odd the onset of senility was. "Does thee think Tilly was aware of Frannie's condition? Thee wasn't in the room when Edwin asked her if she knew, but I was. She never answered him."

Dru didn't speak for a moment. "I think this is entirely possible. Not from Frannie confiding in her, but Tilly has a sharp eye. She notices things, and she carried a child herself. I wouldn't be surprised. Not that we've spoken of it, of course."

What an odd relationship the sisters had, to share a home yet not to speak of something like Frannie's pregnancy. "Then there's the question of who fathered Frannie's child," I went on. Had anyone asked Reuben directly if he'd had intimate relations with Frannie? "Was it a loving Reuben? Or had she been accosted against her will by another man?"

"Like Abial Latting?" Dru murmured.

I looked over at her. "Yes, like him." I supposed in a town this size his wrongdoings would be common knowledge. Why hadn't anyone stopped him?

"Girls are not safe alone around that man." Dru's nostrils flared. "And Tilly told Frannie as much."

If Abial was responsible for Frannie's pregnancy, had he impregnated other girls in town? Fathered other children? And why didn't Tilly suspect Abial of the murder over Reuben?

FORTY-SEVEN

AFTER DRU FETCHED WHAT SHE NEEDED and left, I had an urge to gaze at the bay and revisit the sun setting over the water as David and I had our first evening here. I found it soothing to do nothing but watch a large expanse of water over which I had no control. I carefully locked the house and made my way through last year's dry oak leaves on the path to extract one of the bicycles from the shed. I hopped on, tucking my skirt up in front so it wouldn't become entangled with the spokes. I had a split-skirt cycling garment at home but hadn't thought to bring it on this trip.

I sat on the beach with my knees to my chin, arms wrapped around my legs. Few others kept me company here on the sand. A brisk wind blew the water in at an angle to the shore, and layers of clouds let the sun's light pass through without the sun itself blazing forth. A few minutes later, shimmering pale golden light diffused rays in an inverted fan onto the clouds below. This sight always reminded of me paintings purporting to depict God sitting on the highest cloud. While I wasn't sure God was up there on a cloud somewhere, the effect did look holy and miraculous, and what was God if not Light?

One trim silver-haired lady in a sensible dress with the new slightly higher hems walked purposely along water's edge. She swung her arms as she went. The Calisthenics movement encouraged people to perform a daily healthy exertion. It appeared at least one West Falmouth resident had adopted it. A crew of little sandpipers ran along the beach ahead of her. Once she'd passed, a few of the birds circled around to settle pecking the wet sand in front of me.

I wished I could peck out bits of information as easily. It was a pity that, between Edwin and me, we hadn't solved this case before Frannie's farewell Meeting tomorrow. A resolution, an arrest, would have at least given Tilly the satisfaction of seeing justice served. It would have bestowed peace of mind for all, knowing a killer was securely behind bars.

I doubted I would have a chance to talk things over with my father after he arrived. He'd said he wouldn't get to West Falmouth until noon. He must be taking the same express train the medical examiner had arrived on to examine Frannie's body.

As the large orange orb flattened itself into a half disk before slipping below the horizon, the wind increased, making me shiver. I hadn't attained the peace of mind and absence from thought I'd hoped for by coming here. I removed my glasses and closed my eyes for some moments of prayer.

I'd been working hard on my own to investigate the murder, but I hadn't been calling on God's help nearly as often as I might. I held Edwin and his team in the Light of God, that Way would open for them to put together the pieces of this awful puzzle. I held Tilly, for an eventual peaceful acceptance in her heart of Frannie's passing. I held the killer, whoever it was, for repentance and a cessation of wrongdoing. And I held myself, too, praying I might discern the path to clarity and do so safely.

When the cold breeze caused another shiver to run through me, I donned my spectacles again and pushed up to standing. It was time to peddle home before darkness fully fell. I brushed sand off my posterior and commenced trudging across the beach toward my metal steed. Near the road the sand turned to a narrow dirt track weaving through prickly sea rose bushes. Earlier in the summer the air would have been filled with the sweet scent of their dark pink blooms, but now their rust-colored rose hips matched the turning leaves. Fall was in its ascendance.

At a rustle from the shrubs to my left, I started. My heart pounded as I hurried on. It wasn't a straight pathway. I couldn't yet spy my destination. Was I being followed? Tracked down for getting too close to identifying a murderer, at least in his or her mind? I certainly wasn't close in my own mind. I'd been pursued and attacked during previous cases in Amesbury. While I'd obviously survived, it wasn't an experience I cared to repeat. My palms were clammy, and I nearly tripped over my skirt in my rush to safety.

The bushes rustled again as a huge osprey flew up nearby with a struggling fish in its talons. I slowed, patting my heart. It hadn't been a human looking for prey, after all, but a fish hawk seeking its own prey in a nearby salt pond. Still, I pedaled back to Tilly and

Dru's like a madwoman. Darkness had arrived sooner than I'd expected, and the moon was not yet up. I had to rely on traces of light in the sky and the illumination pushing out from the windows of houses on the route to find my way. Breathing hard, I wheeled the bike into the shed.

Slam. The door shut hard behind me. It wasn't so windy out, was it? I turned toward the door but cried out when I hit my hip on a wooden box next to the wall. *Click.* A gruff curse followed from outside.

What? I finally made my way to the door. I pushed hard. It wouldn't give. I rattled the handle inside. Nothing. I leaned my shoulder against it, set my feet, and pushed with all my might. The door wasn't just stuck. The click had been someone locking me in.

"Let me out!" I shouted.

"That'll teach you," came a hoarse whisper through the crack. "Mind your own business, Midwife Dodge."

FORTY-EIGHT

"OPEN THE DOOR, PLEASE," I pleaded. I pounded my fist on the rough wood.

The noise from a scuffling of leaves trailed away, then nothing but silence answered me.

I slid down with my back to the door to sit on the packed dirt floor. I pushed my bonnet back off my hair and sank my head into my hands. I'd been attacked, after all. At least I hadn't been hit over the head before being locked inside. Who had whispered the threat? It could have been man or woman. Not Abial, because the person had said "you" and "your" instead of "thee" and "thy." So Hazel or Currie. Reuben or even Wesley. Or, I mused, Abial disguising his Quakerly manner of speech. Yes, any one of them could be my jailer.

Why did I do something so stupid as attempt a bicycle ride home from the beach after the sun had set? I could have easily stayed in the house, safe and secure. Or at least left the shore well before dusk. In frustration, I stamped my feet where I sat. But doing so only raised dust, which made me sneeze. Clearly Dru and Tilly's housekeeping didn't extend to the outbuilding.

I had to get out of here. For one thing, I had a need to pass water. I was thirsty from my ride, and a bit hungry, too, but if I had to, I knew I could go without drinking or eating until tomorrow. Surely someone would come looking for me when I didn't meet my father at the train or appear at the Memorial Meeting. Still, I was determined to find a way out. I had no desire to sit in this dusty, flimsy structure for up to twenty hours.

Flimsy. Was it flimsy? I stood. If, in fact, the building was old and poorly constructed, maybe I could push it on its side. Or break down a wall. But with what? The shed didn't include a window, even a small one. My eyes had adjusted to the dark as best they could, which wasn't much.

I braced myself and pushed against the side wall. It didn't budge. So much for thinking I could tip it over. If I could find a sledge or a post to exert extra pressure on the door, I might be able to break the lock. I made my way around the perimeter, feeling for

189

what leaned against the walls or hung from hooks. At the back wall the sharp corner of a high shelf dug into my forehead.

I cried out again. When I felt the wound, my hand came away wet with blood. I patted it with my sleeved forearm. I didn't care about staining my clothing at this point. I stilled. *Crying out.* A house sat to each side of my aunts' abode. Would a neighbor be able to hear my entreaties?

"Help! Please help me," I yelled with all my might and pounded on the door with my fists. I waited, repeating my shouts every minute. "Help!" I pressed my face close to one side of the shed and yelled again, then tried the other side.

After some minutes, my voice grew hoarse from shouting and my fists ached from the pounding. I abandoned my frantic efforts. I sat again, hugging my knees. The other homes were too distant from my prison and they must have already shut their windows for the night. No one was coming to rescue me. Tears welled in my eyes and my throat thickened. This was supposed to have been the happiest week of my life. I was finally married to David. I'd tasted the full fruit of intimacy and found I loved it. I had a new home awaiting me back in Amesbury.

Instead the week was a disaster. I was a failure. I hadn't found Frannie's killer. I hadn't convinced Currie to go see his ailing mother. My dear husband and I were apart, and I missed him terribly. Why did I even think I could go around investigating homicide? I had no training nor a team to back me up. It was dangerous work.

My calling was to a very different occupation. Why didn't I stick to helping pregnant and birthing women? I was good at it, and my services back home were in much demand. Midwifery didn't normally put my life in peril. What did I think I was doing raising the suspicions of a person who had already committed one murder, someone who might be feeling desperate at the thought of exposure? And now look at me. I was alone and locked in a filthy dark shed until tomorrow with no one the wiser — except my jailer.

I closed my eyes, miserable at my plight. I prayed for clarity but found only darkness. When a sob welled up, I choked it back.

No. I sniffed and straightened my glasses, not that they did me any good in the dark. I wasn't going to wallow in self-pity. I had only myself to rely on. I could rest here. I could try to sleep. Except . . . what if my attacker set the shed on fire? Or came back with a firearm. Bullets could likely make it through this old wood. I would be trapped and without defenses. Maybe that was the person's plan all along. It didn't make sense to simply lock me in and leave me until I was discovered.

The better plan was to do my Rose Carroll Dodge best to find a way out. I pushed myself up and smoothed down my dress, feeling the key to the house in my pocket. Could it possibly fit the lock on the shed door, too? I made my way with care to the door and ran my hand up and down the wood at the edge. I shook my head in disappointment. That would have been too easy. No keyhole presented itself. Whoever had locked me in had either jammed a piece of wood in the latch after clicking it closed or had clicked shut a padlock. The door to the shed had been open all week, so I hadn't paid attention to what kind of latch it had.

The roar of a train grew near. It clattered by with a huge noise, being only a few yards from the shed. I took a deep breath after it had passed. I'd stopped my survey of the shed's contents when my forehead met up with the shelf's corner. There had to be something in here I could use as a tool. I felt my way back to the shelf, ducking this time, and continued gingerly around the perimeter. I felt like Laura Bridgman, the deaf and blind woman Charles Dickens had written about in *American Notes*, who learned everything through touch. My blind friend Jeanette had told me about a young student recently arrived at the Perkins School for the Blind in Boston. Jeanette said Helen Keller, also deaf and blind, had acquired language through finger spelling. She apparently had a keen intelligence and was learning to read Braille.

What I needed to feel for was not so fine-tuned. I came across a wooden rake and hefted it, but it was too lightweight to be of use. A hoe leaned against the wall next to the rake. I felt the blade, which was rusted and chipped away. I discovered a small hammer hanging from a nail, a tool far too puny to do me any good. I sighed and took another step. My foot hit an obstacle. I leaned down to feel a rock about the size of the football my nephew played with. Perhaps my aunts normally used it to prop open the door. Maybe it would help me open it once again.

I hefted the heavy stone and tried battering the door at around waist level, where the latch should be, but I couldn't get much leverage. I hoisted the rock over my head with both hands and battered the top of the door, over and over. As someone who believes in nonviolence to her fellow humans—and practices it—I felt remarkably good exerting such force on an inanimate object. *Thud. Whack. Thud.*

The door wobbled more with each hit but remained in place. On my last attempt, one of my hands slipped. The rock rotated. My ring finger came between the rock and the wood. "Ow!" I yelled.

I lowered the stone to the ground for a moment to suck on my finger and catch my breath. This was an old shed and an old door. There might be more than one way to open it. If I pounded on the hinges, maybe I could break them. I felt on the right side but there was no hinge. Of course. The hinges must be on the outside, because the door opened out. Maybe I could loosen them from in here. I used the stone to pound some more, but when I leaned my shoulder into the door, it still didn't budge. I kicked at where the lower hinge should be, resulting only in my big toe aching.

Back at the left side, I set down the rock. I was stronger than many of my sex, but not strong enough to break down a door with a stone. If only I had a prying tool of some kind. *Oh.* I might not have fully explored every inch of the shed. In fact, I hadn't run my hands over the high shelf. On my way back there, my hip clipped the handlebar of one of the bicycles, causing it to fall away from me, taking the other one with it. Wreaking havoc with bicycles was worth it. I returned to the door grasping a two-foot-long metal bar with a flat claw at one end and a hooked one on the other, a tool my father had dubbed a crowbar. Could it act as enough of a lever to help me open the door?

I managed to wedge the flat end between the wide vertical boards at the hinge side of the door. Applying a mighty effort on both my part and the iron crow's, I pried the board closest to the right free from the top hinge. Finally something was going my way. The bottom one screeched as it came away, the board falling toward me, the wind rushing in. I stepped aside to let the wood fall where it may. It hit the bicycles with a thud. I slid sideways through the opening, grateful I had a naturally slender build.

A moment of fright overcame me. Had my attacker waited outside the shed all this time to finish me off? When no one materialized, I raced toward the back door of the house, crowbar raised in one hand, house key in the other. The snick of the lock shutting me safely inside had never sounded so good.

FORTY-NINE

A FIERCE WIND RATTLED THE WINDOWS as I readied myself the next morning, but at least it wasn't an attacker doing so. On my way out the door at around nine, I picked up the crowbar. I'd slept with it next to my bed, in case I would need a weapon at hand during the night. My sleep had been a restless one. A storm blowing in had set a branch to scratching the roof, and all night a door banged somewhere, likely the very shed door I'd left hanging by its locked latch.

Despite the wind, it was oddly warm out. Tropical storms sometimes came this far north, with Cape Cod bearing their brunt much more than where I lived. I prayed this one wouldn't become a hurricane. Maybe they would have news in town of what the weather might bring.

Outside, I glanced all around. If my attacker came back, he or she would know I'd gotten out. I was still in danger as long as I was alone. But I saw no one lurking. After I locked the house door behind me, I first made my way to the shed. The door was a sorry sight, listing askew. I examined the latch. The hasp and plate were rusty, but the padlock my jailer had clicked shut was of a new and shiny metal. I leaned down and peered at the name printed on it: Yale. A piece of the hasp had broken off, leaving a jagged shard of metal stained with something dark. My attacker's blood?

I needed to get to Edwin, and fast. First I set the crowbar inside the small building and rolled the large rock to the outside. I straightened and closed the door as best I could, jamming the stone against the bottom. If we had driving rains later, some would get inside, but this was the best I could do for now to keep the shed's contents dry. I was not inclined to start reattaching the hinges, which would probably need replacing with new ones, anyway.

As a bell clanged furiously from the outer harbor, I made sure my bonnet was firmly tied and hurried toward town, the wind whipping my skirts around my legs. How many times had I entered the law office this week? Nearly daily, I thought.

Young Larkin looked up and jumped to his feet when I approached his desk. "Good morning, Mrs. Dodge. Detective Merritt is out, I'm afraid. Can I help you with anything?"

Alas. "Thank thee, Larkin. Does thee know when he's expected to return?"

"No. He's off on the trail of the murderer, you see, following up a number of leads," he said with excitement.

"I understand." I thought I'd better outline last night's attack for him. If something happened to me, no one would know about the prior attack. "Please tell him I was attacked last evening by an unknown assailant."

His eyes became saucers.

"But I got myself free unharmed. If Edwin arrives before noon, could thee ask him to pay me a call at Huldah and Sadie Gifford's home? He knows where it is."

"I shall do so, of course. I'm glad you are well, Mrs. Dodge."

I smiled at his respectful tone. "I am, and I thank thee. Good day."

Once outside, I thought I might see if the Union Store carried padlocks. I hurried along the walk. From the ever-darkening skies, rain seemed imminent, and I hoped to be indoors at Sadie's when it hit. The train whistle sounded from a few blocks away. I smiled to myself, picturing Daddy already making his way south. Trains traveled in all kinds of weather. I knew even a tropical storm wouldn't delay his arrival. A hurricane might be a different matter, and it would surely delay or even postpone the Memorial Meeting.

Gilbert Boyce greeted me when I entered his store.

"Good morning, Gilbert," I said. *Drat.* I'd forgotten the egg container again.

"What can I help you with today, Mrs. Dodge?"

"An outbuilding on my aunts' property needs securing. Might thee sell padlocks?"

"Indeed we do." He came out from behind the counter, wiping his hands on his long half apron. "Follow me." He led me to an area filled with bolts, nails, wires, and other bits of hardware. An array of Yale locks from tiny to bigger than my hand hung in order of size from hooks. An empty hook marked the spot where a lock the size of the one now fastened to Tilly and Dru's shed would have been.

"Alas, this would be about the size I wanted." I pointed to the gap. "Did someone recently purchase that very one?"

"I expect so, or I would have already restocked it. I can't recall selling a padlock of late, though."

"Perhaps Brigid waited on the person."

"She's the only other one who would have. I'd ask her but she requested the day off. Said she had to work with her father this morning, and she wanted to pay her respects to your aunts this afternoon." He glanced at me. "Sure you can't go up or down a size? We have plenty."

"No, I think the missing one is the size which would work the best. I'll have my aunts check with thee next week, shall I?"

"I can do better than that. I'll deliver it to them when it comes in. Service with a smile is our motto here." His broad grin was the proof of his statement.

"Well, I thank thee kindly." I made my way out. *Good.* I could speak with Brigid before or after Frannie's service and ask who'd bought the padlock in question. Now I wanted to find someone to repair the shed door before my aunts saw the damage. It wouldn't do to worry them with the story of my being attacked. I was sure Daddy could do it if he had the proper tools. I'd be back in Amesbury by the time Tilly and Dru were surprised at the delivery of a shiny new padlock they hadn't requested.

FIFTY

I ARRIVED AT SADIE'S KITCHEN, which was redolent with delicious aromas, to find her, Dru, and Marie preparing refreshments to serve after Frannie's farewell. I grabbed an apron, washed my hands, and insisted on helping. Two chicken aspics already glistened on a sideboard, and dozens of fish fritters drained on a piece of brown paper. Marie sat at the table slicing tomatoes and cucumbers for a salad platter.

"Good morning, Rose," Marie said. "I have been meaning to ask you, do you know Mr. Whittier? He's called the Quaker Poet, isn't he?"

"Indeed I do," I replied as I formed small balls of the sugar cookie dough Sadie had pointed me to and set them on a flat baking sheet. "I'm blessed to call him friend with a small *F*."

"Truly?" Marie asked in awe.

I laughed. "He's a person, Marie. He has every bit as many foibles as the rest of us."

She shook her head in wonder. But it was true. No matter what her church taught, no one was a saint. Each of us had failings and made mistakes, John Whittier included.

"Will thee invite everyone in attendance at the Meeting to gather here afterward?" I asked Sadie.

"I don't see why not. It's simpler that way." Sadie rolled out another small circle of pie dough and nestled it into a six-inch pan. "What does thee think, Dru?"

My aunt frowned. "Tilly might not want certain personages included." Dru was mincing celery and onions for meat pie filling. She sniffed and wiped her eyes from the onion tears.

"Like Reuben, for example?" I asked.

"Yes," Dru said. "Abial Latting's another one she's taken a disliking to."

With good reason, I thought.

"Then we shan't announce the gathering here, instead asking only certain people in confidence," Sadie said, but frowned to herself.

197

"Do you worry about hard feelings, not inviting everyone?" Marie asked.

"Of course," Sadie said.

"Frannie's friend Brigid is going to be there," I chimed in. "I wonder if Hazel will come, too."

Dru frowned. "I hope not."

"Now, Dru, thee knows a Memorial Meeting for Worship is open to the community," Sadie chided gently. "If someone is mourning the loss of Frannie, we always let them join us in worship."

"I know, I know. My sister won't be happy about that."

"I won't be happy about what?" Tilly appeared in the doorway, still in a faded blue flannel dressing gown, her slate gray hair in a messy braid, her face gaunt.

"Well, well. Good morning, sunshine," Dru said.

"Oh, shut up, Drusilla," Tilly snapped.

Dru drew back as if she'd been slapped. I'd never heard Tilly speak in such a severe fashion to her sister, but then, I didn't live with these two ladies who were so different in temperament.

"I can stay in bed on the day of my . . ." She glanced at Marie. "Of my ward's farewell if I want to, especially considering I didn't sleep at all in the night."

She must have been about to say "granddaughter," but Marie didn't know that Frannie had been more than a ward to Tilly.

Tilly came to my side. "Is thee all right, Rose? I had a terrible premonition thee was in trouble last evening." She gazed into my eyes.

Good heavens. How could she have known? I kept my expression as even as I could. I would not add to her troubles by telling the truth about my being attacked. Not now and perhaps never. "I am well, Aunt Tilly. This is a terribly hard time for thee."

"Does thee have any news?" Tilly asked with a burning intensity.

"Nothing of substance, I'm afraid, but I have every confidence Edwin will bring the villain to justice."

"He always was a diligent boy," Dru added.

Sadie dusted off her hands. "Sit, dear Tilly. I'll make thee a plate of breakfast."

Tilly shook her head. "I cannot eat at this time. I would be grateful for a cup of coffee, though." She sank down to sit next to Marie.

Sadie had just delivered black coffee to Tilly and still held the pot when a rapping came at the screen door. The solid door was wide open so the kitchen didn't overheat. Five female gazes swung in the same direction to see Edwin himself standing on the back porch.

"Edwin Merrit." Sadie was the first to speak. "Do come in, Detective."

He entered but hovered near the door, bowler in hand. "I'm sorry to intrude on you ladies." He inhaled, his face taking on a hungry look. "My, but doesn't it smell good in here. Cooking up delicacies for later, are you?"

"Yes, we are." Sadie lifted the pot. "Coffee?"

"I can't help but say yes. Thank you, Mrs. Gifford."

Tilly drew her robe closer around her and tucked a few stray hairs behind her ears. "Please join us at the table, Edwin."

"Yes, do," Marie said, patting the place next to her.

Edwin cast me a look that telegraphed, "I only came to hear your information," but he sat.

Sadie gave him a cup of coffee. She placed a cinnamon roll on a small plate and delivered that, too.

"Gracious sakes, Mrs. Gifford. I'm much obliged."

I cleared my throat and gestured we all should resume our work. No need to make the man nervous. "We were talking about who might attend the service this afternoon."

"Oh?" Edwin asked.

"I hope thee will join us, Edwin," Dru said. "And come here after it is over for some sustenance and conversation."

"I shall be at the Meetinghouse at the appointed hour," he said.

I shot him a glance. He'd be at the service to pay his respects or to catch a killer? Both, with any luck.

"Is thee close to apprehending the villain?" Tilly wrapped both hands around her cup.

"I believe we're making progress in the case, Miss Tilly."

Good.

"But not enough yet to make an arrest, I'm afraid." Edwin bit into the roll, clearly savoring it.

Oh. Tilly stared into her drink. I needed to tell Edwin about what had happened in the shed last night. I finished the cookie dough, then pressed each ball flat with two fingers. A pile of peelings and other vegetable refuse sat in a bowl.

"These cookies are ready for the oven, Sadie." I picked up the bowl. "I'll take this refuse out to the garden. Edwin, could thee help me, please?"

Sadie shot me a look, knowing full well it didn't take two people to carry one container to the vegetable refuse heap. Edwin gulped down his coffee and stood, grabbing his hat.

"I need to be going, anyway. Thank you very much, Mrs. Gifford, for this refreshment. I shall see you ladies again in a few hours."

"It was my pleasure," Sadie said.

The wind blew like a demon outside, but the rain hadn't yet begun to fall. I didn't speak as we walked out back until we were well clear of the house and at the far edge of the garden. "I went by thy office earlier to tell thee I was forcibly locked in my aunts' shed last night after dark."

He gaped. "You what now, Mrs. Dodge?"

"Larkin didn't tell thee?"

"No, I haven't been by the office. When no one was home at your aunts' house, I figured you might be here and wanted to know if you'd learned anything new." He peered at me. "You seem well, but your forehead is cut. Were you otherwise hurt in the attack?"

"No." I gingerly touched the healing wound and proceeded to tell him what had happened the evening before. "The thing is, I couldn't identify the voice."

"Not even male or female?"

I shook my head. The wind whipped a strand of my hair free from its pins, my bonnet being inside the house, and I pushed it out of my face. "Thee knows it's entirely possible for a person to disguise his or her voice and sex by whispering and raising or lowering the pitch."

"This is true, yes."

"I finally managed to get free with the help of a friendly crow-bar."

His pale eyebrows went up. "You are a remarkable lady, I must say."

"Not at all. But I didn't want to spend my night in there, and my entreaties for help were not having the effect I'd desired." I lifted a shoulder and dropped it. "Anyway, I examined the latch in the light of day this morning. A new Yale padlock of a sort sold in the market here in town had secured the door. The latch itself was old and rusty and the hasp half broken. I thought I might have seen blood on the metal shard. Looking closely for a bandaged hand or a bloody cuff this afternoon could prove important."

"I shall do so. It's curious that your attacker knew enough about the shed to bring a padlock with him."

I stared at him. "That's right. I hadn't thought of that. Brigid McChesney might know who bought the last padlock of the exact size now affixed to the shed."

"At the Union Store."

"Yes." I went on. "In addition, after I spoke with thee yesterday, I encountered Abial Latting near his home. I happened to inquire if he enjoyed fishing. He said he hated seafood and never went out on the water. He protested rather too vehemently, I thought. It's something to consider."

"It's a bit of a stretch to leap from that to murder." Edwin cocked his head. "You happened to encounter him?"

"Yes." I raised my chin. "I was looking for Zerviah. Thee knows the Baxter family lives in the cottage behind the Latting mansion."

"I do."

"Abial seemed to know about my detecting, and I'm not sure how. At any rate, I proceeded to the back, where Reuben and his father were arguing. Zerviah was not at home. Joseph left and I had a brief chat with Reuben." I realized I was still holding the bowl of trimmings. I dumped it on a fragrant pile of previously discarded kitchen waste.

"Did you learn something from young Baxter?"

"I think I mentioned earlier he had lost his hat, which is still missing. He also said Hazel Bowman manipulates girls and is possessive of their friendship. Was it she who told thee early on Reuben was seen with Frannie?"

"I'll have to check my notes. The person spoke to Officer Larkin."

"Regardless, Reuben thought Hazel could have killed Frannie because she had turned her affections away from Hazel and toward him."

"Curious, but possible. I have to admit, Mrs. Dodge, the facts of this homicide are the murkiest and most tangled I've ever investigated." He touched his hat. "And now I must get back to it. I shall see you this afternoon."

I said goodbye and watched him go. Tangled and murky the case most certainly was. Impossible to solve? I prayed it wasn't.

FIFTY-ONE

I WAITED UNDER THE RAILROAD STATION'S OVERHANG for Daddy's train to arrive. It was raining with a vengeance now and the sound of it pounding on the metal roof was deafening. Sadie had pressed a large umbrella on me before I left her home, but the wind threatened to turn it inside out as I'd hurried here.

As a whistle pierced the air from the north, I smiled despite how awful the last few days had been. I couldn't wait to greet my father. So much had happened in the six days since I'd last seen him, since my joyous union with David. I couldn't share it in person with my husband — until tomorrow, that is — and I was eager to discuss all the parts of the case with Daddy.

At last he alit, a small valise in one hand and a sturdy sack in the other. When I waved, he hurried down the platform to me. He set down the valise and embraced me.

"Hello, daughter of mine." He beamed, blue eyes atwinkle behind his spectacles. His full beard was as white as ever, and his comfortably padded midsection attested to his love of food.

"I am so glad to see thee, Daddy. How was thy trip?"

"It was a train ride, and I'm glad it's over. Where shall we get ourselves to?"

"Come along to Tilly and Dru's. They've been staying with the Giffords, so I've had the house to myself."

"Thee and David, of course." He picked up his valise and held out an elbow.

"Yes, which was quite a gift to us." I opened the umbrella over both of us and took his arm.

"Where is thy fine husband?"

"Oh, thee doesn't know. Clarinda was taken ill and he had to speed home a couple of days ago. He's already written to say she's on the mend, though."

"Good."

The wind tore at the umbrella, nearly inverting it. I struggled to keep hold of the handle.

"This is some storm thee is presenting me with," he said. "It's much worse down here."

"I know. Daddy, why did we never come to West Falmouth to see Tilly and Dru? It's a lovely corner of the world, and thee must have missed them."

"Thee might well ask. I think thy mother and I were busy raising thee and thy sister, and money was a bit tight for a while. One can't easily leave farm animals, either. I didn't have a brother or other relative at hand to take over for a week while we absented ourselves."

"I understand. I just wish I'd known Frannie better. From all reports she sounded like a lively, creative girl. I think we would have liked each other."

"Yes. Tilly brought her to us on the train only once when Frannie was about three. But it's a long trip, and perhaps the girl didn't take well to traveling."

We didn't speak again until we were ensconced inside the house. The first thing the two of us did was wipe dry our matching spectacles. I got the stove going again for tea and showed him Tilly's room, where he was to sleep, and towels to dry off from the rain. We finally sat with hot drinks, plus a plate of bread and butter. He said my mother had packed him a hearty bag of food to sustain him on the trip and he wasn't overly hungry. Rain battered the south-facing windows, but the house stood firm.

"The ladies have prepared quite the array of foods for after Frannie's service," I said.

"Now, I want to hear all about this very fraught week. Whatever thee wants to tell me."

"There is so much." I bit into a piece of bread and swallowed before speaking. "But what I most want to know from thee is Tilly's past. I've learned she was left pregnant and alone by a man. She went somewhere else to give birth and gave the baby up for adoption."

"Yes." His expression was somber.

"But she was able to keep track of her daughter, who gave birth to Frannie and died, with her husband, in an accident."

"A boating accident. All true."

Boating? I brought my hand to my mouth. "I hadn't realized it was a boating accident. Frannie's death is also connected to a boat."

"What a twist of fate that is." He wagged his head. "I'm sorry, my dear, but my sister swore me to secrecy about her past. Even thy sainted mother doesn't know of Tilly's sad history."

"Why didn't Aunt Tilly adopt Frannie?" I asked.

"She told me she wanted to honor her daughter's married name of Isley. Frannie was the beneficiary of Tilly's will, make no mistake about it, but she didn't want her granddaughter to have to change her name. She felt it was the charitable thing to do."

"I see. This week I met a man named Wesley Stewart who owns two theaters in Falmouth. One is respectable, one not so much. Was he the man?"

"Yes." Daddy spoke in a slow measured voice. "He fathered my late niece. Thing is, he went out to sea. He might not have even known Tilly was carrying his child."

"But he said he would marry her, and she never heard from him again."

"That is Tilly's story, yes."

"Her story? It isn't true?" I stared at him.

He finished a bite of bread before going on. "It was like this, Rose. Thy aunt falling in love surprised everyone, most of all her, I think. Her reserved manner is simply who she is and has always been. Even as a girl she wasn't a fanciful creature. Of course, she is older than I, but I remember her well when she was in her teenage years. She didn't giggle with friends or flirt with the boys as so many others are wont to."

I pictured a young Tilly. "That comports with how she is now, too. So thee thinks perhaps she embroidered the story a bit in her mind?"

"It's possible. Young love can be expressed with great hyperbole at times. Tilly—being Tilly—might have taken as fact what was a flight of the imagination on Wesley Stewart's part."

"And she let herself be carried away by passion with the expectation that a promise underlay it. But Daddy, maybe he was one of many unscrupulous men who lie to women in order to have their way with them."

"That's possible, too."

I sipped my tea and thought. "I wonder if he'll be at the

Meetinghouse today. I'd like to ask him if he knew he was Frannie's grandfather."

"Would thee ask him such a bold question?" He regarded me over the top of his glasses, then threw back his head and laughed. "Of course thee would. My girl Rose wouldn't shrink from such a confrontation."

"Thee knows me too well." I smiled for a moment, but sobered again. "When I first met Wesley this week, he knew about Frannie having been murdered. He must have read Tilly Carroll's name in the newspaper. He didn't show a flicker of recognition. Could he have forgotten her name? Was she so inconsequential to him?"

"Or does he own a theater because he formerly acted on the stage? He could be an expert at disguising his emotions. Did he seem to know Tilly is thy aunt?"

I summoned the memory of our meeting in the opera house. "I think I said I was there to see my aunt whose ward had died, and he then mentioned the murder." How had Edwin described the case? Murky and tangled just got murkier and even more tangled.

FIFTY-TWO

I SLIT OPEN MY EYES to see more and more people enter the Meetinghouse at a few minutes before two o'clock. I sat on the facing bench between Daddy and Dru, with Tilly on Daddy's other side and Huldah flanking her. Tilly hadn't wanted to take such a prominent pew but Huldah, the Clerk of Meeting, had insisted. The pew, normally reserved for the Meeting's elders and recorded ministers and where Abial had been on First Day, was raised a foot higher than the rest, so I could easily observe who was in attendance.

Marie sat with Sadie in a side pew. Brigid had hurried in, brushing rain off her coat, and slid in next to Marie. Hazel appeared in the doorway, surveying the room. Her lip curled as she spied Brigid. She took a seat at the back on the far side. Abial strolled in aiming for our bench. Again in his long coat, he stopped short, nostrils flaring when he saw it was full. He blinked when he saw me, then made for the first pew, which was also fully occupied. He cleared his throat and waited until the West Falmouth Friends sitting there squeezed to the side to make room for him. A quiet hum of conversation went on among the non-Quakers, but Friends sat in silent worship.

The upstairs balcony was full. I'd heard of this happening, that when a young person died everyone in the community turned out to pay their respects. It certainly seemed to be the case today. My eyes widened to see Effie Bugos in the front row of the benches up there, her keen gaze roving over the group below. The divider between the two halves of the building was up today, of course, and I spied Currie and Wesley Stewart come in the far door and take seats. Interesting. If, in fact, Wesley was Frannie's grandfather, I could understand his presence. But Currie's? That remained a puzzle, especially since he'd said he hadn't planned to attend. Tilly didn't seem to notice them.

As Huldah stood to speak, Edwin entered. The door was directly in front of me and I watched as he found a place to stand in front of the back wall. He surveyed the crowd, pausing on each person of note in Frannie's murder investigation.

"We are gathered here today to remember Frances Elizabeth Isley, whose soul was released to God a week ago today," Huldah began. "For those not of our faith, let me briefly explain how we conduct our worship service. As we always do, we sit in stillness seeking God's Light. If one present feels moved to share a message of divine direction, he stands and does so. To be clear, the Religious Society of Friends includes ladies as well as gentlemen in this invitation." He cast a benevolent look around the room. "It is important to leave a goodly period of silence between messages. The difference between a First Day meeting and today is that memories of our dear Frannie may rise up. All are welcome to speak, but please remember to allow at least a few moments of contemplation before sharing thy thought. Rather than ending at a time certain, we shall discern when the worship is completed."

He sat and closed his eyes. I followed suit, listening as the room stilled. As always, I loved this part of worship, the settling into the silence, the calming of the physical body, the quieting of the mind and heart. A rustle from the doorway disturbed my worship. I opened my eyes to see all three Baxters in the doorway. Reuben's eyes were rimmed with red, but the cap he held looked like he must have found the one he'd lost, as it was in good repair. Joseph, bowler in hand, looked tentative. Zerviah made her way to stand by Edwin, but two women on the nearest bench scooted over to make room for the Baxters to sit. I glanced beyond Daddy to see if Tilly had noticed the family come in, but her eyes were firmly shut and her expression somber but not upset. *Good.*

The storm rattled the tall windows as we sat in expectant waiting. After about five minutes, Sadie stood.

"Frannie was a joy to know. She was exuberant and curious every day of her short life. She would pass by as she walked home from school each afternoon, singing with a smile on her face. May her soul rest easy in God's arms." She sat.

That started the flow of messages, some from Friends, some from others who had known the deceased. After a time Aunt Dru pushed up to standing.

"My sister and I loved Frannie with all our hearts. The day she came to live with us changed our lives forever." Her last two words rose and nearly turned into a weeping wail. She brought a handkerchief to her mouth and breathed slowly in and out. "Some of my happiest times were baking with the girl. I shall miss her terribly, and I know Tilly grieves even more deeply than I."

After she sat, I reached for Dru's hand and held it in mine, gently stroking the papery skin with my fingers. I doubted Tilly would speak, but I'd been surprised before. For myself, not a word of inspiration was rising up. Which was no surprise, since I hadn't known Frannie more than distantly.

Brigid glanced around and rose, looking nervous. "Frannie and I were that good of friends. She didn't judge me for being Irish, you see, and oh, did we have fun together. She was a good girl, and let no one say she wasn't."

Something sounding distinctly like a snort came from the area where Hazel sat. I whipped my head toward there to see a local Friend glaring at Hazel, who had the decency to look abashed. Edwin had his gaze fixed on Hazel, too.

"My heart is heavy, but I know Frannie's in heaven with the blessed Lord," Brigid continued, apparently not hearing Hazel's outburst. "May yeh rest in peace, dear friend." She crossed herself and sat.

"Amen," Dru murmured softly.

I wondered if Zerviah would speak, but she held her peace. Or would Wesley contribute a message? I couldn't imagine what he would say short of an outright confession, and that was as unlikely as me converting to Methodism.

Abial stood, smoothing down the front of his waistcoat, the pious look pasted on his face not erasing his florid cheeks and jowls. Was there ever a more pompous Friend, puppy-raising notwithstanding? He cleared his throat.

"I spoke of Frannie's passing on First Day last. It is not right the young should die before the old. May the authorities that be act swiftly to apprehend the scourge who brought about her untimely demise." He stared at Edwin, who returned the stare with a level gaze.

A gasp came from the balcony. I peered up to see Effie, hand to mouth, with alarm drawn on her face. She saw me looking and pointed a shaky finger at Abial. She nodded at me in an urgent gesture. *What?* What was she trying to tell me? She'd said it had been too dark to see identities on Seventh Day morning.

Abial finished. "Young Frannie Isley brought joy to all who met her."

He raised his hand to wipe what I thought was a pretend tear from his eye, and it was my turn to stare. The sleeve of the coat fell away from his cuff. A strip of cloth was wrapped around his palm. I looked frantically at Edwin, who saw me and calmly pointed to his eye, signaling he'd seen what I had.

"She will be much missed." Abial sat, casting me a sideways glance.

Indeed she will, I thought. *But thee will not be missed, Friend.*

Tilly blew out a breath and rose. As she stood, my father offered her a hand but she shook it off. Chin raised, she clasped a black-edged handkerchief between her hands. The high neck of her mourning dress was stark against the pale skin of her neck

"As Frannie's friend Brigid shared, let no one among us speak badly of our Frannie, not now, not ever. She did nothing to deserve her fate. Not one thing." She spit out the words. "I call on the murderer in our midst to rise above his crime and step forward to repent." Her shaking voice came out loud and clear. "This cannot go on any longer."

FIFTY-THREE

A SHARP INTAKE OF BREATH resounded in the room at Tilly's command, not least from Aunt Dru next to me. Tilly remained on her feet for an excruciating few moments. I didn't expect the guilty party to step forth and declare his—or her—guilt, and no one did. When his sister began to sway, Daddy leapt up and helped her sit, then took her hand as I had taken Dru's earlier. My heart broke to see Tilly sitting with bowed head, her shoulders shaking.

Reuben stood and stepped into the aisle. He twisted his cap in trembling hands for a moment. "Frannie was goodness and joy and light." His voice trembled, too.

Tilly looked up. She set her mouth in an iron line with down-turned ends.

"I'm sorry," Reuben blurted, then sat with a thud.

Sorry? For what? Was this the confession Tilly wanted? What would Edwin do with Reuben?

Tilly raised her arm, pointing at him, and opened her mouth. Daddy hurriedly whispered something to her. She lowered her arm and closed her eyes.

The worship room became as quiet as a tomb, which made me realize the rain must have stopped or at least the wind. Was this the proverbial eye of the storm? If it was, we were in for even worse winds to come.

In the silence, Huldah stood. "Please greet thy neighbor." He reached across to the nearest person to his left and shook his hand.

I was glad he'd discerned the meeting was over and equally glad Hazel hadn't said anything shocking about Frannie. I shook Dru's hand, then that of the woman on the end of the front pew.

Huldah approached Tilly and crooked his elbow. "May I walk with thee, Miss Tilly?"

"Thank thee, Huldah." Her smile in return was wan, but she let him help her up. "I should like to leave this place."

Into the hum of low conversation a great crack sounded. The building shook. Dru looked at me with wide eyes. Tilly clutched

Huldah's sleeve. A child shrieked. A man leaning on a crutch, one pant leg pinned up, cringed and sank his face into his hand. I expected he was a veteran of the War for the Union and a person who didn't do well with sudden loud noises.

A young man dashed into the room near where Currie and Wesley now stood. "The big pine toppled. It's blocking both doors!"

"The devil you say," a male voice exclaimed from across the way.

"That one's not a Quaker, I daresay," Dru observed wryly.

I checked, thinking I'd recognized the voice. Indeed, it was Currie who had invoked the Prince of Darkness, as some referred to the concept known as Satan. A mild chaos ensued. Several men of the Meeting hurried into the front hall, while others in attendance milled about. Some of the women—not Friends, by the look of their ruffles and brightly colored garments—looked worried.

"Tilly, why doesn't thee sit again?" Daddy said gently.

She obliged but muttered, "All I want to do is make myself scarce, and God blocks the doors? I cannot fathom it."

"He works in mysterious ways, and thee knows it as well as I do." My father sat next to her.

I stood. I needed to speak with Edwin, and soon. Sadie circulated around both rooms, speaking softly to certain people. I was sure she was inviting Friends and selected others to join the family in the repast she'd prepared. Meanwhile, Wesley seemed to be making his way closer to Tilly. Would she see him first? Was he thinking of speaking to her?

Brigid rose and strode to the door. I followed her. Edwin tried to stop her.

"Let me by." She set fists on hips. "I'm after being as good as any man with a saw and better than many."

I smiled to myself. The broad-shouldered young woman was young and strong, able with heavy fishing lines and boats. Why shouldn't she help clear the obstacle? Edwin let her go.

Joseph followed her out. "We can get the necessary tools from my shed."

"I can slide under the tree and run for the tools if you're telling me where you're keeping them," Brigid offered.

If there was any group under the sun who would accept an offer of manual labor from a girl of sixteen, it was Friends. Joseph wasn't a member of our faith, but he worked for a Quaker. For me right now, my own work had to take center stage.

I beckoned Edwin to a relatively quiet corner in the hallway. "Thee saw what I saw?" I spoke as softly as I could.

"I did, Mrs. Dodge. Someone is a fool to demonstrate such evidence in front of a hundred people."

"He has to be the one who felt threatened by me and locked me in the shed."

Edwin's smile was faint but satisfied. "I would agree."

Effie hurried up, panting, bent over but golden eyes bright. "Mrs. Dodge. That was him."

Edwin's expression grew more keen. "Mrs. Bugos, isn't it?"

"Yes, sir. And you'd be the detective."

"I am."

Effie didn't seem to know Edwin. She must have spoken to Larkin earlier.

"Effie, of whom does thee speak?" I asked.

"That rich old cock who spoke in the service, mind you, about Detective Merritt locking up the villain. My hearing is as good as it was the day I turned twenty, and I have a facility with recognizing voices. I tell you as sure as my middle name is Malvina, that man's is the voice of the person who went out on the boat with Frannie before dawn last Saturday."

My eyes widened. This was the break we needed.

Edwin crouched a little to meet her gaze. "And?"

"He's the selfsame one, him with his coat looking for all the world to these old eyes like a skirt, who came back after sunup with an empty boat."

FIFTY-FOUR

TO THE ACCOMPANIMENT OF SAWING and hewing in the front of the building, Edwin thanked Effie.

"You're willing to sign a statement about what you witnessed?" he asked her.

She scoffed. "Of course." She leaned forward and lowered her voice. "He's a bad one, that Latting."

"Thank thee for this important information, Effie."

"I thank you as well, Mrs. Bugos," Edwin said.

Effie bustled off, hailing another white-haired woman.

To me Edwin murmured, "I have additional information about Latting. This building doesn't have another egress, does it?"

"I actually don't know, but I doubt all these people, including members of this Meeting, would be waiting around for the tree to be removed if they could exit by another door."

"Good point. Where has young Larkin got himself to?" He turned his head right and left, looking. He let out an exasperated sigh. "Well, watch the exits for me, will you, please? Make sure Latting doesn't get out."

Abial was a lot bigger than I was, but I wasn't alone in the building or even here in the entryway.

"I will do my best," I said. I poked my head out the front door and observed the pine-cutting team for a moment. At least the rains and wind had not returned, but the sap oozing out from the fallen growth was making saws stick to hands. I moved to the interior doorway to the worship room on the left. My eyes widened to see Wesley kneeling in front of Tilly. He held both her hands. I couldn't hear what he was saying, but she didn't appear angry with him. This looked a lot like reconciliation. I hoped for Tilly's sake Wesley was offering an apology, and that they both could come to peace with their past as well as their present.

But where was Abial? *Ah.* He stood in the far corner, leaning one arm on a wall, acting far too friendly with Hazel. And she was flirting right back. A raised male voice cracking with emotion drew me away from the sight.

"All I meant was, I'm sorry she's gone, Officer," Reuben said to Edwin a few yards away from where I stood. "I wasn't apologizing. I didn't do anything wrong!"

"Are you sure, young man?" the detective asked.

"I would never hurt her in all my life." Reuben stood tall and serious. "By the sacred eagle, I swear."

Zerviah laid a hand on her son's shoulder, defending him with her silent presence.

Edwin examined Reuben's face. "Very well." He turned away and began to weave through the various knots of conversing mourners toward Abial.

"Mrs. Dodge," a man's voice said at my shoulder.

I glanced up to see a uniformed Larkin. "Where did thee come from?"

He shrugged. "I've been here all along, ma'am. Staying in the background, like the boss told me to." He kept his gaze on Edwin, who had nearly reached Abial.

"Thee is good at it. Is thee the reserve force, so to speak?"

"Yes, ma'am, I believe I am." He sounded both proud and a little nervous as he straightened his shoulders.

Between Abial being as far as he could get from the exit and having Larkin at my side, I figured I could abandon my post at the door.

"Shall we go listen in?" I asked with a small smile.

"Yes, Mrs. Dodge, we shall."

Abial glanced up when Edwin neared him. The Quaker beamed his businessman's smile at Edwin. "Well, well, Detective Merritt. Good news to report, I trust?"

Edwin gestured to Larkin, who hurried the last few steps.

Edwin touched Abial's arm. "Abial Latting, I arrest you for the crimes of homicide, committing violence on a minor, the abuse of a girl, and indecent acts."

Abial's jaw dropped. Hazel went pale and backed away. Larkin reached for Abial's wrist. The older man shook him off, his face ablaze. The entire Meetinghouse stilled, the only sounds being the *scraw-scraw-scraw* of the saws outside.

"This is an outrage. A travesty. How dare you, Merritt?" Abial nearly panted with the exertion of his rage, and his face had turned the color of a scarlet tanager's plumage.

Aha. Abial had abandoned the speech of Friends in the heat of the moment. As he had also done last evening. Perhaps he had not grown up in our faith, or his parents had not used plain speech in the home. In the heat of anger, most people revert to speaking the way their family spoke.

"I am merely carrying out my duties to the full extent of the law," Edwin said mildly, but his mismatched eyes were keenly focused on the accused.

"What is the so-called evidence thee supposedly has to prove my guilt in the matter?" He nearly spat the word "evidence."

"All will be revealed in due time. I would appreciate you not resisting, Mr. Latting. I don't believe that is the Quaker way, now, is it, sir? Larkin, if you please."

The younger officer, looking somewhat terrified, managed to cuff Abial's hands behind his back. I glanced at Tilly, who was gaping and clutching Wesley's hand. I was grateful she'd been able to witness justice being served.

Brigid burst into the worship room, waving a pine branch. "The doors are cleared, ladies and gents."

Applause filled the building for possibly the first time in its forty-seven-year history.

"After you, Larkin," Edwin said, gesturing toward the door. "Mr. Latting, if you would be so kind?"

"Kind?" Abial snarled. "You won't think I'm so kind when I sue you up one side and down the other."

Edwin simply smiled and waved Larkin and his prisoner ahead, the mourners parting to leave them a wide berth.

"Thee will join us at the Giffords' when thee can, I hope," I said to the detective.

"I will do my best. I'm sure you are eager to learn what else we discovered."

"I am, at that."

Larkin and his prisoner hadn't gotten far before Tilly pushed through the crowd to face Abial. When she pointed a bony finger in his face, he cringed.

"Thee! Thee, committing the ultimate act of violence and then pretending to grieve for our girl. Thee, acting as a member of the Society of Friends under false pretenses. Thee, saying thee wished for the killer to be caught." Each time the word "thee" poured out of her with vehemence, she again jabbed toward his face. "Well, thee has been granted thy wish, and thee will burn in hell for it. Thee will have no mercy from me. I hope no one else shows thee any, either, from the police to thy jailers to God Himself. Child murderers have no place in this world of ours. I hope thee suffers for the rest of thy granted days, Abial Latting."

FIFTY-FIVE

SADIE AND HULDAH'S HOME WAS LARGE, but it was packed with people. Tilly sat in an armchair in the sunroom at the back, receiving condolences. Wesley sat next to her without speaking, as if being her rock. She wasn't smiling, but to my mind the tension had gone out of her face. Outside the storm had passed. Puddles dotted the brickwork, and plants drooped from the beating they'd received.

"Tilly looks at ease," I murmured to Daddy as we stood with small plates of food. "It's the first time I've seen her so all week."

He nodded, his mouth full of a fish fritter. Sadie had hired a couple of local women to warm the food that needed it while we were all off mourning and to clean up afterward.

Daddy swallowed. "Tilly told me Wesley apologized for leaving, that he didn't know she was with child. When he returned from being at sea, he pursued an acting career in Boston and never learned about his daughter until this week."

"I'm glad she isn't carrying a grudge against him."

Currie appeared in the doorway from the front and beckoned to me, running his hat through his hands as if he didn't know what to do with it.

"Excuse me," I said to my father and made my way to David's brother in the hallway, curious about what he wanted.

"Rose," he began breathlessly. "You're showing me a different side of what it means to be family. I mean . . ." His voice quavered with nerves. "You've worked so hard to help Tilly, to find Frannie's killer, even staying in West Falmouth when my brother went home. Your father traveled all the way down here to support his sisters." He shook his head in a wondering gesture.

"It's what most families do, Currie." I kept my voice gentle.

He cleared his throat. "I've resolved to patch things up with my mother. I'm taking the four forty train in a few minutes and wanted to let you know."

Good. I took his hand in both of mine. "I'm so pleased, and I know thy mother will be, too. Please give David my love and tell him I look forward to seeing him tomorrow."

"I will, of course." In a rush, Currie leaned forward and kissed my cheek, then donned his bowler and hurried out.

Would wonders never cease? I prayed the reconciliation would go well, and that Currie's change of heart was a long-lasting one. I turned back to the sunroom.

Brigid knelt in front of Tilly. "May I come to see you on occasion, Miss Tilly? I'm not Frannie, but she used to tell me how much she loved you, and I'd like to know you better."

Tilly brought her hand to her mouth, her eyes filling. "She said that?"

"Oh, yes," Brigid said, her expression serious. "You were the center of her universe."

"I didn't know," Tilly whispered.

Brigid laughed. "You know, we girls get silly in these years as we're becoming women. Sure and she might have forgotten to tell you, but I speak the truth. She loved you, and that's that."

"Please do call on me." Tilly patted her eyes with her hand-kerchief. "I'd very much like to see thee again."

"I will, then. Both me own grans are back in Ireland. I miss them terribly."

Tilly regarded Brigid. "Thee is a good person, my dear. I see this."

I wiped my own eye and turned away. The world held more than one spot of hope today. I passed by knots of people talking, eating, some waiting to see Tilly, some making chitchat. Before leaving the Meetinghouse, I had invited Zerviah to join us. She'd thanked me but declined.

I'd taken her hand. "I very much enjoyed meeting and learning from thee. I hope we'll see each other again."

"I hope so, as well." She frowned. "I'm not certain what will happen to us, my husband and son and I. If Mr. Latting is hanged for his crimes, what will happen to the house for which we are caretakers?"

"I don't know. He has children. I would imagine they would inherit the property."

Her frown disappeared. "I suppose so." She squeezed my hand. "I would like to write to you, Rose, if I may."

"Please do, and I shall write back. We live on Whittier Street in Amesbury."

Now I spied Dru in the parlor. She was surrounded by women and looked happy. All was well there. Marie sailed in holding a platter of cookies.

"Rose, dear, you might as well taste your own wares." She smiled at me.

"I thank thee, but I haven't had any savory food yet. I'll wait on the sweets. Marie, we were all so busy this morning I didn't inquire about thy mother."

"She's actually doing somewhat better. She's at least more comfortable, and my sister is with her. Thank you for thinking of her."

"Of course. I'll be traveling back to Amesbury tomorrow, but I hope to see thee there."

"I expect you shall." Marie beamed her smile at me and returned to cookie duty.

I went back into the hallway to find Edwin, hat in hand, standing in the open doorway.

"Precisely the person I wanted to see," he said. "May we talk somewhere?"

I gestured with my thumb. "Not in there. It's full of ladies. How about a walk outside, now the storm is gone?"

"Excellent idea."

I'd stashed my bonnet in one of the bedrooms, but decided I could go without. The detective and I strolled together down the quiet lane.

"Our criminal is safely locked up, I trust?" I asked.

"Indeed he is. He's not a bit happy about it, either."

"Did thee notice he addressed thee as 'you' in the heat of his anger? The person who attacked me did, too, from the other side of the door."

"Oh? I hadn't noticed. You'll like this one. When I asked him how he'd cut his hand, he claimed it was from attempting to repair something in his house. I daresay the man has never fixed a thing in his life."

"Not recently, anyway. He wouldn't know where to start except by summoning Joseph. Now, Edwin, I'm sure a cut hand and an old woman saying she heard his voice getting into a boat with a girl will not be enough to convict him of Frannie's homicide."

"And you would be correct. However, Miss McChesney attested to Latting buying the very size of padlock that shut you into the shed. And based on your recommendation, we had a thorough interview with the wharfmaster."

"Who goes by Mr. C."

"He's the one. Apparently Joseph Baxter owns a rowboat he docks at the wharf. Mrs. Bugos says she saw Latting come back alone, and so did Mr. C. We scoured the boat and discovered traces of blood on the gunwale."

"But there's no way to determine if it was Frannie's blood."

"If only there were."

"Perhaps in the future the police will have a way at their disposal to analyze blood," I said.

"At any rate, one key piece of evidence is a button my man discovered stuck in a crack in the boat's bottom."

"Abial's button?"

"Yes. It matches the missing one on his tailored suit jacket. These buttons are unique to a particular Boston tailor."

My eyes widened. "I noticed a missing button on First Day. I thought perhaps he'd simply neglected it when he buttoned the coat."

Edwin shook his head. "He didn't forget to fasten it. Make no mistake about it. Latting was in that boat."

"It seems the height of arrogance to go about in public with a missing button—which was lost while he committed homicide—and then a hand bandaged in the commission of an attack on me."

"I daresay Latting is nothing if not arrogant. He had another button sewn on since Sunday, but it didn't match the others."

"I told thee he said he never went out on boats."

"All a ruse, Mrs. Dodge. A criminal's ruse, one of many. Once we presented him with the evidence, he blew up and told us the whole story. Larkin got it all on paper.

"I suppose he must have fathered Frannie's child and she told him. She wanted him to marry her, I expect. Or at least support her child."

"Latting is a man who relies on his reputation," Edwin said. "He told us being exposed to the world as a man who impregnated a sixteen-year-old girl would have hurt his business prospects."

"Not that men have never done that." I raised my eyebrows.

"Right you are, more's the pity."

"Perhaps his business prospects aren't as solid as he likes to make out," I said. "He could be in financial straits and wouldn't have been able to manage the additional expense of supporting a young wife and baby."

"We'll find out. Have no doubt about it."

"Was Abial the one who lied about seeing someone in Tilly's boat with her?" I asked.

"Yes. Larkin reminded me of that this morning, and it was Miss Bowman who lied about Reuben taking Frannie out. I now regret having suspected him on such a flimsy thread." He shook his head. "So many prevarications this week."

We walked on in silence for a moment. Marsh grasses nearby waved mauve-colored feathery plumes six feet tall, looking like ladies at the opera. On the ground under a wickedly thorny stem holding red rose hips, poison ivy leaves turned a deadly reddish purple. In the distance a giant white egret tiptoed through shallow water, its long pointed beak ready to grab unsuspecting prey. Abial hadn't used a beak, but he'd certainly preyed on the young and innocent.

"I'll be returning home tomorrow, Edwin." I stopped and held out my hand. "I wish I hadn't had the need to work with thee, but I enjoyed it. I very much appreciate thy openness to my assistance."

He shook my hand heartily. "Your Detective Donovan is a lucky man to have such an able assistant."

I laughed and shook my head. "I'm certainly no detective. Midwifery is my calling, not police work."

"You have a talent for the latter, I must admit, and I daresay for the former. My own wife is carrying our first child. I wish she could have you to watch over her when her time comes."

"Tell her to seek out Zerviah Baxter's services. Thy wife will be in excellent hands."

"The Indian lady?" He stroked his chin. "Well, why not? You Quakers have opened my eyes a bit this week. I shall pass along your recommendation to Mrs. Merritt."

We turned and reversed our steps. "I will say I am relieved my brother-in-law was not involved in any way," I said. And I truly was.

"Currie Dodge is a bit of a rake, but we found no criminal wrongdoing associated with him. Nor serious crimes by young Miss Bowman. Taking laudanum isn't against the law. I suppose I could charge her for impeding an investigation, but it's unlikely the sheriff has the heart to do so."

"I doubt it would change her behavior, anyway," I said. "Hazel's a difficult and likely deeply unhappy girl. I'm glad she wasn't the murderer." I thought some more. "I was thinking about why Aunt Tilly seemed evasive when she first talked with thee about that morning. I think it might be because her own daughter—Frannie's mother—was killed in an accident on the water. And when you mentioned Frannie's death and Tilly being out on a boat, it might have deeply upset her, especially if you thought she was to blame for Frannie's death." I was ashamed I'd ever entertained the notion she might have harmed Frannie.

"Maybe you can ask her, by and by, once her grief has ebbed."

"Perhaps I will."

As an osprey beat its wings above the inlet, the sun shot a bright silver streak across the water from under gray clouds. I knew it was a natural phenomenon, but I preferred to think of the streak as a symbol of hope. Some among us on this earth perpetrated evil deeds, but most people carried God's Light within them. They shared love and help and wisdom. It was the reason we as humans kept going, kept reproducing, kept teaching and learning and standing up for justice.

Tomorrow I would travel homeward. To my husband and my new life as a wife in our shared home. To my calling of midwifery. To becoming a mother myself if I were blessed with that gift.

I also expected I would become involved in more murder investigations back home. Blessedly, this one was over.

223

ACKNOWLEDGMENTS

For all my avid fans who have been asking me over the years, after they finished each of the five previous books, if Rose and David will ever be able to marry — enjoy!

I very much appreciate Bill Harris and the team at Beyond the Page Publishing, who now publish the Quaker Midwife Mysteries. Thanks to my agent, John Talbot, for steering me in their direction.

Huge gratitude to Ramona DeFelice Long for deep reading this manuscript, as she has done with each book in the series, and for enriching it in so many ways with her suggestions and critiques. I couldn't do it without you, my friend! She also leads the seven o'clock online "sprint" group, which starts every morning with an hour of focused creativity and gets my day going in the best of ways.

Thanks again to mystery fan and midwife Risa Rispoli, my consultant on all things perinatal, for keeping me accurate, birthwise. I named one of Rose's aunts Drusilla so her nickname would be Dru, in honor of the fabulous Dru Ann Love, a mystery reviewer, blogger, and enthusiastic supporter of the genre. I also borrowed the maiden name of my longtime friend (and gardener) Janice Bugos Valverde for Effie, the old woman who lives and tends flowers across from the wharf.

Blessings on the West Falmouth Quaker retreat cottage, where I regularly spend a week in solo retreat during the off-season and where I finished the first draft of this book, my twenty-third mystery. I was there in September 2019, which was perfect for checking details of light, weather, flora, and history. West Falmouth Friends generously helped me with local research for this book, as did the West Falmouth Public Library. All errors are of my own making.

I wrote the first quarter of this book at the Women's Writing Retreat at Pyramid Lake in the Adirondacks. Thanks to the Pyramid Life Center for letting eighty women writers of all types occupy your camp and share creative energies for a week. Writers — check it out. It might be the best mid-July week you've ever spent. I last went to this retreat in 2001, and my first published full-length story sprang from a Pyramid Lake prompt. I was delighted to be back in 2019 with eighteen published books under my belt.

Amesbury resident Marie Deorocki was the high bidder at the Merrimack River Feline Rescue Society Auction to have her name included in the book. Thank you for supporting the kitties, Marie, and I hope you like your made-up historical self.

Gratitude to my fellow Wicked Authors—blogmates, dear friends, and lifeboat. Readers, please join us over at wickedauthors.com and meet these fabulous authors: Jessie Crockett, Sherry Harris, Julie Hennrikus, Liz Mugavero, and Barbara Ross (and all their alter egos). I hope readers will also find my two contemporary mystery series, which I write as Maddie Day.

Thanks as ever to my family—Allan, Alison, John David, Barbara, and Janet—and to my fellow Amesbury Friends, for your support and joy at my successes. Hugh Lockhart—antique house restorer extraordinaire as well as my life partner and kitty co-parent—helped me figure out the crowbar scene after I had placed the door hinges in the wrong place. Whew!

I'd like to offer deep and special thanks to my dear friend and Friend, the late Annie Tunstall. Even during her own serious health struggles, she never failed to ask about my writing and my books. She taught me about gratitude and celebrated life's graces with me. This series was her favorite, and her soul was released to God—as Rose would have put it—during the writing of it. I miss Annie very much, but after a long life well lived, she slipped the surly bonds of earth and sailed away (to quote Emmy Lou Harris) knowing she was loved and that she would soon rejoin her beloved late husband, Richard Gale.

ABOUT THE AUTHOR

Agatha Award-winning author Edith Maxwell writes the Amesbury-based Quaker Midwife historical mysteries, the Lauren Rousseau Mysteries, the Local Foods Mysteries, and short crime fiction. As Maddie Day she writes the Country Store Mysteries and the Cozy Capers Book Group Mysteries.

A longtime Quaker and former doula, Maxwell lives north of Boston with her beau, two cats, and an impressive array of garden statuary. She blogs at WickedAuthors.com and KillerCharacters.com. Read about all her personalities and her work at edithmaxwell.com.

Quaker midwife Ros̶̶ ̶̶gative skills on her own family when a young woman's murder stuns a New England community . . .

Following a long betrothal, midwife Rose Carroll and her beloved David are finally celebrating their marriage with friends and relatives, when a most disturbing telegram interrupts the festivities: the young ward of Rose's aunt has suffered a mysterious death, and Rose's help is needed urgently on Cape Cod. Reluctantly agreeing to mix her honeymoon plans with murder, Rose embarks on an investigation that will expose family secrets and a community's bigotry.

As Rose does her best to comfort her aunt in her loss and also learn as much as possible about the poor young victim's death, she discovers that each new clue points to a confounding list of suspects: a close friend of the victim who may have harbored secret resentments, an estranged brother of David's with an unsavory reputation, and the son of a Native American midwife who supposedly led the young woman astray. And as Rose grows closer to identifying the perpetrator, the solution rattles her assumptions about her own family and faith . . .

Praise for the Quaker Midwife Mysteries:

"The historical setting is redolent and delicious, the townspeople engaging, and the plot a proper puzzle, but it's Rose Carroll — midwife, Quaker, sleuth — who captivates in this irresistible series . . ."

— Catriona McPherson, Agatha-, Anthony- and Macavity-winning author of The Dandy Gilver series

"Edith Maxwell's latest Quaker midwife mystery teems with authentic period detail that fascinates as it transports the reader back to a not-so-simple time. A complex, subtle, and finely told tale . . ."

— James W. Ziskin, author of the award-winning Ellie Stone Mysteries

Agatha Award-winning author Edith Maxwell writes the Amesbury-based Quaker Midwife historical mysteries, the Local Foods Mysteries, and short crime fiction. As Maddie Day she writes the Country Store Mysteries and the Cozy Capers Book Group Mysteries.

BEYOND THE PAGE
PUBLISHING

ISBN 9781950461547

90000

9 781950 461547